'If you like forensics, interesting settings, great characters and terrific storytelling, I commend Fox's first and her strong writing to you.'

Linda Fairstein, *New York Times* bestselling author of *Death Dance*

'Fox forgoes conventional plot twists for far darker ones that are genuinely surprising. With an appealing heroine, informative forensic detail and a strong sense of Sydney, *Malicious Intent* is an excellent first effort. *Baltimore Sun*

'Highly rated . . . It's a tale littered with suicides and the real fascination, I found, was how the women were persuaded to kill themselves.' *Lovereading.com*

'An investigation with baroque twists and turns, and a thrilling denouement.' *Independent*

'Rather than stalling the pace of her novel, the moral layer adds an emotional depth to the often stony genre of crime fiction. Crichton is not your average hard-arse investigator . . . She's together enough for us to trust her and weak enough for us to care'. *TNT*

'It is a wonderful moment when you track down something that's really worth reading. And Kathryn Fox's first novel, *Malicious Intent*, is just that. A forensic thriller, it has just the right balance of pathological detail and tight plotting. Think *ER* meets *CSI: Crime Scene Investigation* . . . a fine novel. Gripping from its very first page, it carries you breathlessly through its deftly plotted twists and turns.' *Vogue* (Australia)

'Fox is clearly in her element on the scientific side of things . . . Her slow build-up of forensic evidence linking all these women is absolutely fascinating and, forensically speaking, *Malicious Intent* is top-notch in its genre.'

Sunday Telegraph (Sydney)

'Highly recommended reading.'

Daily Telegraph (Australia)

Also by Kathryn Fox

Malicious Intent

About the author

Kathryn Fox is a general practitioner with a special interest in forensic medicine. Her bestselling debut novel, *Malicious Intent*, received international acclaim and was awarded the 2005 Davitt award for best adult fiction. Kathryn currently lives in Sydney, Australia.

KATHRYN FOX

Without Consent

HODDER

*To the doctors, police and health care workers
who work with victims of sexual assault.*

Acknowledgements

Once again, many people have offered their expertise and time to help with accuracy in this book. Although the story is fictitious, the work done by the professionals and the psychology of the characters is as true to life as possible. It is sobering to discover that very little research continues to be done in forensic science due to poor funding. Victims – alive and deceased – don't carry much political power, it seems. Crime shows and novels belie the lack of attention paid to such an important field.

Dr Jean Edwards, Dr Caroline Jones and Dr Guy Norfolk have all selflessly contributed to authenticity about sexual assault examination and the work of forensic physicians. For that, and their tireless contribution to victims, I hope I have been true to you.

Thanks also go to Dr Jo Du Fluo, forensic pathologist, extraordinaire, the great legal mind (and humour) of Siobhan Mullany and the superlative investigative skills of Chief Detective Inspector Paul Jacob.

In addition, appreciation to Cathie Barclay,

Lyn Elliott and Kerrie Nobes for being astute and informed readers, and once again for the outstanding teaching skills of Marg McAlister, from writing4success. Marg, I promise to 'pass it on'.

Thanks must go to the exceptional staff at Hodder, especially Sara Kinsella, Leni Fostiropoulos and Isobel Akenhead for their belief, tireless efforts and friendship, and to Euan Thorneycroft, my wonderful agent.

Finally, I would like to acknowledge close family and friends, who have been so supportive and positive through every step in the writing process. Please know that you are never taken for granted!

1

Temporarily blinded by the flashing bulbs, Geoffrey Willard stepped through the gate. Immediately, the onslaught began.

'Over here,' a man called.

'No, this way,' cried another.

'Geoff! What's it like to be free?'

A microphone lurched forwards and grazed his chin. The impact caught him off balance.

'Do you think you're rehabilitated?'

Cameras click-clicked.

'Mate, look this way! Show us those baby blues.'

'Sunny, over here!'

Geoffrey instinctively shielded his eyes, the ones that caused inmates to nickname him Sundance, after Robert Redford, only before he turned old and wrinkly. With his forefinger, he touched a bit of newly shaved scalp and took half a pace backwards, wishing he could retreat to the safety of prison.

More flashes exploded in the twilight. Not knowing which way to turn, he hid his face with his knapsack. What felt like a fist plunged into his side. As he pulled away with the pain, someone shoved from the other side.

The prison guard held out a baton and opened a narrow pathway. 'Come on, back off. Give the guy a break.'

'Yeah, like he did for Eileen Randall?'

Geoff tensed his considerable shoulders and clenched his fists.

'Everyone settle down,' the officer warned. 'We don't want anyone getting hurt.'

More cameras fired and someone lunged forwards and yanked at his pocket, almost pulling the trousers down in the process. He didn't even see her face, just a mop of dark shiny hair. Shielding his eyes from a spotlight coming from where they were headed, he called out, 'Someone make them go away.'

'We'll take it from here,' boomed a deep voice. 'Car's waiting.' Geoffrey saw two men in suits holding back the throng. They looked like cops.

'I didn't do anything,' he said.

'This is for your own protection,' the deep voice growled. This man sounded even angrier than the others.

Suddenly, Geoff felt a whack on his back and stumbled, landing with a thud on both knees. A boot quickly caught his right thigh. The tattered knapsack fell just out of reach.

Bodies and legs surged forwards. He could barely breathe.

'Bring back the death penalty!' a woman screamed, and a cheer went out.

Hands dragged him to his feet and forced him, limping, to a white sedan. The door opened from inside and Geoffrey felt a sweaty weight on his crown, shoving him into the back seat. The bag of special belongings followed. The door slammed and he felt safe – like a fish in its bowl. Not safe enough, though, to show his face.

'Stay down, you little fuckwit,' the huge man beside him growled through closed teeth and swiftly clipped Geoff on the right ear. 'And put this on.'

A black cap struck his face.

The front doors slammed and the car screeched away before anyone had time to put on a seatbelt.

'It's our job to take you to a safe house,' the ear-clipper said.

'Are you taking me to see Mum?' Geoff's ear burnt with pain as he put on the baseball cap.

'The press found out where your Mummy Dearest lived and beat the community into a frenzy. Seems no one wants you in their neighbourhood.'

'Is my mum okay?'

'Fellas, Mumma's boy is all upset,' the driver sniped.

Geoffrey plucked at his trousers, provided by the social worker for his first day of freedom. They were far too loose around the waist and thighs. 'Stop making fun of me! Stop it!' He covered his ears, and started humming.

3

The suit in the front passenger seat turned around, red-faced. 'Listen you motherfucker, shut the fuck up!' His nostrils got bigger and a thin top lip disappeared. 'If it were up to me, I'd have let that mob tear you to shreds. So like I said, you little piece of shit, shut the fuck up!'

Geoffrey kept his ears covered but stopped humming. He didn't like these men. They were arseholes.

'Reporters two cars back,' the driver announced. 'White van and a blue hatchback. Hang on.'

The car braked at an amber light then sped through it, turning with a skid into a side street. Geoffrey sat in silence as the car weaved through traffic, like something out of a TV cop show. He didn't recognise this area with tall buildings and people everywhere. It was nothing like the old home in Fisherman's Bay. No sand, no water and no trees. *This place sucks.*

He pulled a cigarette from his shirt pocket and fumbled for the lighter.

'Not in here, you don't.' The hand next to him snatched and crushed the last of Geoffrey's nicotine supply. 'Looks like we lost them,' the man added, peering out the back.

The car felt hot and stuffy, like solitary confinement, but Geoff didn't dare open the window. He thought about his mother. She hadn't made the trip to visit last week. She'd said she was

4

getting things ready. He began to grind his thumb along the palm of his other hand, over and over again.

He wasn't supposed to get out until tomorrow, but this afternoon an officer had ordered him to get his things and see the social worker. No one ever explained why. He didn't even get to say goodbye to his friends, the blokes who'd kept an eye out for him for so long. His thumb moved faster and deeper. Who were all those people outside the prison and why were they all so angry? It was just like in Fisherman's Bay before he went to jail, only he had known most of them back then.

After a long time, the car slowed outside a row of weatherboard houses. They drove past then did a U-turn and parked in the driveway of a grey house with a dead lawn at the front. A lady with streaky brown hair in a long ponytail came out and opened the car door.

'Hello, Geoffrey, I'm June Bonython, a friend of your mum's. Best not be seen hanging around out here too long.'

The woman sounded kind – nothing like the dickhead 'pigs'.

'She's waiting inside.'

Geoffrey clutched his canvas knapsack and scrambled out of the car. Both legs cramped but he couldn't wait to get away from his captors. The woman put her hand gently on his back and looked around as they went inside. She made him a bit nervous.

The pair entered, and to Geoff's relief he saw his mum stand up, straighten out her crisp floral apron and walk slowly towards him. She looked old, really old, and shuffled more than before. Different from how she did when she came to visit. But, he thought, she usually sat down in the prison courtyard and didn't leave until he'd been taken back to the unit.

He didn't know what to say so he removed his cap, stepped forwards and wrapped his arms around her shoulders. Lillian's arms remained rigid by her side.

'I'll pop the kettle on, then,' she said, breaking the embrace with a pat on Geoffrey's arm. 'And you'll be growing that hair right back.'

Out of the kitchen stepped Nick Hudson, Lillian's brother's son. With a giant grin, he made up for his aunt's coldness.

'Welcome home, mate!' Two muscled arms grabbed the newcomer, slapping his sides with considerable force. 'You've been working out a fair bit by the looks of it. Check out those lats!'

Geoff hugged his favourite cousin and hung on tightly.

'I'd have put up balloons but I ran out of time,' Nick said, letting go. 'You still like balloons, don't you, Geoff?'

Geoffrey nodded, unsure whether anyone would make fun of him if he admitted it. So he chose the moment to announce, 'They call me Sunny.'

Everyone stayed quiet, as if something were going to happen. Geoffrey replaced the cap and studied the floral carpet, worn thin to brown strands in front of the lounge. He always noticed floors. They were more interesting than lots of people, and no one bothered him whenever he looked down. Not watching had saved his life at least once in jail.

Miss Bonython smiled. 'How about a tour of the place? I'll show you where everything is. We had to organise alternative accommodation at short notice, once the press found out where you'd be living. At least here the toilet and bathroom are separate. Nice and close to your bedroom.'

From the corridor, the sight of a bright blue toilet seat made him chuckle. The towel next to the yellowish hand-basin had frilly lace on it.

'Where's the paper towels?'

'What do you mean?' his mother asked from behind the procession.

'To wipe my hands on. I always use paper towels.'

'We use proper towels here, Geoffrey.'

'I always use paper.' He began to rub a thumb along his palm. 'I *always* use paper.'

Miss Bonython touched his back. 'No problem, Sunny, we'll get some for you.'

In the next room, a coloured quilt lay on an old-fashioned wooden bed. In between two shelves at

7

the head was a panel of white glass with a switch in front.

Geoff reached over and clicked the light on and off, on and off. A big wooden wardrobe covered part of a brown stain on the carpet. The whole space was huge, but the best thing had to be the window. It had a view of the neighbours' paling fence. Even better, it was open, with no bars. Fresh air and the sound of children playing could get through. He hoped there were kids next door.

'What do you reckon?' Nick slapped him on the back again. 'Once you put your own stuff in, it'll feel more like home.'

Geoffrey swallowed. 'It's good.'

The tour finished with Nick's bedroom. On the other side of the corridor was a pink room. He knew better than to go in there. His mother would never allow it. Besides, the curtains were all closed on the front side of the house and it smelt musty. It had that old-people smell that reminded him of Grandma – before she got sick and died.

'Smoke?' Nick pulled out a brand-new pack and tipped out two cigarettes. Using one match, he lit the first, then handed the second to his cousin.

After bumming the light, Geoffrey inhaled deeply and blew a series of smoke rings through his mouth.

The kettle boiled and June Bonython excused herself to help with the tea.

8

'So where's Brown-Eye?' Geoff asked.

'Geez,' Nick said, 'he died years ago.'

'No one told me.' Geoff took a long drag. 'He was like your shadow.'

'In a way, he still is.' Nick laughed heartily. 'Had the ugly mongrel stuffed for posterity.'

'Right,' was all Geoffrey could think of to say, and he stared back down at the floor.

'Hey.' Nick clapped and flicked the hair from his eyes. 'Got a surprise for you, in the backyard. Want to see?'

'Sure.'

They passed the inside laundry and opened a screen door that led to a small grassed yard. Attached to the clothesline, a golden labrador puppy strained at his lead.

'Meet Caesar,' Nick announced. 'He's all yours.'

Geoffrey turned around to see Miss Bonython arrive with two full cups of tea.

'Is he shitting me?'

'No,' she said, smiling. 'This is your pup. Donated by a charity that helps people adjust to life outside prison.'

Geoffrey squatted down and received a face-licking. For his trouble, Caesar got a rough pat and a roll in the dirt.

From around the side gate, two of the men in suits reappeared and approached Miss Bony-thon. Geoffrey quickly retreated towards the back door.

The one with flared nostrils spoke. 'No sign of trouble. We're off.'

The kind woman put her cup down on the back step and followed him out. 'Isn't anyone staying in case the press finds the family? You know what they're like, with all the publicity about the release.'

'Listen, lady, I've got a kid the same age as the one that bastard raped and hacked to death.'

'Detective,' she said, 'he served his time, twenty years in fact, and by law has earned his freedom.'

'Earned?' He stood with his face over Miss Bonython's. 'That prick isn't cured of anything. And the reason he served the whole damn sentence is 'cause he showed no remorse. He didn't earn parole and doesn't deserve anything from me. Besides, murdering paedophiles don't rehabilitate. They just go on to rape and kill again. If you've got kids, you'd better lock your doors and windows.'

The woman refused to back down.

'Like I said, he's done his time. And so has his mother, being forced to leave her home all those years ago and being driven away when anyone discovers who her son is.'

'Our job is to protect the community, not nursemaid pervert child-killers.'

June Bonython put both hands on her hips, but still looked small compared to Bully-Boy.

'Detective, I'm afraid you're missing the point.

10

Whether you like it or not, the judicial system released Geoffrey Willard back into our community. That makes him someone you are obliged to serve *and* protect.'

2

Dr Anya Crichton detested work-related functions, especially ones that raised money and profiles. Milling around making small talk with people you barely knew – what worse way could you waste an evening? She silently cursed the 'social' committees who deemed it part of every job to mix with colleagues on pseudo-social occasions. They should cut out the pretence and just leave a jar in the office for donations.

If she were being completely honest, the real reason she disliked these functions was that they made her feel completely inadequate. Just like she did when she picked up Ben, her four-year-old son, from preschool, and had to chat to the other mothers. Giving birth didn't automatically bond you with every other mother, a fact few women seemed to appreciate.

She also had to admit that being seen by colleagues was good public relations for her private consulting business. And it never hurt to stay in touch with the politics of forensic pathology as much as the knowledge base.

Glancing around her side of the room, she

wondered what she could chat about with someone who played golf, attended overseas conferences and whose children left home years ago. Unfortunately, that covered most of the people there.

After an acrimonious divorce, seeing her son every second weekend meant that overseas trips were out of the question unless paid for by a client. She wasn't going to rely on that ever happening. Having left the public pathology system, she no longer had the security of sick leave, paid holidays or study leave. And definitely no access to conference funds. She was saving every spare dollar to challenge her former husband for shared custody of their only child. Private forensic medicine was nowhere near as lucrative as she had hoped.

The other side of the foyer comprised the usual advocates for victims of crime. A local politician, social workers, psychologists and families who had been devastated by crime all stood uncomfortably in a group herded together by Bob Reynolds. Bob had campaigned for victim recognition for over twenty-five years and was widely acknowledged as an expert in sentencing law. He was also Anya's father.

She sipped her Verdelho and played with the condensation on the glass, glancing around the room for an ally. The deputy coroner had just legalised his second, or maybe third, marriage. Secretaries fawned over the new wife's bauble as the men exchanged not-so-humorous anecdotes and laughed louder than the jokes deserved.

Forced to manoeuvre past a raucous raconteur, she relaxed when she spied Peter Latham, her mentor and friend. Headed for sanctuary, she slowed as she noticed that Peter was involved in what looked like a serious and very intense conversation with another pathologist, Alf Carney. The current directors of the state's leading forensic centres stood with their heads close together. Aware that Peter Latham had known Carney a long time, Anya was still surprised to see them so involved in such a private discussion.

She didn't notice her secretary sidle up.

'Sorry I'm late. The phones went crazy just as I was about to lock up.' Elaine Morton pulled a compact from her bag and checked her face. Her newly permed and set hair smelt like ammonia. 'Nothing that can't wait. How do I look?' She preened odd strands from her forehead. 'Oh, and Dan Brody wants you to call him tomorrow.'

'Fine. You look fine.' Anya couldn't avoid noticing the musk perfume, a sure sign that Elaine had smoked on the way. 'What did he want?'

Elaine licked her teeth and grinned. 'Your opinion on some case he's involved with.'

Anya took a breath. She hadn't spoken to the high-profile defence barrister for months. The previous year he had been the only one sending her work, which had kept her business afloat and meant she could pay alimony to her ex-husband

14

while paying off the mortgage on her home and office. Then her world had almost crumbled when Kate Farrer, a homicide detective and close friend, was kidnapped and both their lives were threatened.

After that, Kate had gone on long-service leave and Dan had lost touch. Anya's professional name had been poison for a while, with whispers that lawyers feared her forensic evidence would be tainted because of media interest in her past. Luckily, a job as acting director at a sexual-assault unit meant that she was at least able to maintain her income and slowly rebuild her reputation.

By the time cases she was now involved with came to trial, there would be no doubt that she was still one of the most qualified and experienced forensic physicians in the country. No court could tarnish that, or so Anya hoped.

'Looks like Brody's grown up and come to his senses.' Elaine snapped closed the compact mirror. She'd spotted Peter Latham and headed straight over. A middle-aged woman on the prowl had no qualms interrupting secret men's business, Anya thought. She watched with anticipation as to how Peter would handle the situation. Married more to his work than his wife, she'd never seen him flirt until he had met Elaine. As innocent as it seemed, Elaine had developed an almost adolescent interest in any meeting Peter was likely to attend, and the new hairdo was obviously for his benefit.

Anya thought about what her secretary had said about Brody. If she were honest, she missed the banter and arguments about ethics versus the law. The last time she saw him he had brought champagne. Instead of accepting his dinner invitation, Anya had rushed off to see Ben and her ex-husband. Dan hadn't rung her about work – or anything else – since.

The chief coroner, Morgan Tully, excused herself from a zealous police sergeant and lifted a hand to Anya. In her late forties, she could accessorise classic suits with a scarf or necklace and look like she'd been dressed for a fashion magazine. The tastefully cropped silver hair drew attention straight to Morgan's large green made-up eyes.

'Do you find these things as boring as I do? The old boys' network in full swing?'

Anya mused, 'Agony would be a better description.'

A master of discretion, Morgan Tully spoke softly. 'I'm glad you came tonight. I wanted to see how you were. The fiasco in the papers a while back about you and your family was appalling.' Laying a hand on Anya's shoulder, she lowered her voice further. 'I tried to call you to offer support, but your secretary said you'd taken some time off.'

The weekend of Kate Farrer's kidnapping, a hatchet-style article in the country's biggest-selling newspaper had implied that Anya had helped her husband escape a murder charge in England. The journalist even suggested that Anya might have been involved in the abduction of her sister, who disappeared at the age of three. At the time, Anya was a mere five years old. The savagery of the article almost cost her access to her own child.

It had taken a lot of time and effort since then to convince her ex-husband that her work would no longer compromise their son.

'Couldn't imagine any sane lawyer employing me as an expert witness, so I spent some time with my son down on the south coast.' Anya sipped her wine. 'Turns out, I was right.'

'The article was outrageous and we all knew it. Just like all supposed scandals, everyone forgot about it when we found out about another politician who got caught with his mistress milking taxpayer funds.' Morgan lifted a mineral water from a passing waiter's tray. 'I've always had a lot of respect for your work, you know. So much so, I wanted to talk to you about a rather sensitive matter.' She motioned towards a leather lounge adjacent to a large indoor plant just inside the entrance. It was the most privacy anyone could expect in a crowded foyer.

The pair sat down and Morgan Tully began.

'I would appreciate your help on what really could be a political time-bomb. It's come to my attention that one of your colleagues has made some, shall we say, controversial decisions, and I'd like you to review some of the cases. I don't know if I'm over-reaching with my lack of expertise in your field, but I have questions about some of his findings that perhaps you could answer.'

Anya nodded. 'How many cases are we talking about?'

The chief coroner frowned. 'I'm not really sure. I'd like you to look at a dozen to start with.' She poured the mineral water into the wilting pot plant. 'I don't want this to look like a witch-hunt, which is why I would like it to stay just between us for now. And I don't expect this to be pro bono.'

Anya knew she could use the extra income. Twelve case-reports were the equivalent of about three weeks' work. 'Fine, but why me? Why not someone like Peter Latham?'

Morgan looked around, presumably to ensure no one was eavesdropping. 'For a couple of reasons. You're the only fully independent forensic pathologist in the state, so you're removed from the locker-room talk within the departments. And if we're being honest, because you're a woman.'

She seemed to anticipate Anya's offence at that comment. 'This isn't an affirmative-action thing. I thought about Peter, but unfortunately he's part of the problem.'

Anya couldn't believe what the coroner was saying. 'I know Peter *and* his work. He's above any kind of reproach – professionally and personally. Did you know he is my son's godfather?'

Shifting to stand, she added, 'I won't help you undermine him.'

Running a finger around the rim of her empty glass, Morgan smiled. 'Don't worry, I wouldn't put you in that position. I agree with you. It's not Peter I'm investigating, it's his mate over there, Alf Carney.'

Morgan perused the room and rose. 'Can I rely on you and your discretion?'

Investigating a colleague was never going to make her popular, but getting the coroner offside would be the worse career move. Anya nodded. 'Courier the files to my office and I'll let you know what I think.'

Morgan's eyes widened. She gave a half-smile then turned and embraced an elderly man who seemed more than willing to escort her in to dinner.

Never a fan of Alf Carney, who had deliberately tried to block her accessing vital information for a potential homicide case, Anya watched him finish his conversation with Peter Latham and make a direct line for the exit. She wondered what he had done to warrant a clandestine investigation.

Anya hoped that, just maybe, Morgan's concerns about Carney's work were unfounded. Becoming a 'whistle-blower' was the last thing Anya needed.

3

Louise Richardson sat on the blue lounge, body trembling. Mary Singer, the counsellor on duty, had draped a cotton rug around the woman's shoulders and locked the door leading to the rest of the sexual-assault unit. Anya knocked and waited. Mary stepped outside to speak in private.

'She's been assaulted with a knife as she left work and headed for her car. Thankfully, the wounds are superficial, but she's pretty traumatised.'

Anya pulled an elastic band from her wrist and swept her uncombed hair into a ponytail. 'Did he threaten to kill her if she called the police?'

Mary nodded. 'Took her credit cards and told her he'd be watching and would come back if she told anyone.' She glanced over her half-glasses. 'You look tired.'

'I was asleep on the lounge when you called.' Troubled by the prospect of investigating Alf Carney, Anya hadn't felt like going to bed when she arrived home after speaking to Morgan Tully. She had begun watching a movie and dozed off before the ending. Anya took a deep breath and braced herself. This examination could take hours.

Louise Richardson barely acknowledged the two women entering the room. She hugged the rug and trembled.

'Are you cold?' Mary asked.

'No,' she muttered, 'I just can't stop shivering.'

'That's pretty normal at this stage. It'll pass in a little while.' Anya sat on the coffee table. 'I'm Doctor Anya Crichton. I've come to see if you're okay, and to make sure you're safe.'

'How can I be safe after what he did to me?' Louise grimaced and pulled the rug tighter.

'You are safe here. No one can get in, we've locked the door from the inside.'

'What about my husband?'

Mary sat on one of the chairs in front of the coffee table. 'I've spoken to him and he's on his way. You can see him when he gets here if you'd like, or after we check you out. Whatever you'd prefer.'

'I'm not sure.' Tears welled in her eyes. 'I don't want him to see me like this.'

Anya moved next to Louise, careful not to disrupt the blue-backed waterproof sheet beneath. 'It's okay, we can get you a bit more presentable. You're in control here, even if you may not feel like it right now. No one is going to make you do anything. You have choices and we're here to let you know what they are.'

The counsellor handed Anya a large yellow envelope from which she pulled a white booklet.

21

'Thanks.' She lowered her head into Louise's field of vision. 'First thing you should know is that I don't work for the police. I'm independent and my duty of care is to you. That means what happens here today is confidential and doesn't leave this room if that's what you want.'

Mary Singer nodded agreement.

Louise Richardson sat back, hands still trembling. 'Can I have a drink of water, please?'

'If you don't mind, we should probably go through a few things first. They might be important later on. After that you can have a drink. There are, if you like, two separate parts to what I do if you consent to an examination. The first is to check you out medically, to make sure you'll be all right physically. The second part is that I can collect physical evidence that the man who did this might have left, while I examine you. I'll only do this if you agree, and you have the choice later as to whether or not that evidence is handed over to the police for an investigation.'

'I don't know. I can't think straight right now.' Louise began to cry.

Anya looked at Mary. This woman needed a little time, but the sooner they examined her, the better the chances of getting effective specimens.

'What I should say, though, is that if we are going to collect forensic evidence that could be used to catch or convict this man, we'll need to do it now, before some of that evidence disappears. Even before you have a drink.'

'I just want a sip of water. My mouth is so dry.'

'That's partly your body going into survival mode, and the shock of the whole thing.' Anya touched the woman's elbow, very gently, careful not to invade her space right now. 'If this man bit your lip, made you perform oral sex, or even kissed you, there could be vital evidence in your mouth.' She tilted her head and spoke more quietly. 'Did he do any of those things?'

Louise closed her eyes and more tears fell. 'He did everything.' With a startle, she stood up and examined the red gush on the blue sheet. 'Oh, God, I'm bleeding.'

'When was your last period?' Anya began to take notes.

'When we went to the Blue Mountains, a couple of weeks ago.' Louise Richardson's face became pale. 'God, I'm not on any contraception. We've been trying to get pregnant.'

Sperm lasted longer in the vagina for the first two weeks of a woman's cycle, and that meant increased risk of pregnancy. Anya wrote the regimen for the morning-after pill in the treatment section.

'We can give you some medication that minimises the risk. Do you know if he used a condom?'

'I don't know. I couldn't see what he did, just felt how much it hurt. How could I not know?'

It wasn't uncommon for women not to know what their assailant had done. In a fight for survival, they had little or no chance of seeing

23

what the attacker did or whether he used a condom. The smarter ones used a condom then took it with them.

'That's pretty common too,' Anya reassured. 'I think it's important that I look at where the bleeding might be coming from and how severe it is – that is, if you'll let me.'

Louise wiped her eyes with a tissue from the coffee table and began to talk – although not directly at either of the other women in the room. 'Tim was in Berrima. He's an art assessor for Christie's and got a call about a Whitely self-portrait, one where he used his own hair. Tim was so excited, he wanted to have breakfast with the owner first thing this morning . . . that's why he stayed the night.

'I was about to close up when a family came in with a script. The little girl was in pain with an ear infection and needed antibiotics. The pharmacy assistant and I normally leave together, but there didn't seem any point in her staying. She's got kids to get home to.'

Mary nodded sympathetically. She was the best SA counsellor Anya had ever met, always knowing exactly when to speak and when to listen.

'I park in the vacant lot opposite the hospital. I was about to get in the car when he grabbed me from behind.'

Anya glanced at bruises on Louise's knuckles – evidence she'd fought back and might have captured some of the offender's DNA.

A large bruise extended from her left eye to her cheek. On the same side, both lips were swollen and blackish-blue. A straight line of blood ran downwards from her jugular vein, and disappeared towards the nape of her neck.

She pulled a strand of brown hair behind one ear. 'He said he had a knife and would cut my throat if I didn't do what he wanted.'

Louise paused, snuffled and stared at the ceiling. 'He raped me, every way he could. I tried to fight him, but he was just too strong. He did things I don't even do with my husband.'

Mary interjected. 'There was nothing you could have done. In fact, fighting more may have got you killed.'

Louise Richardson stared at the coffee table again. 'I thought he'd finished. Then he dragged me across the gravel with the knife stuck at my throat. I was so scared. All I could think about was my husband and how he'd cope if I died.' She put more hair behind her ear. 'While he held me down, I couldn't see. He said he knew where I lived and how he'd kill me if I told anyone or went to the police. Then he stuck the knife into my throat and said, "If you can't be hurt, you can't be loved." That's when he took off his gloves . . . and . . . raped me all over again.'

Anya gently patted Louise's elbow. 'Before I can examine you, I need your written permission. Even if we collect evidence, you still have time to decide whether or not you want it released to the police.'

Louise dropped the rug behind her shoulders and revealed a dirt-stained white blouse and navy skirt. Her jaw tightened and she sat up straighter, as though garnering strength.

'All right, I'll sign, but I need time to think about whether I want the police to know.'

4

Geoffrey Willard sat at the table in his donated clothes, waiting for his breakfast. Six a.m. came and went and the rumbling in his stomach got louder. Still, he stayed at the battered wooden table and waited for someone to tell him what to do. An hour later, his mother appeared in the kitchen in a pale blue dressing gown.

'Good morning,' she said, and brushed his forehead with her lips.

'I'm hungry,' he said, annoyed, 'and thirsty.'

'Oh, of course you are,' Mrs Willard said. 'I didn't expect you to cook something for yourself.'

Her youngest son stood and pushed the chair back. 'I'll be watching TV.'

She put the already full kettle on the stove. Each evening, without exception, she put water into a jug in the fridge and the stainless-steel kettle. That way, if the pipes froze overnight, there would always be a cuppa in the morning. She thought about the social worker's predictions. This wasn't going to be easy, but no one knew how difficult it would be for her, and always had been. Life was cruel, delivering her a pathetic spineless husband

and a deviant child. If it hadn't been for the pregnancy she would never have married Geoffrey's father. He could never cope with a child who was different and left the first chance he got.

Geoffrey had always been different, and no amount of discipline stopped him behaving that way. She would never know what had happened to him in prison, or why he did that vile thing to end up there. Her son always was and always would be evil. There was no other explanation.

And now, after twenty years of respite, he was here again, living with her.

Locating a frying pan in a cupboard beneath the oven, she opened a carton of eggs then went to the fridge for some butter. Suddenly, she became aware that she only knew what Geoff liked as an eighteen-year-old boy. Not a man – as he now was, with stubble for hair and lines etched on his long, angular face. Her child was almost forty – a middle-aged man. At least he still had his pretty blue eyes – a blessing and a curse.

The thought of all those years missing, wasted, brought an ache to her chest. How do you begin to get them back? If only she'd had a normal child.

Now she had to make the most of things, starting with bacon and eggs. She cracked the eggs into the pan as the kettle whistled. Making a pot of tea seemed the only sensible thing to do. She began to wonder whether Geoffrey still drank tea. A quick search through the cupboard made her realise that she hadn't put coffee on the shopping list for the social worker. What sort of a mother didn't know what her own child drank? She tried to block out the guilt.

Never mind, she'd make do, just like she always did. And, Lord knows, it had never been easy. She grabbed a spatula from the second drawer and turned over the eggs. She'd make sure he ate something, so she put two pieces of bread, one white, one brown, in the toaster.

Geoffrey reappeared and sniffed the air, without saying a word.

'What would you like to do today? There must be so many things you've been wanting to do and see?'

'I want the TV in my room.'

Lillian Willard quietly buttered the toast and put the eggs on top. Her son didn't thank her. Instead, he shovelled food into his mouth, as though he hadn't eaten for days. She studied his face – how hard it seemed. His teeth had yellowed and one in the back had either rotted or been knocked out. She hadn't dared ask how or why he had lost it.

'We can get a small one for there, if you like. Maybe with some of the money you saved. Televisions are a lot cheaper now than they used to be.'

Geoffrey nodded.

'I thought we could go to the main street shops and get you some clothes one day this week. The bus takes you right there. But we don't have to go today if you don't want. You might like some time just getting used to the place. At least, that's what June said.'

'All right,' he replied through a mouthful of egg.

'I'll just clean up and get dressed, then.' Lillian checked her watch. 'If you decide you want to go, we should wait until peak hour's finished. That way we'll have less chance of drawing attention to ourselves.'

'Can I watch TV now?'

Before waiting for an answer, Geoffrey hurried out of the kitchen, bumping into Nick in the corridor. His cousin carried a basket of dirty washing.

'I'm just doing a load. Anything you'd like washed?'

'Looks like you've already got it all.' Lillian put the frying pan in the sink and dried her hands on her apron. 'It's a godsend having you here after so long.'

The older woman had been relieved when Nick had agreed to move in to keep an eye on Geoffrey. Lillian knew she was no physical match if her son was violent, and Nick would not hesitate to keep Geoffrey in line. With a divorce behind him, her nephew was happy to have free rent for as long as he was needed.

'We modern men are all like this. Just have to train Geoff up a bit and you'll be laughing.'

Childish giggling emanated from the lounge room.

'Speaking of laughing, what is it your cousin's watching?'

'Sounds like *Scooby-Doo*.'

Lillian ventured into the lounge room and found her son lying across the recliner chair with a pile of junk mail on the floor. He'd torn out the underwear sections from the Kmart catalogue and lay snickering at the scantily dressed models.

Less than twenty-four hours out of prison and her son was ogling innocent young women. Maybe prison had made him worse.

The thought made her heart palpitate.

5

Exhausted after the late-night rape examination, Anya had to be at court by ten o'clock. This time a young woman needed all the support Anya could muster.

'It's almost over,' she said, squeezing the teenage girl's hand. 'You've come so far. I know it's not easy, but for your own sake you have to try to keep it together just a bit longer.' Anya stroked the dry, flaking skin, a barometer of the young woman's level of stress. She'd never seen dermatitis that bad.

'I think I'm going to be sick,' Naomi said, releasing Anya's hand before running to the court toilets. Her mother quickly followed.

Anya could see that the prosecutor, Jennifer Beck, seemed distracted when talking to her assistant counsel. Jennifer excused herself from the conversation and walked the few feet across the gravel drive to Anya.

'We can't afford for her to lose it now.' She tugged at her bar jacket. 'Any hysterics she shows today will just make her look unstable and give the defence the gift they're after.'

Anya sensed that the usually sympathetic prosecutor was feeling the pressure. Today's closing argument had to convince the jury that the men on trial had deliberately drugged and raped the young woman.

'She hasn't got over the cross-examination and knows it doesn't look good for a conviction.' Anya lowered her voice. 'What do you think?'

'If we had more physical evidence this case wouldn't have been a farce. I'm recommending a review of evidence collection procedures in all SA units. You have to give us more evidence, or we're telling the community it's easier to get away with sexual assault than shoplifting.'

Anya sighed inwardly. This wasn't the time or place to debate the introduction of more invasive investigations for assault victims.

Jennifer Beck obviously disagreed.

'If you doctors hadn't pushed so hard to minimise evidence collection—'

'The invasiveness of examinations is what we fought hard to reduce, for the victims' good.'

'What you've done is weakened our ability to present solid, irrefutable evidence. Sexual assault cases are tough to get up even with that evidence. Take it away and you hog-tie us, but still expect a good result.'

As acting head of the Western Regional Sexual Assault Service, Anya Crichton had discovered that so often in the politics of policy, administrators, police and lawyers lost sight of the purpose of medical examinations after an assault. It was to provide the best possible medical care, not treat victims as a human crime scene and little more than a forensic reservoir. Even so, she appreciated the prosecutor's point.

'We'll try to calm Naomi down before she goes back in,' Anya said. It was the best she could do.

Anya had first met the traumatised nineteen-year-old the morning after her school's farewell dance. Naomi had awoken naked in a strange hotel room with two boys from her class. She told a typical story of a date rape: having a drink or two then feeling woozy and losing a large block of time. All she knew was that she wouldn't have voluntarily gone to a hotel room, or had sex with the boys.

'At least you've got the carpet burn to her nose. It's not easy doing that to yourself.'

'Pity she scrubbed herself raw in the shower and destroyed anything more tangible,' Jennifer answered, adjusting her wig and bar jacket. The fidgeting looked more like a nervous gesture than essential grooming.

Anya felt very sorry for the young victim but knew the chances of a conviction were slim, despite examination supporting the girl's story. A carpet burn to her nose and top lip, and finger-mark-sized bruises on her upper arms, were consistent with her being dragged along the floor to the bed while unconscious.

Her mother had found Naomi at home, scouring her bleeding skin with steel wool, and immediately brought her in to the sexual-assault unit.

Anya was quick enough to contact the hotel to secure the room before it was cleaned. Crime scene discovered semen on the sheets and DNA pointed to one of the boys in the room. This turned out to be the most damning evidence. Mysteriously, the sheet had disappeared from the evidence room during the trial. Whether it was deliberate or through sheer incompetence, the prosecution's case had been irrevocably damaged.

The wig and jacket managed another readjustment as Jennifer watched people move towards the courtroom. 'I'd better go in.'

The only evidence the prosecution had was a urine sample that showed the presence of Rohypnol, a powerful amnesic benzodiazepine.

'Good luck,' Anya said, more to herself, at the prospect of calming Naomi.

The young woman walked back from the toilets, wiping her face with a tissue. Her mother held a protective arm around Naomi's shoulders. Anya thought about Louise Richardson and others like her who had experienced every moment of their assault, but felt particularly sad about Naomi's situation. Not knowing what happened that night was in some ways even more traumatic. With the effects of the benzodiazepine, it was as though her mind was like a video camera without the record button. No memory had been laid down to recover, no matter how hard she tried. All that the

35

girl had was her imagination and anxieties, which could be more frightening than the attack.

'Will you please sit with me just for this?' the girl pleaded.

Anya sighed. 'I'm sorry, but I still need to be seen by the jury as being independent. If I support you in there, they start doubting my evidence. That just hurts your case.' She gently touched Naomi's arm. 'Mary is due any minute. She'll be here for you for as long as you need her.'

The sexual-assault unit's most senior counsellor arrived outside the court puffing, apologised, and led her charge into the courtroom. Jennifer Beck was already at her table when Anya quietly slipped in and took a seat at the back.

Within minutes, Jennifer's closing argument had begun.

As she listened, Anya thought about the humiliation Naomi had endured both in the hotel room and in the multiple statements she'd had to make to police, as well as in the witness box. The young men had hired Veronica Slater, a defence barrister known for being ruthless.

Veronica's cross-examination of victims was like watching a wolf dissecting a lamb. Anya could imagine Naomi faltering with each question. How could she do anything else? She couldn't remember any of the events that night, which is precisely what the perpetrators wanted.

Jennifer Beck concluded the case for the prosecution and sat down.

Veronica Slater stood, a little over five foot tall, in heels that even a supermodel would baulk at.

'The alleged victim thinks something terrible happened to her in that hotel room. Actually, she isn't even sure that's what she thinks. You see, she cannot remember anything about the hotel room or the defendants, whom she danced with at the graduation dance. She can't identify people she thinks attacked her, and the physical evidence doesn't prove she was in any way violated. We've heard about the carpet burns to her nose from Doctor Crichton. This young woman passed out on the floor of the carpeted hotel room. No one disputes that. These two young men, *friends* since childhood,' she emphasised the word, 'helped lift her onto a lounge to be more comfortable. Lifting an unconscious woman who weighs, what, around eighty-five kilograms?' She paused and pointed in Naomi's direction for effect.

Great, Anya thought, the girl's weight was now on trial.

Veronica continued. 'These young men aren't experienced in carrying a drunk woman. So they did the best they could, awkwardly lifting her onto a lounge.' She paused and clasped both hands. 'I don't doubt that Naomi Gallagher is distressed by her own behaviour that night and panicked at the thought of what she might have done. But to save face, she vindictively accused these two young men of a heinous crime. Teenage girls are

37

renowned for their melodramatics and cattiness, but this accusation goes way beyond that.'

Anya watched the predictable palms-up for emphasis. Next there would be counting points on one hand.

'It is malicious, vicious and completely unfounded.' The hands obliged.

Veronica Slater continued with the usual spiel about false accusations being so easy to make, and told the jury they had no choice but to acquit her clients and restore their good names.

That line always amused Anya, given the names of the accused in sexual-assault cases involving minors were not disclosed in the media. Even so, the jurors nodded in agreement.

Anya had heard enough. The files from Dan Brody had been delivered that morning and there were more departmental meetings to attend. Part-time work with a sexual-assault unit really meant full time, only part pay. She stood, followed protocol and nodded at the judge before slipping out the back door.

Naomi's father sat on the step outside, covering his face with large, calloused hands. Anya pretended not to notice his moist, bloodshot eyes when he looked up.

'After everything my little girl's been through, those bastards are gonna get away with it.' He wiped his nose with the back of his hand. 'What sort of justice is that?'

Anya never knew what to say in these situations, no matter how many times she went through it with family members and victims. Undecided whether to stand or sit down with him, she was almost relieved when her pager went off, reminding her of a meeting.

'Tell me this, Doc. What sort of a message does it send those lying, raping pricks? That they can get away with anything? Jesus, are we supposed to thank them because they attacked her when she was unconscious and didn't bash her? Should we be grateful she *can't* remember a bloody thing?' He bowed his head, silenced by the procession of people filing out of the courtroom. The distraught father stood, wiped his hands on his shirt and greeted his family with a forced smile.

There was nothing more Anya could do here. She quietly left, with a sense of foreboding. Judging by Veronica Slater's performance, the boys were about to be acquitted, and Naomi would spend the rest of her life trying to deal with it.

6

After a week of television punctuated by nightly walks with the labrador pup, Lillian Willard persuaded her son to venture out to the shopping centre.

They waited patiently for the bus with a couple of other people, and Geoff kept his head down, hoping not to be noticed. Luckily, no one looked twice at them. The bus wasn't crowded, and his mother chose a seat near the back. He sat behind, just like he had when he was younger and they'd gone to town. After what seemed like hundreds of stops, they got off in the middle of a group of shops.

Geoffrey stared at the traffic buzzing past. It was so much busier than Fisherman's Bay: more cars, more trucks, more people. Horns honked and tyres screeched, just like in the movies. Everything seemed so noisy – much too loud. And the place smelt like diesel. The air stank, nothing like the salty air at Long Bay Jail. His mother led him by the elbow, past a library and a bank with an armed guard outside. Geoffrey flinched when he saw the man and suddenly wanted to be back home.

'He's just here to protect the bank,' his mother said.

A few doors along, they entered one of those church donation places, with clothes, toys and blankets. Behind the counter a pretty girl looked up and smiled at them. Geoffrey stopped and watched. He liked her face. She didn't stare at him or yell, or run away, not like the people outside the prison when he came out. Her long, blonde hair looked soft and he wondered what it smelt like.

'How about this one?' His mother suggested a denim shirt from a long rack of men's clothes.

'All right.' Anything was better than green tracksuits, he thought.

Sorting through another rack, Lillian presented him with a number of pairs of long pants and held them up to his legs. The smiling girl added a couple of black T-shirts to the collection and asked if he wanted to try them on behind a sheet-curtain at the back of the store. Inside, he saw a mirror and stripped to the pair of white Y-fronts his mother had bought. He could hear the pair chatting outside.

'You don't often see a mother and son shopping together,' the pretty blonde declared.

'Yes, well, we thought we'd spend some time together for a change. He's been through a very tough few years.'

'Let me know if I can help,' the shop assistant said.

Geoffrey chose the striped shirt and tucked it

41

into black jeans; a bit baggy in the backside, but the right length. One glance in the mirror and he proudly opened the curtain for approval.

'They'll do, let's try the others,' his mum said.

He wanted her to say how good he looked, but she kept quiet.

The girl smiled again. 'The shirt matches the blue in your eyes,' she said, leaning forwards to catch his gaze. 'They're amazingly blue.'

Lillian flapped about, shoving Geoff back into the changing room. She kept handing clothes over the sheet until he was sick of being a shop dummy.

An hour later, Geoffrey had more clothes than he'd ever owned, in two large paper bags. He handed over sixty dollars and the girl gave him five dollars change. 'We have some hats and baseball caps over there that just came in, if you're interested.'

Geoffrey followed her to a table but was quickly distracted by a pile of comics lying on the floor nearby.

'I love *The Phantom*! Can I look at them?'

'Of course,' she said, blonde hair swishing as she bent over, exposing the tops of her breasts under her shirt. 'I used to love comics when I was a kid, especially the *Archie* ones. You can take the lot for five bucks if you want.'

'Geoffrey, we need to save money for the television, remember?'

'I want the comics, Mum. You always reckon I need to read more.'

He'd handed over the money and collected the pile before his mother could object.

'This is a great shop,' he said, and smiled at the girl. 'I'll come back here again.'

It was the first time Lillian had seen her son smile in years. And it made her wish he'd never been let out of jail.

7

Thank God for screw-top wine bottles, Anya thought, as she poured a glass of Chenin blanc from a bottle she'd opened a few evenings ago. After a day of meetings with the Department of Health, arguing about evidence collection techniques, Anya wanted some peace. Sitting cross-legged on her lounge with a large red pillow supporting her back, she opened the first of the reports Morgan Tully had asked her to review.

This case from 1998 involved the death of a three-month-old girl who was taken to an emergency department after being difficult to rouse in the morning. The mother had been out drinking with girlfriends the night before and left her twenty-four-year-old boyfriend babysitting. The next morning she had noticed vomit stains on the little girl's pillow and tried to wake her. Instead of calling an ambulance, she put the child in the car and drove to the nearest hospital.

The emergency doctor's statement said that he suspected child abuse as soon as he saw bruising on the child's upper arms and back. The child was already in a coma and didn't respond to painful stimuli. She had suffered significant brain damage. A cerebral CT scan confirmed the large intracranial bleed. According to the notes, the child was placed on a ventilator but died before anything could be done to relieve the pressure on her tiny brain.

So far the story sounded like a dozen other cases Anya could remember. Each one indelibly etched on her memory. The boyfriend said that the infant had gone to sleep at her usual time and slept through the night. He hadn't heard any vomiting and had no reason to suspect anything was wrong.

Anya sighed. She'd heard that so many times. Amazing how a carer could have no idea what went on in a house when most parents reacted to the slightest noise where their children were concerned. She turned to the post-mortem report.

Alf Carney had described the gross findings. Multiple bruises ranged from 0.5 cm in width to 3.5 cm. On a tiny body, those bruises were anything but normal. The photographs showed round black bruises on both upper arms, consistent with finger-marks. The largest were at the front of the arms, where thumbs would have dug in if the child were held in an upright position. There was also bruising over the right collarbone and ribs.

On the back were red circular lesions that, although enhanced after death, looked exactly like cigarette-burns. The PM X-ray report showed multiple fractures – clavicle and posterior ribs,

45

and a partially collapsed right lung. Anya closed her eyes and imagined the horror this tiny child had been forced to endure in such a short life. She thought of her own son Benjamin at the same age. He would giggle, babble and smile at everything he saw. And she clearly remembered how much affection he had been given, even from two parents who were emotionally detached from each other.

Anya took a sip of the wine and searched for the mother's statement as to how she explained the wounds and injuries. Apparently, she believed that the lesions on her child's back were eczema, and thought bruising was normal in children.

Unable to conceive how a mother could be in that much denial, the more disturbing thought occurred. The mother may have been a willing partner in torturing her baby, or even the sole abuser.

The post-mortem appeared straightforward, and Carney had documented retinal haemorrhages, small dot-like bleeds at the back of the eye, usually found in shaken-baby syndrome. Microscopic findings were barely commented on, and those in the report were consistent with the effects of severe physical abuse. Notably absent were histology reports on the lung and blood slides, or blood cultures. Apart from that, everything seemed routine and Anya suspected she'd been sent the wrong case to review, until she read Alf Carney's final comments.

46

A swab of the right lung had grown a small amount of E. coli, a common finding at autopsy, thanks to contact with the bench surface; but the pathologist deemed that sepsis and overwhelming infection was present at the time of death.

Cause of death: Intracranial haemorrhage with cerebral oedema, resulting in severe brain-tissue damage. The precipitating factors are:

1) *E. coli pneumonia and sepsis. The endotoxins released by the backteria are the most likely cause of the increased bleeding tendency, which resulted in the skin bruising, retinal haemorrhages and the large intracranial bleed.*

2) *Probable scurvy, from chronic Vitamin C deficiency or an accelerated metabolism of Vitamin C. This would account for the excessive fragility of blood vessels, exacerbating bleeding problems, and the increased tendency for bones to fracture. Metabolism of Vitamin C would have been rapidly increased in the presence of sepsis and intercurrent viral infection. The history of recurrent respiratory infections can be attributed to scurvy, which significantly reduces the effectiveness of the immune system.*

3) *Fractured ribs due to excess force during cardiac massage in the failed resuscitation attempt, irrespective of pre-existing brittle bones.*

In conclusion, the child died from natural causes. The history of recurrent viral infections, bleeding and bone fractures are most likely the effects of chronic Vitamin C deficiency. This death would have been prevented if the emergency doctor had administered large doses of intravenous Vitamin C on the initial presentation.

Anya re-read the conclusion in complete disbelief. Not only did Carney ignore the possibility of child abuse and murder, he accused the treating physician of negligent homicide! He had failed to state that cardiac massage could cause fractures of the front, not the back ribs. There was no comment at all about the suspicious marks on the child's back, and no slides were taken to confirm the pathology. In this case, all the physical evidence pointed to severe physical trauma from child abuse. A statement from Community Services mentioned that the family was under investigation following a complaint from the child's maternal grandmother, who suspected abuse. Another, from a neighbour, claimed that the night before the child died she had heard a male voice screaming at a crying baby.

Based on the pathology report, the police would have been unable to pursue a case of abuse. Anya put the report on the rug and unpacked her laptop. She plugged in the power cord just as the phone rang. Unable to locate the handset, she pressed the microphone on the base station.

'Mummy!'

'Hi, Ben! I've just been thinking about you.'

'Hey, me too.'

'How are you feeling? Yesterday you sounded terrible.'

He took a deep breath to prove the lack of snuffles. 'All better.'

'That's great news. Did you go to preschool?'

'Yeah, but it's a little bit boring.'

Ben rarely talked about preschool over the phone. There was no point asking any more about it.

'Mummy, what are we doing when I come to sleep over?'

'Well, I've been practising a new song on the drums. Maybe we can play it together. And we might go to the Powerhouse Museum again. There's a huge *Star Wars* exhibition.'

'I love *Star Wars*! How did you know?'

'Maybe I just know you.'

There was silence for a moment. Then Ben's voice almost whispered,

'Love you, I miss you.'

'Me too, Speedie. Me too. Love you all the way to forever and back again.'

'And way past there . . . Uh, Dad's calling. It's bath-time.'

'Then you'd better go and get clean. I'll see you tomorrow.'

'Okay. Bye.'

Before hanging up, she waited to hear the click at the other end.

At least her son was over his latest head-cold. Like other preschoolers, he had a constant runny nose, ear-infections and skin rashes that could only be described as 'viral'. Any mother knew that the first years of contact with other children brought an endless string of respiratory and gastric infections. He was owed more swimming lessons than he'd been well enough to attend.

She wondered whether Alf Carney had children. Surely not, she thought, otherwise he would have known that was a normal process in young children, not pathological, and certainly not diagnostic of scurvy.

She picked up the second autopsy report – of another child, an eight-week-old boy, with the same surname as the first. Retinal haemorrhages, bruised chest and forearms; the pattern of injuries was disturbingly similar. This time, Carney concluded even more strongly that the child had died from natural causes, with a familial case of Vitamin C deficiency. After all, Carney had examined the baby's sister, who had died of the same thing a year before. He referred to the previous report as confirmation. Again, the police were unable to act without a PM report that showed abuse or interference.

Anya began to type her report on these first two cases. Two hours later, she had referenced all her comments and felt satisfied that the cases should be reopened, based on the overwhelming evidence of abuse. In developed countries, scurvy was virtually unheard of, except in cases of severe malnutrition associated with abuse. Even milk contained Vitamin C, so small children were extremely unlikely to get this condition, even on a diet lacking fruit and vegetables.

With ten more files to review, Anya glanced at the clock. Too early to sleep and with only reality shows on TV, she decided to find out how many more cases of scurvy Alf Carney had stumbled upon.

In each of the next four cases, microscopic examinations had been minimally performed. In the sixth file, the slides had been provided for an elderly man found drowned on a beach at the south coast. The man had a number of lacerations to the head, which Carney explained as being post-mortem injuries, despite bleeding from the site. Although some head lesions oozed serum, especially in water, despite no blood flowing through a body, a large amount of blood from a wound suggested arteries still pumped blood at the time of the injury. Anya collected the slides of the biopsy of the skin from the laceration site and headed to the front room, her office. For economy, Anya did her private work downstairs in the front rooms of the terrace house and lived upstairs. During work hours, the kitchen, bathroom and lounge room were shared by her secretary. Once inside, she switched on the light and carried her small microscope over to the desk. After focusing the lens, she could make out individual characteristics of hordes of tiny cells fixed to the glass. The skin specimen showed a rim of early inflammatory changes around the wound. Double-checking, she noted the infiltration of neutrophils, part of the body's defence system essential for preventing infection while the wound heals.

For these cells to be around the site, the elderly man had had to be alive when the wounds were inflicted. The injuries could not have been sustained after death, by knocking against rocks near where he was found. The diagnosis of accidental drowning needed to be reviewed in the presence of multiple lacerations to the scalp, and they were unlikely to have been self-inflicted. The death had to be deemed suspicious, and the case reopened.

Anya sat back in her chair, astounded by the conviction with which Carney excluded foul play in the most suspicious cases. The implications were enormous.

Could one pathologist possibly be that incompetent, or did he have his own agenda? If Carney's evidence had stopped murders being investigated, how many killers had escaped prosecution? Like every pathologist, he had worked on thousands of cases over the years. The ramifications for the legal system were enormous. Morgan Tully's 'political time-bomb' was set to go off.

8

Anya arrived early at the unit to catch up on paperwork. She checked the time – seven a.m. Four hours before her meeting with Dan Brody.

Within minutes, Mary knocked on the door with a cup of steaming black coffee.

Anya looked up after smelling the brew. 'What did I do to deserve this so early?'

'Actually, it's what you're about to do. Sorry, but there's a call-out and no one else is on duty yet.'

Anya slumped and accepted the bribe. 'How long before she arrives?'

'She's already here, in room two. It won't take long. She doesn't want the police involved, just wants emergency contraception, and get this, a book list of references so she can read about rape. A real "type A" personality.'

After gulping down the coffee, they entered the counselling room. Anya greeted 'Just Elizabeth', who paced the room.

'Good, you're here. I've got to be at work by eight thirty, so could we please make this quick? I've got someone waiting in the car and a science excursion this morning with sixty kids.'

'I'll do what I can. I'm Doctor Anya Crichton. You asked to see me?'

Mary excused herself and retreated.

'All I want is a script for emergency contraception, whatever that is these days. I can't afford to get pregnant. I'm not on anything at the moment.'

'If you were assaulted overnight, you're probably going to feel pretty sore and uncomfortable at the very least.'

'I'm fine now. He must have seen me through the open window. I was watching a movie and fell asleep on the lounge. I woke up with him on top of me. When he'd finished, he left. That's it.'

The woman continued to pace with her hands in her trouser pockets, shoulders raised, the way a small animal tries to make itself bigger as a form of defence.

'I'm healthy and I understand there isn't any point in screening for infections just yet, so I'll come back when it's time. I don't need anything but the contraception.'

Experience told Anya there was no use pushing a victim who refused to be examined or counselled. She had to respect every decision, not just the ones she agreed with. Elizabeth's behaviour was almost as if she knew her attacker – keen to quickly get on with life and loath to discuss any details. Most of all, it was the way she almost took responsibility by emphasising the 'open' window.

Anya sat at the desk and opened a drawer. She

removed a pill packet and cut four tablets from the sheet. She added this to an envelope containing anti-nauseants. 'Are you allergic to anything?'

'Nothing.'

'This contains written instructions. Take two tablets now along with one of these capsules. The hormones can make you nauseated, which the capsules counteract. In twelve hours, take the rest of the tablets at the same time. Here's my mobile number. If you vomit within a few minutes of taking the tablets, please let me know and I'll arrange more for you.'

'Is that it? I've got to get to work.'

'Elizabeth, you've been through a traumatic experience. I understand you want to get on with your life, but maybe you should take a day off to recover. I can give you a certificate for work. That way we could at least discuss your options.'

'Thanks, but it's not necessary. I'm fine.'

'Can I at least call you later and see how you are on the pills?'

The woman, who looked like she'd run a marathon, rummaged through her bag and retrieved a notepad. Anya noticed she wore a turtleneck jumper despite the warm weather and wondered what injuries were being disguised. Worried that there was more to the assault than Elizabeth admitted, she had to concede that every victim had his or her own coping mechanism. It was their right to choose treatment or refuse it. All she could do was offer to be there if things went even more wrong.

'You're not responsible for what happened.'

'I left the window open.'

Anya handed over the envelope. 'That doesn't make what he did any less of a crime. He forced his way into your home and assaulted you. You did not give him permission or the right to do that. If someone goes through an open door and steals the stereo, it's no less of a theft than if he'd smashed that door to get in.'

'This is where I'll be staying.' Elizabeth scrawled the numbers on the notepad and tore off the lower half of the page, minus the letter-head. 'You can get me after school,' she blurted, and left.

Anya glanced at the piece of paper. On it was written the phone number for her own unit's crisis line. Clearly, Elizabeth – if that was her real name – didn't want to be contacted. She doubted they would ever see the woman again.

9

Anya enjoyed the decor of Dan Brody's chambers. Wall-to-wall books and the smell of leather-bound law tomes gave it an old-fashioned and authoritative feel.

A pot of freshly brewed tea sat on a glass tray on the sideboard – Irish Breakfast by the aroma, her favourite.

Dan returned with a matching jug of milk and bowl of sugar. No food in the room, because that inevitably left crumbs and mess, something the barrister was averse to.

He poured two cups and fumbled with the sugar cubes. For the first time, he seemed uneasy about being with Anya, which made her feel on edge. Pulling a file from her briefcase, she wondered whether his uneasiness was because he felt awkward seeing her, or if it had something to do with his mother's recent death.

He put down the cup and saucer on a coaster within reach.

'Thanks.' Anya handed him the file of the original case notes. 'There's a fair chance the eye-witness who identified him made a mistake.

There is a definite possibility your client didn't expose himself to all of those women. There's nothing on the forensic examination I performed after his arrest to suggest he'd recently had intercourse or ejaculated.'

Dan stirred his cup and picked up a gold fountain pen from its stand. He listened as Anya continued.

'The prosecution could argue that he either didn't ejaculate after exposing himself in the park or that he washed himself before they picked him up. But I can't see how he could have washed himself that thoroughly in a public toilet.'

'Any other possibilities?'

'Swabs don't always pick up the semen or saliva, given the shape of the penis. I can explain how I took the specimen to increase the yield, but they still have the very real possibility that I missed it. Where humans are involved, error is always a possibility.'

'Precisely,' he said, drawing an exclamation mark on the legal pad.

'There's something else about your client that's significant.' Anya sipped her tea and leant back. 'He has what's known as Peyronie's disease. If he supposedly exposed himself to all of those women, someone should have noticed.'

'How would you define that in layman's terms?'

'Simple. He has scar tissue underneath the skin of his penis, which causes it to bend in a sharp curve if he has an erection.'

The lawyer pulled a face, which she ignored.

'If a woman was staring at his erect penis, she may well have noticed.'

'May I ask how you know, if he didn't have an erection when you saw him?' He paused. 'Please tell me he didn't—'

'Dan, he *told* me after I declined to see his "party trick". Not many men would boast about something that made them the butt of jokes in the locker room. Besides, I didn't just take his word for it. I couldn't feel much scar tissue when I examined him so interviewed some of his team-mates who admitted they liked to masturbate in the showers after a winning game. From what they described, he definitely has Peyronie's disease.'

'Anya, your conscientiousness knows no bounds.' He raised an eyebrow, and doodled more small boxes, something he did when digesting information.

'Okay, so we know he has it. What sort of issues could arise out of your report?'

'Apart from the deviant behaviour in the showers?'

Dan closed his eyes. 'Even the innocent ones don't make it easy.'

'I have to say women may not be too sympathetic to a group of muscle-bound sportsmen who masturbate together, boast about each other's sexual conquests and even "share" women. They thrive in a culture of misogyny and lack the insight to see it's not acceptable to anyone else.'

Brody frowned. 'Then I have to find inconsistencies in the eye-witness's testimony. I'll work on it.' Brody seemed preoccupied, not his normal cocky, aggressive self.

'Is that everything?' Anya stood to leave, keen to escape the awkwardness.

'Actually . . .' He rose and pushed the leather chair back. 'Fancy a walk? I can buy us lunch.'

'All right.' Anya collected her jacket and Dan held it for her to get into.

In the foyer, Dan grabbed an umbrella and they headed through a revolving glass door into Castlereagh Street. A gust of papers circled ahead of them. Anya buttoned up her jacket. Dan didn't seem to notice the cold through his shirt.

'I'd like to talk to you about something sensitive.'

She tried to deflect the conversation with humour. 'I think you'd already know if you had Peyronie's.'

Dan remained stony-faced.

They walked for a while and crossed at the lights into the Pitt Street Mall. Descending the escalators to a food hall, they found an empty plastic table and deposited the umbrella.

'Have a seat. How about a beef kebab?'

'Chicken—' Although the possibility of food-poisoning from under-heated chicken didn't appeal. 'On second thoughts, beef sounds good, thanks.'

Brody quickly returned with two doner kebabs and four serviettes. Anya waited until he'd finished wiping both chairs to sit.

'I meant to say sorry about your mother. She must have been an amazing woman. I mean, with all her accomplishments.'

He studied the foil wrapping. 'In spite of her art and writing, she was very private. She was one of the kindest, most intelligent people I've ever known, and had one of the driest wits as well. Now that I think of it, she was actually a lot like you.'

Anya had a mouthful of beef and stopped chewing. She swallowed, unsure how she felt about being compared to Dan's mother.

'How is your father handling it?' Muzak filled the food hall but had competition from crying children and frustrated parents.

'It's hard to tell. He seems all right in the nursing home, but finds it difficult to communicate. We never really had heart-to-hearts even when he could speak. How are you and your son going?'

'Ben is enjoying preschool, I think. I guess he feels a bit confused sometimes.'

Dan wiped his mouth. 'That's understandable, though.'

'In some ways, with both parents apart. Not many four-year-olds have two homes. With me he likes books and craft, but with his father he kicks a ball and does all kinds of sports. It's like he divides himself into two separate people.'

61

'Weren't you thinking about starting him early at school?'

'Right now, Ben needs to mix with his peers and learn to socialise. Being a boy and having fun is what's most important at the moment. Academic stuff can always wait, but missing out on social skills now could cripple him for life.' Anya took another bite, suddenly self-conscious. 'It's about the only thing Martin and I agree on.'

Dan cleared his throat. 'Does that mean you two are getting on?'

'Nothing's changed. He's still looking for the right job, whatever that is, and keen on having a great life. As far as he's concerned, I am antisocial, which is why I lock windows and deadlock doors. He'd rather let anyone and everything in, no matter how mangy.'

'Sounds like my ex,' Dan laughed. 'Yin and yang.'

There had been a time last year when Anya could have fallen for Dan Brody. He had brought that bottle of champagne to her home and asked her out to dinner, which had never eventuated. Since then, this was their first personal conversation. It felt strange, but good at the same time.

A loudspeaker announced a lost two-year-old boy wearing a Spiderman shirt and matching pants.

Anya's heart raced.

The announcer then said that the child was

located at the information booth and asked the mother to collect him there.

The pair sat quietly finishing their lunch when Dan ventured, 'Any word about your sister?'

For some reason, Anya didn't recoil from the question. 'After all the publicity last year, a psychic contacted Dad, saying he knew where Miriam was buried, but it was another crank. After thirty years, we don't really expect to ever find out what happened to her, but you still live in some sort of hope. You can't help it, I suppose.'

'Losing my mother to breast cancer was bad enough,' Dan said. 'Not knowing what happened to an abducted child is, I can only imagine, inconsolable grief.'

Anya was unsure whether he had meant to speak out loud or not.

Brody checked his watch. 'I'd better be going. Walk you back?'

Drizzle fell and they wandered back in silence, sharing the umbrella. Anya wondered what was bothering Brody. He seemed agitated, not his usual confident, obnoxious self.

'Before lunch, you mentioned a sensitive matter.'

'Oh, nothing that can't wait,' he said as they approached his chambers. Outside, Veronica Slater paced beneath cover. 'Where have you been? I've been waiting five minutes!'

'Sorry, I had a conference.' Brody turned to

Anya. 'Have you met the newest addition to our chambers, Veronica Slater?'

'Yes, I have.' Anya forced a smile. She didn't know that Veronica had wormed her way into Brody's chambers. Maybe that explained the high heels. Without them she wouldn't even make it to Dan's chest.

Veronica put her arm in Brody's and held the umbrella handle with the other hand. 'I'm starving. Let's go celebrate my latest win.'

Like a lapdog, the oversized barrister obliged. 'Thanks for the advice on that case,' he said, and wandered off for his second lunch.

Anya stepped out into the rain, trying to hide her disappointment.

'Celebrating' meant the verdict in the drug-rape trial was in. She shuddered and hoped that Naomi and her family could accept the news. She didn't know what annoyed her more – Veronica gloating after humiliating a victim or the sight of Veronica's talons in a colleague like Dan Brody.

As she stepped around a puddle, she thought about putting victims through even more detailed forensic examinations. Somehow, it didn't seem worth it when all that offenders suffered was an over-inflated bill for a high-heeled lawyer.

For the first time, Anya felt glad she didn't have a daughter. She loathed the Veronicas of this world – people intent on beating the system at any cost. They ensured rapists and murderers walked free – to rape and kill again – for nothing but ego and money.

With bile rising in her throat, Anya wondered how she could continue to work for and support a system she was fast losing faith in.

10

Anya arrived at the Department of Health Quality Assurance Committee with just enough time to check her make-up before entering. Not in the habit of wearing foundation, she needed the extra war paint to cope with the bureaucracy and empire-building administrators at the meeting. Most people thought of working in sexual-assault units as providing an essential service, others saw it as a career-making prospect and were prepared to cut down any threats to their ascendancy.

In the third-floor bathroom, the most aggressive in the pack, Dr Lyndsay Gatlow, applied the finishing touches to blood-red lips. Co-ordinator of the southern regional SA unit, she was not known for subtlety of any kind, and the canary-yellow suit was testament to that fact.

'Should be an interesting meeting.' She smirked at herself in the mirror. 'The department's putting more pressure on to replace us with nurse practitioners. If we don't act quickly, some of us could find ourselves redundant by the end of the year.'

Anya washed her hands to remove the remnants of the greasy make-up. 'It's been a budgetary disaster in the UK. Three nurses doing eight-hour shifts cost more than a doctor on call for twenty-four hours, seven days a week. When you factor in nurses' holidays and superannuation, costs blow out.'

'I couldn't agree more. Good to see we're on the same side.'

With that, the lioness in canary's clothing took her leave, to stalk some unsuspecting prey.

True to form, Lyndsay materialised in the boardroom on the stroke of nine with an excessive pile of papers.

'Welcome everyone, we've got a lot to get through today. So if we can get seated.' She deposited herself at the head of the table. 'Today we'll be joined by Jennifer Beck, from the Office of the Director of Public Prosecutions, whom we all know. She wants to discuss ways to increase the effective collection of evidence.'

Complying, the six doctors and four social workers took their places alongside a Detective Inspector from the Physical Evidence Section and the department's own representative.

Anya glanced at Mary Singer, one of two people present she deemed allies. Mary responded with a wink.

A document was immediately passed around the table with Anya's name on the top. She felt her pulse quicken as she recognised the correspondence. This was a private letter written to her by a leading UK forensic physician on the topic of photography in sexual assaults – Lyndsay Ga-tlow's favourite agenda. The one agenda she hoped would make her National Director of SA units responsible for hiring and, in Anya's case, firing.

So far, Gatlow had managed to convince the police that photos would be ideal for court. It sounded good in theory: if a photo of a crime scene was convincing, photos of anatomy should be far more effective than an expert's verbal evidence. Worse still, she believed the evidence would be irrefutable.

Anya's experience suggested the opposite. Photos could be misinterpreted and it was too difficult to control access to them. She felt that lawyers and even the attacker viewing photos of genitals added to the victim's abuse.

Detective Chief Inspector Haddock flicked through the handout and clearly focused on the underlined section. 'The president of the International Association for Forensic Physicians seems to think that photography of all wounds is likely to result in more convictions. Isn't that what we all want?'

Lyndsay Gatlow interrupted, barely able to contain her excitement. 'I think we should do things properly, and according to the agenda, so everything said can be documented in the minutes, don't you agree?'

For the first time, the group unanimously con-curred, delaying the inevitable fight Anya was bracing herself for. Her name was back on the menu.

Feeling the heat on her neck rise, she couldn't believe Gatlow had got hold of private correspondence to her from a colleague, then had the gall to present it publicly. Predictably, Gatlow had taken his comments out of context. The missing pages in the letter outlined why photography had been unsuccessful when trialled in the UK.

Anya controlled her irritation as the agenda covered the usual – rosters, specimen collection, chain of evidence and inadequate storage facilities in SA units for the number of assaults seen. This inevitably led to disposal of vital evidence that could be useful in the future, something which frustrated police and lawyers, but didn't increase the funding for the units.

'Now,' Lyndsay announced, 'I'd like to table a document by one of the world's foremost proponents of something we must embrace if we are to move into the next era of evidence collection – colposcopic photography.'

Mary Singer interrupted, 'Excuse me, but why are you tabling this?'

'That's what I'd like to know,' Anya started. 'It is a private letter never intended for public dissemination.'

Anya had written to colleagues in the UK discussing the advantages and disadvantages of using the equivalent of a microscope on a flexible tube to examine and photograph inside women's vaginas.

Lyndsay Gatlow smiled – insincerely. 'Why, I phoned the author personally and he gave permission for me to use his opinion to precipitate discussion on the subject.'

Anya could imagine how the conversation had gone. No doubt Gatlow argued that the controversy here about colposcopic photography continued, but omitted to mention she was the sole instigator of the debate.

'We've covered this before.' Anya dug her fingernails into her palms. 'The trial in the UK failed, if you read the rest of that letter, which, incidentally, appears to be missing from the copy you gave us.'

The other committee members shifted in their seats.

Anya continued, 'As doctors, we're advocates for patients, or in this case, the victims. We do whatever we can to collect forensic evidence, but only with the victims' informed consent. We've gone out of our way to make the whole experience less sterile and invasive, which is why we don't do colposcopies. Now you want us to film and photograph victims' genitalia, for potentially hordes of people to see in a courtroom.'

'We owe it to them to get a conviction wherever possible,' Lyndsay interrupted.

'That is not our purpose.' Anya placed both palms on the table. 'Our role is to empower them, not turn them into a freak show, where people stare at their genitals and give varying opinions as to whether or not an assault took place.'

The predatory smile returned. 'I hate to say it, but I think Doctor Crichton is being overly sensitive about this. As with medical records, we can restrict who has access.'

Anya felt the rash on her neck rise. No one patronised women better than women. 'Don't think that we can control who sees the images. If admitted, they'll be viewed by police, judges, lawyers, juries, and even the perpetrator in the victim's presence.'

'I don't see the problem,' said the detective inspector. 'If the assault is particularly brutal, the defence lawyers could argue that photographic evidence is prejudicial, and have the images excluded.'

'Taking that argument alone, any images that fail to show trauma could be used as evidence that no assault took place. As everyone at this table knows, the majority of sexual assaults don't have signs of genital trauma. In those instances, any photos that appear normal will be prejudicial to the prosecution's case. We'd be disadvantaging the victims.'

'Sorry I'm late,' announced Jennifer Beck as she entered the room, pulled a spare chair from the corner to the table and sat down. 'Who's disadvantaging victims?'

Lyndsay Gatlow gushed, 'We were just debating the merits of photographing genital injuries.'

'Good, that's why I wanted to speak with you today.' Jennifer pulled up the sleeves of her pale blue cardigan and glanced around the table. 'You've all heard by now that prosecutors are losing the fight against sexual assault. With only twenty per cent of assaults reported to police, what we see is the tip of an enormous iceberg. With other crimes declining in recent years, sexual assault stands alone as the one crime category in which the number of offences is on the increase. Even with the evidence doctors collect, and the statements of the victims, the majority of offences don't result in a formal investigation. Most trials don't lead to convictions.'

She locked eyes with each person before continuing her speech. 'What we estimate is that 199 out of 200 incidents will not result in a conviction. That's a hell of a lot of scared and traumatised victims we've all let down.'

Lyndsay frowned. 'If there's virtually no chance of being caught, there's no deterrent. Unless we help the police and prosecutors, we're telling offenders that sexual assault isn't a crime.'

Mary Singer stopped studying her fingertips. 'We could start by doing away with feeding the media terms like date-rape. Rape is rape, irrespective of the social circumstances. And what does "domestic violence" suggest? That violence in the home isn't as bad as if it occurred on the street? Violence is violence. We don't label men fighting in a bar "social violence". So why belittle violence against women? We've got to change a whole cultural mentality before we'll see any difference in the crime rates of sexual assaults.'

One of the other social workers added, 'What about that famous drunk actor who was killed in that fight at a party?'

Anya remembered the public outcry about the tragic loss of someone so talented. Even though he'd had a reputation for being aggressive after a few drinks, no one suggested the 'celebrity' contributed to his own death by starting a fight with a blood-alcohol level multiple times the legal limit. The other man involved in the fight was charged with manslaughter. His family suffered death threats and had their lives ruined.

'Exactly,' Mary added. 'Compare that to what happened to the woman who was sexually assaulted by the visiting athletes. We all remember – the media vilified her for participating in "group sex"! We're supposed to think that every woman wants to have intercourse with a pack of steroid-abusers who'd be lucky to have the combined brain capacity of an amoeba.'

'We're missing the point,' the prosecutor interrupted. 'This isn't just about cultural change. It's about doing more to convict the perpetrators of sexual offences. I want to talk about ways to get more solid, irrefutable evidence I can use in court. After the recent debacle where evidence disappeared during a trial, we were sunk. We can't rely on only one piece of DNA. We need more – a lot more – if we are to convince a jury of what took place. That's up to you, who see the victims when examination's most likely to yield results'.

Jennifer pushed her sleeves higher. 'Recently we won a case when a physician managed to get a perpetrator's skin cell from a bruise he caused on a victim's neck. From now on, I want everyone to swab bruises, no matter how insignificant they seem. We could just get lucky and get saliva, skin cells, anything! I need a lot more solid evidence to convict.'

A male doctor from the rural service broke his silence. 'An expert witness can refute or cast doubt on the veracity of *any* piece of evidence. If we're being honest, what we collect contributes very little to your case. Even if a perpetrator leaves his wallet, fingerprints and sperm all over the scene, it's still a case of "he said, she said". You still have to deal with the issue of consent. Without a confession, juries are going to tend more to acquittals if there's a trial. If all a defendant needs is reasonable doubt, the odds are in his favour about two hundred to one, I'd say.'

'If you feel this negative, why are you doing the job?' Jennifer shot back at him.

'Because the victims need us. We don't work for the police. We work for the victims. That's why we'll always differ on viewpoints about evidence collection.'

Well said, Anya thought.

Lyndsay Gatlow tabled the document initially addressed to Anya.

'Jennifer has already seen this letter and agrees it's worth introducing across the state. All the doctors here are adept at colposcopic examinations and, with digital cameras, photography is easy and doesn't require particular skill.'

'I would like to state that I fail to see the validity in Doctor Crichton's objections to photography,' the detective inspector began. 'Normally in crime, the police are the first ones called. The problem we have is that in sexual assault, others are involved first and traipse all over the evidence. From our perspective, photos of dishevelled clothing, dirt on the victim, bruises, would all help get the message across to a jury. Hell, we don't care if the victims take the photos themselves. Something is always better than nothing.'

Although that sounded reasonable, Anya knew that there were a few problems with the theory. The first was that forensic physicians – and victims, for that matter – weren't expert at photography and the equipment didn't produce perfect images. Secondly, it was a lot different looking at a 2D photo without seeing the whole area first-hand. A photo could be misleading, just like a picture of a car didn't explain how fast the car was travelling.

And normal photos didn't exclude sexual assault having taken place. Besides, there was debate as to what constituted normal and abnormal, given that couples having consensual sex didn't tend to agree to have their genitals photographed after the event for plenty of minor injuries.

Mary Singer studied the finger where her wedding ring used to be. 'These people have already been abused. Imagine the degradation and emotion involved in displaying photos of them to strangers, and maybe even the perpetrator.'

'It's no different from presenting pictures of a homicide victim.'

'It's very different,' Anya replied. 'Dead is dead. You can't argue over a body that death didn't occur. The onus here is on the victim to convince a jury the assault took place. He or she is still alive, reliving the horror of the assault, for years if there is a trial, not to mention appeals. Without a victim giving evidence, there is no trial.'

'What's the alternative, presenting nothing?' The policeman threw his hands in the air.

'No, there are other alternatives,' Anya emphasised. 'We can work better with the analytical laboratories and determine the most effective means of collecting evidence when we do our examinations. Should we use dental floss to increase the yield of DNA more often? Should we be taking more swabs for the presence of condom lubricants? That's what we need to do. There is no study in existence showing what is normal on colposcopy after consensual intercourse, so showing photographs we "think" show the effects of non-consensual sex would be laughed out of court. If you use science to prove a case, you need it to be impeccable.'

Jennifer Beck studied the papers. 'I take your point. Perhaps Lyndsay's team could perform a pilot study. But for now, why don't you try taking photos of the victims' state – clothing, and any visible injuries on their faces or hands. Anything that could help us.'

Mary Singer refused to look up or comment, but the others tentatively agreed.

Anya wasn't that restrained. 'If the victims are properly informed about photography and its potential uses, fewer women will consent to examinations and you'll have even less evidence.'

'That's a risk I'm prepared to take,' the prosecutor proclaimed.

It always astounded Anya that lawyers and police didn't feel the need to understand the science behind the evidence they depended on. They just wanted to manipulate it for their own advantage. The lack of scientific studies on post-intercourse physical findings would sink any prosecution's case. So Jennifer Beck wanted victims to have invasive procedures done and photographed, for no real benefit.

Beck and Veronica Slater had more in common by the minute.

Lyndsay moved on to the next item on the agenda: nurse practitioners performing sexual-assault examinations and having the doctors interpret the evidence.

Anya decided this battle could wait. She collected her papers and left the meeting.

11

Geoff watched his mother leave for bingo at the senior citizens' club and immediately announced his need to buy more underwear at the shops. Nick thought it was a good idea and drove his cousin to the centre. For the first time since leaving prison, Geoff had a few hours to himself.

Alone, Sunny checked the buttons were done up on his shirt. He didn't want to appear sloppy, and so he rubbed the tips of each shoe on the backs of his trousers. It's what he'd seen men do in the movies before they saw their girls. His palms sweated on the tissue paper keeping the flowers together and some of the purple dye came off on his hands. He looked up and down for somewhere to wipe them and chose a bus-shelter a few doors down. He checked his watch. She'd be coming out the door any minute now. The same time dinner got served at the prison.

He'd only been out a couple of weeks, but his hair had already grown. He didn't really need the cap, but he felt safer wearing it. Watching the traffic, he counted the cars going past and sang the theme from *The Jetsons* to himself. Nervous about meeting his girl, he mustered a mouthful of spit and landed it on the ground in front of the bench. Someone on the bench gave him a dirty look before moving. Geoff sat down. As it turned out, it was a good move. A bus came along and Geoff pretended to tie up his shoelace, so he could look up the skirts of girls getting off the bus. This was one of his favourite tricks.

Out of the corner of his eye, he saw his girl come out of the shop and bend down, facing the shop. Approaching, he could see the thin V-shape of her undies showing under her trousers and he felt excited. Hopefully, she had that low top on too – the one that made her breasts stick out. She stood up and locked the door.

'Are you closed?' he said, from behind her back.

'Yeah, come back tomorrow. We open at ten.'

'Do you have any more comics?'

The girl turned around. 'Hey, it's you. You're the one who came with your mum.'

She remembered. Geoff felt his heart beat harder. 'You helped me get some good stuff.'

'Well, that's my job.'

She attempted to move past him, but he held up the flowers, unable to take his eyes off her chest.

'These are – um – for you,' he said.

'Thanks, but I already have a boyfriend,' she replied. 'Look, I'm sure you're a nice guy. Maybe some other girl would like them.' She sidestepped and started walking. 'I've gotta go.'

'Wait. I picked these especially for you. Don't you like them?'

80

Her heels clomped faster. 'Look, I told you. Thanks, but no thanks.'

This wasn't the way Geoff had imagined it. She was supposed to take them. She had been nice to him when he bought the clothes. Now she was being rude.

He hurried to catch up. 'I don't understand. You acted all nice; now you're not.'

'I was doing my job. What did you expect?' She stopped and glanced around. After looking him up and down, she softened.

'If it makes you feel better, I'll take the flowers.'

He handed them over.

'But don't get the wrong idea. I told you I've got a boyfriend and he is really jealous. You'd better not come around again. If he catches you, he's likely to do something stupid.'

'They'll die if you don't put them in water.'

She waved the bouquet in the air and walked away.

Geoff followed her down to the corner and watched as she walked down the next street. Outside a block of units, the girl walked up to a rubbish bin, opened the lid and tossed the flowers away.

Nick Hudson stood with his empty glass. 'Another beer?'

Geoff kept his face buried beneath his cap. 'I want coffee.'

'You're kidding, aren't you? This is a pub,

mate. The first one you've been in for twenty years. Remember Pat French and Tom Bowles from school? They moved here from the Bay a few years ago and bought the place. We get mates' rates.'

'Geez. Did every bastard from home move here?'

'No real choice, mate. When the mines closed up north, all the work dried up. Reckon half the Bay came here looking for a job because of the chicken factory opening up. C'mon. How about another beer?'

Geoff dug the tip of the knife into the wooden table, chiselling a divot.

Nick sighed. 'Coffee it is.'

Geoff didn't look up. The remains of his second schooner had sloshed out when he bumped the salt-shaker.

He didn't understand why everyone in prison reckoned alcohol was great. After someone got caught making moonshine, they were only ever allowed to have a couple of pieces of fruit in their cells. Geoff didn't get it. He'd never really liked the taste of beer, wine or spirits. And then there was having to go and take a piss every time he drank the stuff. It just went right through him. He'd already fought his way to the men's toilet three times and they'd only been here for one hour and three minutes.

This floor was sticky and covered in spills from the drinkers standing around, waving their arms as they crapped on about something they thought sounded smart. He didn't like the smell, either. Stale beer smelt worse than piddle, he reckoned.

Nick returned with a cappuccino and a small glass with a brown and white drink.

'Thought I'd have a cock-sucking cowboy to get things moving. Pat says hello,' he said. 'She's at the bar if you want to—'

'I'm hungry,' Geoff grunted.

'Mate, food's on its way. They'll bring it when it's ready. Pat's organised a double-size feed for you.'

It was past dinnertime and Geoff didn't like it. He was only here because Nick had brought him to meet some of the old gang from Fisherman's Bay.

'Do you like being out? I mean, it must be kinda strange being free after all this time.'

'I like *Gilligan's Island, Hogan's Heroes,* and all the good shows.'

'That's great, mate, but how about the other stuff, like meeting people?'

With the cap firmly over his eyes, Geoff confided about the girl and the flowers.

'So that's why you looked so down when I picked you up. You don't need a bitch like that. She's probably so far up herself she'd disappear if she sneezed.'

Geoff snickered. The thought of someone being blown out her own nose made him laugh. Just like that guy from the *Cat in the Hat* movie.

'Mate, I need to ask. Is there someone special you've been keeping a secret?'

'Nah.' Geoff sneaked a look at the women around the bar. 'I'm not good at talking to girls.'

'Well, who's this?' Nick pulled a photo from his wallet. 'You left it in one of your pockets. I found it in the laundry basket.'

Geoff studied it. So that's where it had gone. 'She is special. She wrote me a letter and put it in my pants when I got out. When all those people were yelling at me. I didn't even see her.'

'Why didn't you tell me?'

'I thought you'd take her away.'

'Man, if she approached you, that's different. What did the letter say?'

'Dunno, stuff about how she liked me. And how she liked to play rough.'

'Jesus, mate!' Nick grabbed the photo. 'Her address is on the back.' He gulped the cocktail. 'If you don't call, I sure will.'

'Who you harassing now?' A stranger in a black T-shirt and jeans sidled up, beer in one hand, other hand anchored in his coin pocket. He looked like the bad guy in a spaghetti western waiting to draw his six-shooter.

Following him were three other guys who stood around the table.

Geoff didn't like being crowded. He put his head down, grabbed the photo back from Nick and put it in his pocket, not wanting any trouble.

'Luke. Great to see you.' Nick stood up and

slapped his friend on the shoulder. 'Hey, Badger, Gazza, Carrot, remember my cousin?'

They all sat down, cramping the small table.

'Geoff, remember Luke Platt? Used to live up the coast. Thought we could have a bit of a reunion, like the good old days back in Fisherman's Bay.'

Geoff refused to acknowledge them, but had already sized up the visitors. Prison had taught him to check men out to see how dangerous they were. Luke – average height, weight, athletic. Pigeon-toed, too. Could be a good runner. Badger had a head like a busted toilet, looked like a boxer with his cauliflower ears and had the build for it, too. At least that's what his cellmate would have said about the 'new boys'.

They both looked familiar, but neither had ever been a friend.

Gazza used to work in the mines and he was the sort of guy you wouldn't look twice at, the kind who stood with his arms crossed to make himself seem bigger. Carrot-red hair, freckles; used to be a dickhead when he worked in the boat shed. By the way he sat down with a dopey grin on his face, he still was.

'How's it going?' Luke held out a hand to shake.

'It's past dinnertime.' The table scored another divot.

'Don't mind him,' Nick explained, 'he's got the shits because a girl from the local Vinnies shop gave him the brush-off.'

A plate of steak and chips arrived, along with a bowl of pasta.

'Thanks, darling,' Gazza said, winking at the bargirl.

Geoff noticed her face and smiled. 'Are you Pat? You look just like Daisy in *The Dukes of Hazzard*. She's really pretty.'

The young girl blushed and grinned while she rearranged the salt and pepper shakers. 'No, I'm Maddie.'

'Well, mate.' Luke stood up. 'I better be off. If the wife asks, I was at work late again. All right?' He stood up, scraping the floor with his chair. 'It's the only way I get a leave-pass these days.'

Nick started on the spaghetti. 'No worries. Thought a baby on the way would give her something else to focus on.'

'Hell, with these pregnancy hormones, she's a mess. Suddenly she wants me there all the time when I'm not at work. Even worse, she's obsessed with washing everything – curtains, floors, clothes. I can't even fart without her wanting to clean up the smell.'

Nick laughed. 'She's nesting.'

Carrot chimed in, 'You're under the thumb, mate. Have been from the moment she got her hooks in. You ought to show her who's boss.'

'It's not that easy. Marriage is like living with your mum.'

Geoff looked up. 'What's that supposed to mean?'

Nick licked some sauce from his upper lip. 'Nothing. Mate, he didn't mean anything. Want another coffee?'

'No.' Geoff put down his knife and fork and thought about the girl in the picture. She was pretty. Long dark hair, big brown eyes and bright red lips. Then he had to take another piss.

Luke tapped his fingers on the table and leant over Nick.

'Aren't you supposed to be keeping an eye on your cousin? After what he did to that girl, aren't you worried he might just cut up another one?'

'That was a long time ago. He was just a kid himself, and Eileen Randall was a fucking bitch to him. She had it coming.'

'He's never been the full quid, and he sure as hell is weird. Look at the way he reacted when I made a crack about my mum.'

Nick nodded. 'I know, but he's paid for what he did.'

'All I know is I wouldn't want him hanging around my sister.'

A couple of tables away, voices got louder. The pair turned to see Geoff, head down, blocked by a group of men.

'I'm talking to you. Hey, aren't you that fucking child-killer? The one who's been on all the news?'

Geoff clenched both fists by his sides and side-stepped back to his seat at the table.

'What's this? A meeting of the child-fuckers' union?'

Luke spoke first. 'We don't want trouble. We were just leaving.'

'I haven't finished my dinner,' Nick said.

'You have now.' The angry one tipped the remainder of the meal on Geoff's head. Deftly, Geoff seized the man's outstretched arm with one hand and threw Nick's drink in his face. The man reeled, grabbing his eyes, as Geoff leapt to his feet.

The other men at the table stepped back. Badger landed a right-cross on the guy with the drink in his eyes. Someone knocked Luke to the floor and he felt a foot connect with his side, just as a bouncer intervened, grabbing the kicker in a headlock. Nick was standing between Geoff and another man who was being held back by a second security guy.

'Break it up,' said a loud voice. The gawking crowd dispersed.

On the floor, Luke realised his father's crucifix was missing from his neck. He sat up and scanned the floor.

'Is this what you're looking for?' The waitress bent down. In her palm was a large cross-shaped amulet and its chain.

'Your friend – the one with the big blue eyes – is cute,' she whispered. 'I know what they say about him, but he looks so gentle.'

Beneath the amulet was a piece of paper with her phone number on it.

Luke, Geoff and Nick left the pub under security escort. They sat in silence on the way back to the Willards' home. Geoff's mother didn't say a word as they came in.

Luke cornered Nick. 'Can we have a quick word? Now you're home safe, I've got to get going.'

'No worries.' Nick led his friend into the hallway.

Inside, Luke spoke quietly. 'I know he's your cousin, but you've got to watch him. That waitress thought he looked gentle after his chat-up Daisy Duke crap.'

'He can't help the way he looks. Nature had to make up for his brain, I reckon. Besides, some girls just have a thing for guys who've been in prison.'

'Yeah, but he isn't in jail any more. He's out. And I reckon it's only a matter of time before he hurts someone again.'

From the lounge room, Geoff called out, 'Come quick. *Baywatch* is coming on. It's the bit where they run real slow.'

Suddenly, they heard the crash of glass breaking. They rushed to see Lillian Willard lying on the floor, blood dripping from a gash on her head. A rock lay beside her. The window had been smashed from outside.

'Turn off the lights,' Nick commanded, 'and the television!'

He knelt next to his aunt, who was breathing hard. 'She needs a hospital.'

Luke stood to the side of the window, flipped open his mobile phone and dialled emergency. 'We need an ambulance. An elderly woman's been knocked out by a rock thrown through the window . . . Of course it's a fucking emergency! She's just sort of lying there, not moving. Hang on . . .' He turned to Nick. 'They want to know, does she have a pulse?'

'Yeah, but it's weak. And tell them to send police, too.'

'Hello? Her pulse is weak and there's trouble outside. We need the police. There's a crowd outside and, oh shit, they're fucking angry.'

The crowd began to chant, 'Get Willard out. Get Willard out.'

Someone with a loudspeaker shouted, 'Leave our neighbourhood tonight. We don't want sex offenders near our kids.'

Geoff crawled to the back door. He wanted to protect Caesar.

'Come here, boy.' He opened the screen door but the labrador pup didn't move.

'Quick boy, get inside,' he urged, but Caesar stayed asleep. Geoff clambered across to where the dog lay and put a hand on his back. That's when he knew something was wrong. Caesar wasn't breathing. Putting his ear to the dog's chest, Geoff couldn't hear or feel a thing, but he could smell the vomit. It was all around the dog.

Beside him lay a stinking piece of meat. Caesar wasn't sick. He'd been baited and poisoned.

'NO! You bastards!' he screamed.

Luke hurried to his side. 'Oh Jesus,' he said, pulling Geoff inside the back door to the laundry.

Geoff paced, his eyes welling with tears. He punched the inside wall, puncturing the plaster.

'The police will be here any second,' Luke offered. 'You'd better get out of here.'

Geoff didn't acknowledge his cousin's friend. He was too angry. All he wanted to do was kill the bastard who did this. Fucking coward, picking on an innocent dog.

He ground his thumb into his palm. What the fuck was happening?

Everything was going wrong. His mum was lying inside bleeding, his dog was dead. And it was his fault. He had to get away.

He took off out the back door, scaled the back fence, and ran. As fast as his legs would allow.

12

Melanie Havelock couldn't believe her luck. Landing an advertising job so quickly with the company she wanted to work for was a dream come true. She practically skipped home from the station, for the first time noticing how fragrant the gardenias were at this time of night. After a celebratory drink with her best girlfriend, she had caught a late train, all the while planning her career. First thing, it would mean a whole new wardrobe. Nothing too conservative, maybe something a little funky. And new shoes, too. Lots of high heels. After all, she was an advertising consultant.

How good did that sound?

Unable to stop smiling, she cut through the park, even saying hello to a jogger. She crossed the road, and for the first time felt the humidity. Perspiration beneath her new suit made her slow a little as she turned the corner into her street and wondered how she'd break the news to her mother. A job would mean moving out, new friends and holidays away from the family. Somewhere nearby, a dog barked, interrupting her thoughts. She pulled her keys from her bag and fumbled with the old wooden door. It had stuck again and needed a bigger push than usual.

'Mum, I'm home and I've got great news,' she said, dropping her keys on the table in the hall.

'Hello?'

Silence.

She threw her bag on the kitchen bench and found the note.

Her sister was studying, Mum was at work and her father's plane had been delayed. He wouldn't be back until the morning. Dinner – leftover pizza – was in the fridge. All it needed was ten minutes on medium heat in the oven.

The one time she had brilliant news and there was no one home to celebrate. Just a note. Typical Mum, no mention of the interview, just a lesson in how to reheat food! How did she think teenagers survived?

Melanie slipped the pizza into the microwave and pressed three minutes. With the house to herself, she flicked on the lights in the main living area, along with the air-conditioner, stereo and TV.

Being alone had an upside. She could have more than one appliance on without anyone carrying on about the cost. 'Do you think we own shares in the electricity company?' her father would always say.

A moment later, the air-conditioner, microwave,

stereo and TV clicked off. She checked. Even the alarm clock in her room was powerless. At least the lights stayed on.

The safety switch must have triggered, she thought. With the porch light on, she went out the front door and around the side of the house to the fuse box. Lifting the metal lid, she flicked on the kill-switch and the air-conditioning kicked back in. Once inside again, she decided to unplug the stereo just in case that was what had over-loaded the system.

As she reached down, a rubber glove covered her mouth and her knees buckled with a weight from behind.

'This isn't funny!' she said, grabbing for her boyfriend's hand.

'Don't turn around or think about screaming.' The voice was not familiar. Without meaning to move her head, she saw the knife blade just before it stung her cheek.

Heart drilling in her chest, she struggled for air. Panic rose like a tidal wave.

God, was she about to die?

'Don't hurt me,' she mumbled. 'Please don't hurt me.'

'Tell me where your money is and I won't.'

The hand around her mouth loosened.

He just wants money, that's all. Melanie felt her body relax a little. She pointed at the kitchen.

'I don't have much in my purse, just a few dollars until I get paid.'

'You do as I say and I'll be out of here real quick.'

She turned this time to see a black cap covering most of his face and felt the knife at her throat.

'You stupid bitch. Don't look at me!'

'I didn't see—'

Suddenly, he had her off balance in a headlock. He tightened his grip around her neck and the knife hovered in front of her eyes.

She could feel his hot breath in her ear, deeper and more rapid as she fought to breathe.

'Where's your bed?'

'I don't have any jewellery.'

No answer.

She struggled to get her balance, but her leather-soled shoes offered no resistance on the tiled floor as he dragged her into the main bedroom. With one swift move, he threw her on to her back, pinned her arms with his knees and pushed her face to the side. The knife moved back to her throat.

'Don't look at me!' His free fist exploded across her face.

Dazed by the pain in her nose and cheek, Melanie took a moment to focus.

'My – my boyfriend – he'll be home any minute.'

'Liar! You fucking liar.' With a quick movement, he ripped open her shirt and pushed up her bra. The gloved fingers exposed her flesh then dug into her, kneading and squeezing until it hurt.

Unable to inhale properly, she didn't dare struggle. She stared at the floral curtain hanging over the locked window.

He snapped off the rubber gloves and she saw a flash of white as he took the knife in one hand while the other groped at his trousers. He took some weight off her arms, but not enough for her to get free. Too scared to look, she thought he pulled out a condom and tore off the wrapper.

'God, no, please don't. I've never done this before.'

'Shut your fucking mouth!'

'Please don't hurt me.'

He ripped off her trousers and panties then lifted his hips and lowered his jeans. First he stuck himself in her mouth, kneeling on her elbows the whole time.

She gagged and tried to pull away. He just got harder. Then he stopped and moved down between her legs.

Bending forwards, he whispered in her ear, 'Relax. If you can't be hurt, you can't be loved.'

With that, she felt pain shoot from her thighs through to her back. It felt like she was being ripped open, but the knife remained pressed at her neck. Sobbing, she thought she'd pass out, but closed her eyes and thought of her mother's grief if anything happened to her. After a few minutes, he stopped and pressed his face into her chest.

She could smell his cheap aftershave and mint breath.

Instead of leaving, he rolled her onto her stomach and raped her again, pressing her face into the pillow. This time she thrashed her head, gasping for air. She couldn't feel the knife but knew it was still there. It had to be. The pain kept on, but now it was as though it was happening to someone else.

Overcome by a strange numbness, she felt as though God was saving her from any more physical pain.

If she did what he said, he'd let her go. She hadn't seen his face, just felt his weight. And his smell.

She wanted to gag. When he'd finished, she closed her eyes and waited to die.

He threw the bedclothes over her limp body and lifted her head by the roots of her hair, waving the blade across her throat.

'I'm going to get something to eat. Don't think about running away. If you try, I'll slice you, starting with your eyes and nose. They won't even be able to identify your body.'

Grabbing at the covers, she slowly lifted them up to her shoulders as her entire body shook. The window was key-locked. He'd see her if she tried to leave the bedroom. Too paralysed with fear to move, all she could do was listen. The fridge door opened, followed by the clink of bottles.

Oh God, he's staying. He's getting something to eat!

After what seemed like hours, he came back and sat on the bed.

'Don't look at me.'

This time his voice sounded calm, which scared her more. For sure, he was getting ready to kill her. He pulled off the bedclothes and stared at her half-naked body, twisting the knife in his hand.

Then he rolled her onto her back and pressed the blade hard against her breast. He unzipped his pants, climbed on top and raped her again. This time the smell of beer and garlic doused her with each grunt.

When he'd finished, he made her take a shower in the en suite and forced her to scrub all over.

'Now, where's that handbag?' he said, while the shower still ran.

When he returned, through a misted screen-door she saw him shove something into his back pocket.

Cat-like, he pounced and opened the screen-door, pulling the cap further over his eyes. 'I have to go now, but I'll be watching from around the corner.'

Ashamed and still afraid, she tried to shield herself from his burning stare and turned away. 'Please don't hurt me any more.'

'Listen, you fucking bitch. I know everything about you. If you call the police or tell anyone, I'll be back. If you try to hide, I'll find you. And next time, I'll finish what we started.'

13

Anya stared at the Department of Health directive that instructed all physicians to photograph assault victims on presentation and during examination. The accompanying consent was in addition to the other two forms that victims had to sign before evidence could be collected. No wonder victims' groups demanded better treatment.

Anya wished she'd argued better at the meeting. Survivors were different from murder victims in two important ways. Unlike homicide victims, they had a choice in whether or not to come forward. Secondly, they remained alive and vulnerable, often feeling as though the offender had committed 'unfinished' murder.

Mary Singer entered the tearoom.

'Thanks for coming in again. The poor girl seems more terrified about how her mother will take it. Apparently, her mum was mugged last year and has been over-the-top protective of her kids ever since.'

Anya could relate to that. Having a four-year-old son was worrying enough. She tested the charge on the digital camera and put it on the trolley outside the examination suite.

Inside the room sat a straight-backed young woman, with mascara smudged around her eyes and a large swollen bruise on the left side of her face. She wasn't crying now.

'I'm Anya, the unit's doctor.'

'Melanie,' the woman uttered with a hoarse voice.

Mary Singer sat in the armchair next to Anya's.

'I'm here for two main reasons,' Anya explained. 'The most important thing is to look after you; to make sure you are safe and all right. The second reason is to conduct a forensic exam, but only if you want it. I won't do it unless you consent to it. You do have power and choices here tonight. Your attacker may have tried to take them away from you, but you are in control now.'

Melanie looked intensely at Anya. 'What does a forensic exam involve?'

'An examination to see whether your attacker transferred any DNA material from his body to yours. That means taking cotton swabs of areas he might have left some of his "genetic fingerprint", if you like. That happens if he licked, bit or kissed you, or even pressed hard on your skin with his fingers. It can also be left in the form of semen, hairs, or if you scraped his skin with your fingernails.'

'I think he used a condom the first time. It sounds stupid, but I'm not sure about the other times.' Her voice trailed to almost a whisper.

'Nothing you say will sound stupid. You'd be amazed how many people don't know if a condom was used. How could you when you weren't able to see?'

'The police already know I was attacked. I didn't know what to do, so I called emergency. A policewoman brought me straight here and said I'd have to be examined.'

Anya referred to her clipboard and booklet. 'There is no "have to" here. I won't do anything without your permission, and you can change your mind at any time at all. But, if you think you might want to make a police statement, it's better to look for any forensic evidence now rather than later. If you go home and decide you don't want the police involved, we can dispose of the evidence. If you agree to my collecting evidence, you have time to decide whether or not you want it handed over to the police. I can't do anything with it unless I have your written permission.'

'I've never even had a Pap smear.'

'I wouldn't do that tonight, but it's important to check you for injuries and treat you if necessary. We need to talk about the risks of pregnancy and infections as well.'

Melanie bit her bottom lip.

'If I let you examine me, is that all?'

Mary Singer cleared her throat. 'We offer you medical treatment and ongoing counselling whether or not you have an examination. There's no pressure either way.'

'It might help if you can tell me how you were attacked, and where you were hurt,' Anya added.

Melanie paused, 'I just got home after catching a late train. The power went off and I checked the fuse box and came back inside. That's when he grabbed me from behind. I thought it was my boyfriend kidding around. Then the knife dug into my face.'

Anya noticed a small wound on the right cheek and a stream of blood heading towards her chin. She was upright when the knife pierced the skin.

Melanie continued talking, and, taking brief notes, Anya documented key points of the story.

Oral, vaginal, then anal penetration. Offender left the room to eat and when returned, repeated vaginal penetration. Made her shower.

Anya asked, 'Have you had any bleeding since the assault?'

'Kind of like a heavy period.'

'It's important that we look at that, to make sure you haven't got any damage to your bladder or bowel as well.'

'I didn't fight him. I was so scared, I couldn't move.' Melanie hung her head. 'It was like being paralysed.'

'Whatever you did during the attack was the right thing,' Mary emphasised. 'You survived. Don't ever forget that. You did the right things.'

The young woman gazed at the pot plant on the coffee table and seemed to drift into a daze.

'I once saw one of those wildlife shows where a

surfer was attacked by a shark. He said that out of the corner of his eye he saw something grey, then felt a tug on his leg. When he looked down he saw blood in the water but didn't know he was missing half his leg. It didn't even hurt. It was as though the first bite wiped out all feeling of fear and pain.' Her voice faltered and her hand dabbed the swollen cheek. 'He paddled to the shore and didn't collapse until someone helped him onto the beach.' Her voice became raspier, but she kept talking. 'Maybe it's nature's way of trying to help animals that can't save themselves.'

The calm facade started to slip. She bit her lip again. 'That's kind of how I felt after he started to rape me the first time.'

Melanie Havelock sat forwards and stared at the pot plant for a good few minutes before making her decision. 'I survived for a reason. I want to have the forensic exam.'

Anya admired the strength of this woman. She should do well with support and counselling.

After signing the consent form, Melanie asked about the other forms. Anya explained what they meant, and how she documented the findings. 'This last one,' she added, 'is a request to photograph your injuries, and what you look like now.'

Melanie sat back and crossed her arms. 'Why do you need photos? My doctor always draws stuff.'

'If you decide you want a police investigation, photos may be helpful. At least of your injuries.'

'Would they hide my face?'

Mary shook her head. 'No, they would need to be identifiable.'

'I don't want anyone seeing me like this. God, what if someone I know saw them?'

Anya acted quickly to reassure her. 'It's fine, only people concerned with the case will see them.'

'You mean like the Paris Hilton video?'

'It's your choice. We don't need to take any photos. It won't affect anything we've discussed at all.'

Mary glanced at her colleague. 'I'm a witness to that. No photography.'

'Let's get this over with,' Melanie announced, standing. 'Where do I go now?'

The phone in the room buzzed and Mary answered it.

'Melanie, your mother's outside. What would you like to do?'

Tears filled her eyes. 'Can she hold my hand?'

Mary moved to open the door. 'Sure, if that's what you'd like.'

Anya tore open the bag of the assault kit and began labelling the collection vials. She pretended not to notice the mother and daughter standing together.

'I'm afraid you can't hug your daughter until we've collected the evidence,' Mary tactfully explained.

'I know.' The mother moved some hair out of

her child's eyes. 'You're in very good hands here.' She turned towards Anya.

She seemed familiar, but Anya couldn't place her.

'I don't expect you to remember,' she said. 'I looked a lot different then.'

'Gloria Havelock.' Anya smiled, out of genuine respect. 'Now I remember. Very clearly.'

How could she forget? It was the first time Anya had been on call for the unit, and the night she had first worked with Mary Singer. Gloria was lucky to have survived a vicious assault. Frightened for her family, the mother behaved stoically and did not want anyone knowing about the rape. Instead, she wanted them all to think she had been mugged.

'Ma, how do you know the doctor?'

Gloria turned to her daughter. 'We can talk about that later. Right now, we need to look after you.'

Anya suddenly felt the hairs on the back of her neck prickle.

What were the chances that the women were both victims of random attacks?

14

With Gloria waiting in the front office, Anya moved into the adjoining room and Mary laid down a fresh blue sheet on the bed. 'I'll stay if you like, or be just next door if you need me.'

'I'm all right with just the doctor,' Melanie said.

Anya closed the sliding door, locked it and placed a sheet of white paper on the floor. She opened a pack of size-five latex gloves and stretched them over her fingers.

'I'll need you to gently take off your clothes over the paper. It's the best chance of collecting dirt, fibres, hairs and anything else he transferred to you in the attack.'

Melanie complied. Anya helped her into a white hospital gown, observing more injuries as she tied up the back. She then folded the underwear and placed it inside a brown paper bag.

'We'll get you a drink in a minute, but first I need you to spit into a container.'

Melanie tried her best to muster some saliva. Anya pipetted out the contents into another screw-top vial.

'I'm going to give you a tiny amount of water. I

want you to swish it around your mouth and spit again.' This time, the result yielded more.

'Lastly, flossing your teeth after an assault might be a more effective way of getting DNA evidence.'

'If it helps get rid of any part of him, I'll do it.'

With the dental floss labelled and placed in another jar, Anya began to take notes of the injuries. The face was swelling more, but there was no bagginess when she pressed it to suggest a fracture. Oval-shaped bruises on the right-hand side of Melanie's neck were consistent with those caused by finger pressure. A thumb-sized mark on the left suggested his hand had spanned Melanie's throat, his four fingers embedded into the flesh on her right side.

'Did he take off both gloves?' Anya asked.

'I think so. I'm not sure. I remember seeing a flash of white as he punched me. I didn't see the hand again.'

Anya took both wet and dry swabs from the fingermark bruises, in the hope they'd uncover some of the offender's skin cells. Chances of a result were low since Melanie had been forced to have a shower, but worth the try.

The attacker had punched Melanie in the right breast, causing a large black haematoma beneath the skin. Anya measured the width and breadth of the bruises and copied the shapes in her notes. From the left breast towards the collarbone was a linear narrow bruise, consistent with the impression left by a knife blade and part of the handle. She measured the dimensions and drew them as accurately as possible.

The mark was alarmingly similar to the bruise left on another victim she had recently seen, Anya realised. The pharmacist attacked in the car park near the hospital.

Two raps on the door meant that Mary had a drink ready. Anya unlocked and opened it enough to take the foam cup for Melanie, who continued to thank her. It always amazed Anya how grateful sexual-assault victims were for even the most minor act of kindness or consideration.

Next task was to take a dry swab from under the fingernails, in case the offender's tissue had transferred in the struggle. Anya repeated this with wet swabs and then asked if she could cut Melanie's rather long nails, a job she didn't enjoy. To most forensic physicians' surprise, studies showed that swabs from beneath fingernails were more likely to yield DNA than the cut portions. Anya suspected that was due to the fact that the clippings often projectiled across the room. In the process of hunting the specimens down and recollecting them, it was hardly surprising that some of the DNA matter would be lost. So much for high-tech processes shown on shows like *CSI*. Reality was far more clumsy.

She opened a new pair of scissors and carefully clipped each nail before discarding the utensils in a sharps bin.

'Do you throw all the equipment away?' Melanie asked. 'Is it all contaminated?'

Anya was glad the young woman had spoken. It felt more comfortable to explain procedures than endure the silence.

'Anything metal needs to be soaked, scrubbed and sterilised in an autoclave. The protocol says to soak scissors in alcohol, but when I tried that, they turned into a pile of rust, which would be great for spreading tetanus.'

Melanie offered a half-smile through a swollen mouth. 'What made you want to do this kind of work?'

Anya slowly lowered the head of the bed.

'Now, I need to feel your tummy, then it's time to see where that bleeding is coming from.' Repositioning the pillow for comfort, Anya added, 'It's something I feel strongly about – that this job is done right and people like you get the best possible care.' After covering Melanie with a rug across her upper legs, she swabbed the area around the vagina for semen, smeared the swab onto a glass slide and replaced it in its labelled tube. 'I need to do the same for the back passage. This shouldn't hurt.' Anya noted no obvious injury to the perineal area and carefully collected the next specimen. Finally, she warmed the smallest metal speculum with running water from the adjacent sink. 'You're actually in control here, although you may not feel it. If you feel tense or it hurts, please let me know and I'll stop straight away.' Anya walked over and stressed, 'I don't want to cause any more pain.'

Melanie gritted her teeth and her thigh muscles automatically tightened, revealing bruising of the inner thighs.

'By the way, breathing really helps you to relax. Holding your breath makes every part of your body tense.' Anya walked over, gently inserted the speculum and opened it. 'I've found what's causing the bleeding. Along the back wall of the vagina there's a small tear. It looks like it'll heal by itself in the next couple of days.'

'Is that bad?'

Thigh muscles contracted again.

'Not at all. It means there isn't damage to your bowel or bladder, or other organs.' Anya took some more swabs and removed the speculum.

Melanie's eyes welled with tears again. 'Can I get up now?'

'The shower's all yours. There are some unglamorous black tracksuits in the cupboard, and new underwear, too. Consider the lot disposable.' She threw out the used speculum in a yellow contaminated-waste bin.

While Melanie sat up, Anya thought about the similarity in injuries between the two rape victims. 'If you didn't see your attacker, was there anything else about him that you remember? Something he said or did?'

'Apart from taking a break to eat? Actually, there was something. He seemed to think he was

110

doing me a favour the first time. Just before he raped me, he told me that if I couldn't be hurt, I couldn't be loved. It was almost like he loved me and pain was part of that.'

Anya shuddered with the realisation that a serial rapist was on the loose in their area. 'You've done brilliantly.' She helped the woman down and into the en suite. 'I'll leave you in peace, but if you need anything I'll be in the lounge room. You just have to call or press the buzzer in the cubicle.'

Closing the sliding door, Anya returned to Mary.

'Can you give her a few minutes? We still need to talk about emergency contraception, infection screening and follow up.'

Mary agreed. 'Are you okay?'

'Just tired. We've got a serial rapist this time. I get the feeling we're going to be seeing more of his handiwork.'

As the sound of the shower continued, Mary left to comfort Gloria, the second victim of Melanie's sexual assault.

15

Before Anya left the unit, she sat down to re-read Louise Richardson's file. Her offender had used the exact phrase, and the pharmacist had suffered an almost identical bruise near her collarbone. Her attacker had also carried a knife, but Anya assumed the police already had those details. Checking the logbook for the evidence fridge, she saw that the specimens had been removed but not collected by the police. They were listed as destroyed. Anya hurried to find Mary Singer, who was writing up her own notes in the main office area.

'Do you remember Louise Richardson, the pharmacist attacked near the hospital?'

'The one trying for a baby.' Mary glanced up. 'Husband was into art, I think.'

'Yes. What happened to her specimens? I thought she wanted to go to the police.'

'Ah, she called a couple of days later and wanted us to destroy the samples. Said she didn't want the police involved.'

Damn! 'Do you remember the name of the pharmacy?'

'It's in the lane behind the specialists' centre, I think.' Mary returned to her notes.

Anya used the Internet to locate the pharmacy and phoned, asking for Louise. The man on the phone said Louise had left work and was not returning. He offered to help, but Anya knew that if Louise had voluntarily disappeared, like so many victims did following an assault, there was little chance of eliciting more information about the attacker. Telling the police about Louise Richardson was a breach of confidentiality but they somehow had to be warned about a violent serial offender. In Anya's experience, the violence would only escalate.

In her Annandale office later that day, Anya put down the receiver in disbelief. After wading through the next six cases Morgan Tully had sent, she had called the president of the College of Pathologists. Each file she reviewed suggested that Alf Carney found remote and even theoretical reasons to deem each of the deaths from natural causes. No wonder Carney was under investigation by the Coroner's office. Despite highly suspicious circumstances surrounding each death, the police's hands were tied once Carney had labelled the deaths due to vitamin, mineral or some other deficiency.

Her secretary knocked on the door with a coffee and a slice of chocolate cake.

'You're quiet today. Everything all right?'

Anya took the offerings and put them on the table beside her paperwork. 'Thanks. I could do with more caffeine.'

'Your lawyer conference is rebooked for Thursday.' Anya instantly recognised Elaine's concerned-mother expression. 'Long night?'

'You could say that. But this lot . . .' Anya waved her hand over the case-files, 'has got me stumped. I can't see why someone with Alf Carney's experience and renown can come to conclusions like this. Don't suppose you've heard anything on the grapevine about his health?'

Elaine blushed, just perceptibly. 'Are you asking me to make some discreet inquiries?'

Anya felt awkward discussing Peter Latham with Elaine, even more so since the older pair had begun playing bridge together once a week. She didn't know whether the relationship was platonic or not, and didn't really want to know. She ate the icing off the cake.

'No. I don't know what I'm asking. It just seems so odd.'

Elaine sat in the chair across from Anya's desk. 'Peter said he'd spent some time with Alf recently. I think he feels sorry for him. His wife died a few years ago. After that, he took up with some alternative-health practitioner, but that didn't last long. Sounds as though the man thinks the world is against him at the moment.'

'Why don't I know this stuff?'

'His wife died about the time you were away in

114

England. No one talks about it any more. Besides, if I wanted the latest gossip, you'd be the last one to ask.'

'Fair enough. I can sympathise with him, but the reports speak volumes about his lack of knowledge and dubious interpretation. Based on the objective findings, I can't agree with any of his conclusions about cause of death.'

As though anticipating her next thought, Elaine offered, 'You don't have to worry about me telling anyone what's going on.'

'I appreciate that. Apparently, Alf didn't ever sit or pass the college exams. He dodged the training and all the exams by being in rural areas without any pathologists. He started doing autopsies and working with the police because there was no one else to do it.' She sipped the coffee. 'Years later, he was awarded an honorary fellowship by the college, so no one ever questioned his qualifications.'

'But if his findings are so controversial, why haven't they been challenged before?'

'That's what I don't understand. These cases go years back. There weren't any complaints before, which means that lawyers and police loved him. His opinion helped convict a lot of people.'

'Didn't you say he finds cause of death natural in those cases?'

'That's what doesn't make sense. Somewhere he's switched allegiance. Maybe it had something to do with that alternative-health practitioner you said he was involved with?'

Elaine crossed her legs. 'A man under the influence of a siren?'

'Hardly, but he might have been influenced by an evangelical belief in vitamin and immune deficiencies as causes for all ills.'

Elaine stood and straightened. 'Does the college think there's a problem with him?'

'There has been some concern from other pathologists, but no one's made a formal complaint. That's how he's managed to keep practising. No one's game to ruin his career.'

Elaine left the room but returned a few minutes later with a knock. 'There are two women here to see you.'

Anya took the time to close the files and move them into a drawer before she greeted Gloria and Melanie Havelock in the corridor. Melanie didn't make eye-contact as they found seats in Anya's office.

'We need to speak with you,' Gloria began. 'We found your address in the phonebook.'

'I'm glad you came. How are you feeling, Melanie?'

The younger woman stared at the table. 'How am I supposed to feel? Mum gets raped, lies about it and doesn't tell us that there were photos of us in her bag, along with our address. Then I get raped in our own house. How do you think I feel?'

'I imagine very angry, which is absolutely normal right now.'

Gloria fiddled with the collar of her plaid shirt.

'It's my fault, what happened to Melanie. I thought I was protecting her by not making a police statement.'

Anya leant forwards in her chair. 'You had to do what was right for you at the time. Every rapist tells the victim he knows where she or he lives, and threatens to come back if the police are called. It's their way of trying to control you afterwards as well.' She stood up, unable to wheel her chair around to Melanie. Instead, she sat on the desk near her. 'Sexual assault has nothing to do with sex. It's all about control.'

For the first time, Melanie Havelock looked back.

'Can we find out if whoever did this to Mum did this to me too?'

'That's difficult,' Anya said.

'What about the forensic evidence? Mum said you examined her at the time.'

Gloria looked away and closed her eyes again. This must have been so painful for her. She did not just suffer herself. She had to relive it with her child.

'I asked them to destroy it all,' she almost whispered.

'What?' Melanie asked. 'What does Mum mean? You can't destroy evidence! There must be something left.'

'I can't send the SAI kit – all the notes on the examination and specimens collected – on to the police without written permission. Your mother didn't give it. That means she chose not to make a police statement or be involved in an investigation.' Anya paused, and clasped her hands. 'Because she didn't want to do either of those things, she wanted us to destroy the samples, which we did.'

'So what you're saying is that whoever did it to Mum got away with it? And maybe came back for me too?' The young woman stood and dug her fingers into her scalp. 'How could you do that?'

Anya understood the frustration, but tried to make it clearer. 'It's the law. Your mother had the same choices you now have. We have to respect her decisions. Just like we respect yours.'

'I'm nothing like my mother.'

Gloria Havelock buried her face in her hands and began to cry.

Her daughter leant on the desk, ignoring the older woman's distress. 'I want this bastard to pay, whether my mother likes it or not. I want the police to get the evidence you took from me last night and find the bastard. He is not going to get away with what he did to me.'

'He said he'd come back and kill you,' Gloria sobbed.

Melanie stood straight and spoke calmly. 'Not if I find him first.'

16

Anya sat on the bench outside the police forensic labs, watching the crime-scene police file out of a meeting. She had mixed feelings about being here. Technically, what she had to say could be considered a breach of confidentiality, but she also had a duty to the community to help the police prevent major crimes from taking place.

Eventually, Detective Inspector Hayden Richards broke free from the group surrounding him outside the brick building. A compelling speaker, Richards had more experience investigating serial sexual assault than anyone else in the state, and always took time to pass on his expertise.

He'd been morbidly obese most of his life, but the junkfood addict had shed a spectacular proportion of his bulk and now merely bordered on 'overweight'. The change in his appearance took Anya by surprise, not having seen the detective in over six months.

He greeted his visitor with a proud smile and shook her hand firmly. Anya half-expected him to pivot to show off the new physique.

'You look healthier than ever,' Anya blurted, before she stopped herself. What if the weight loss had been because of illness or even cancer? She bit her tongue.

'You're looking well yourself.' Hayden grinned through his dark moustache. 'There's nothing like diabetes and a cancer scare to make you wake up to yourself.'

'I'm sorry to hear that,' Anya managed.

'Don't be, nothing else could make me give up the smokes. I even discovered vegetables were edible!' He offered a seat back on the bench. 'I'm lucky it happened when it did. Lectures start again after the break and I guess this isn't social. What have you got for me?'

Anya smiled. She liked the man's directness and knew she could rely on his discretion.

'A possible serial sex-offender. He's confident, brazen, and has taken time to eat at one scene we know of.'

Hayden pulled out a pack of chewing gum and offered some to Anya, who shook her head.

'Is the SA Taskforce investigating?'

'Not yet. Technically, I can't go to them yet. So far only one victim's made a police statement. The other, a pharmacist, just changed her mind. I'm concerned we may not get any others to come forward, or if they do, they might not even consent to being examined.'

Hayden frowned, popping a piece of gum. 'He says he'll kill them if they talk to anyone?'

'Exactly. The "I know where you live" routine.'

He rolled his eyes. 'The first thing they learn in rape 101. Why do you think they won't be examined if they turn up at one of your units?'

'We now have a directive to photograph victims and injuries, especially the genital ones.'

'Bullshit! Since when?'

'This week. Of course, the victims can refuse, but just asking has caused some refusals of consent even to examination. The mere mention of photography really spooks someone who's already vulnerable.'

Hayden did his blowfish impersonation, both hands on hips. Sitting down, the effect was lost.

'And with intimate stuff all over the Internet, no one smart is about to trust photos staying in police hands. What dickhead came up with that one? Can't be anyone who's ever spoken to a victim?'

'Officially, it's come from the department. Lyndsay Gatlow's been pushing for it and obviously has the backing.'

He shook his head slowly. 'That she-devil would devour her own offspring if she thought it would help her career. I'd like to photograph her where the sun don't shine and see how she likes it.'

Anya smiled again. This was one of the reasons she respected the detective. He was a perceptive judge of character. It was also what made him a great investigator, especially in sexual assault. If another detective managed to record a one-page statement from a victim, Hayden would go back and elicit ten times that amount of information. His ability to get victims to remember the most obscure detail could lead to an arrest and prevent further assaults.

'So what have you got exactly?'

His eyes sparkled. He was more than interested.

'Two women with similar injuries but different stories. One was attacked just after she got home from the train. My guess is he followed her, but her mother was raped a year ago and had her bag stolen. The rapist might have already known the address. The other was grabbed in a car park opposite the pharmacy she'd just closed.'

Anya ticked off the facts with her fingers. 'Physically speaking, both attacks involved a knife and both women had similar genital injuries – minor bleeding in both cases, no permanent damage.'

'How violent is he?'

'Punches them in the face when he thinks they've seen him. The knife he's using leaves an impressive bruise on their chests.'

'But he hasn't used it on them.'

'Only to scratch and frighten.'

'Has he changed his MO? One outside, one inside?'

'Maybe not. They were both attacked near train stations so he may be on foot. They're both in the same area.'

The detective chewed his gum, seemingly deep in thought.

'Any distinct characteristics?'

'He wears a dark cap, jeans, T-shirt. One mentioned a white hand so he's probably Caucasian.'

'Then he doesn't wear gloves?'

The detective delivered a penetrating gaze. He was processing every minute detail.

'Yes, but he has taken them off during the attacks.'

'Interesting. He is careful about leaving evidence, but just has to feel skin once he's got them under his control. Leave any semen, hairs, fingerprints?'

'Not that I've found, but I've only had one kit to send off. But here's the interesting part: he does have this thing he said to both of them: "If you can't be hurt, you can't be loved."'

'A penny fucking philosopher.' Hayden continued chewing. 'We can rule out Shakespeare and every other genius in town. Obviously fancies himself as smart. Anything found at the house?'

'Not that I've heard.'

'I'll check it out with crime scene.'

One of the hovering constables waved to the detective and pointed to her watch.

'Thanks for filling me in. I'll run a check and see if there have been any other similar assaults reported in the area in the last few months. And, if you see any more women . . .'

'Unless they go to the police, I can't give you much.'

'Yeah, yeah, but ethically you can ask them whatever you want. Think of yourself as a conduit. I'll make up a list of questions in case anyone else comes in.'

'I can't interrogate victims. I'm their advocate, remember?'

'You want this guy off the streets more than any of us. You've seen first-hand the damage he does. If no one else goes to the police, you're the best shot at catching this animal.' He stood up, hitched up his trousers at the waist and grabbed his lecture materials. 'If he's already hitting them, the violence is only going to escalate. The reality of rape never lives up to his fantasy. He'll be killing before he's finished.'

Hayden swallowed the chewing gum and headed off to teach the next batch of investigators.

17

Later that afternoon, Anya pulled into the preschool car park, barely avoiding a four-wheel
drive partly blocking the entrance. Finding a
designated place to stop, she checked her watch.
A few minutes early shouldn't matter. She
couldn't wait to see Ben and had trouble waiting
until his finishing time. Other mothers milled
outside the childproof gate, parading the latest
fashions in gym gear. Judging by the perfect
make-up, hair and figures, most of the day was
spent preening and exercising. Anya wondered if
they had trouble living up to their own images.

Inside the gate, she entered the preschool building and did a quick check for her four-year-old.

'Can I help you?' offered a woman wearing a
cardboard crown covered in glitter.

'I've come to pick up Ben.'

'Of course, Mrs Hegarty. Sorry, I didn't recognise you.' She sat back down at a small table
covered in scrunched-up paper. Three toddlers
with busy hands stuck the paper to coloured
cardboard. 'He's outside, playing with the other
boys,' she said. 'He's had a fantastic day.'

Anya didn't bother to correct the 'Mrs Hegarty', her former married name, and wondered if a child's day was ever described as anything other than 'fantastic'. Even so, she knew her son enjoyed his time at preschool. In the vast outside play area, she scanned the climbing frame, swings, fort and bike-track. In the distance she saw a group of boys playing chase and watched the unmistakable frame of her child, running around, laughing and calling out to the others. She cherished these moments – the ones that most mothers took for granted. Day-to-day things that she rarely got to see, let alone share, like a little boy running as fast as his short legs could manage in the company of friends. No fears, no concerns, just being himself.

She walked over slowly, dodging a tricycle and soccer ball. The boys seemed oblivious as she stood nearby. They paused for a rest.

'What are we gunna do next?' panted the one with the reddest face.

'How about playing ninjas?'

'Can I play?' asked a larger boy.

'No. We don't want you to play,' Ben announced.

The other boy started to yell, 'I wanna play too.'

'No!' Ben stood defiant.

Not sure why he would behave like that, Anya waited until he'd spun around in a fighting pose before she called his name. Ben froze, a guilty look on his face.

126

Anya moved forwards and hugged him. 'Hi boys, what are you up to?'

Ben answered, 'Playing Jedi knights.' As the six other boys ran off to face some evil character, the boy her son had confronted stood staring.

Ben approached his mother and wrapped both arms tightly around her waist. 'Mum, I love you.'

'Love you too.' She knelt down to his eye-level and whispered, 'I'll go inside and get your bag.'

Inside, she found the teacher Ben chatted about most. Miss Celeste was a pretty young woman dressed in bright yellow overalls. Large sparkly spheres hung from her ears. She sat on the floor, singing nursery rhymes with the kids as they picked up pieces of confetti, Lego and other toys.

Anya waited for a break in the song, and Miss Celeste stood up.

'Hi, I just thought I'd ask how Ben's going, particularly with the other children?'

Miss Celeste's expression became serious. 'I've been hoping to speak to you. He's very social and enjoys playing, but he needs some work with cutting. His scissor-work is behind the others, and it's very important to work on that for when he goes to school.' She had a look almost of pity on her face.

Anya tried to absorb the wider implication of the problem. 'How is he going otherwise?'

'Fine, but we do have to make him come in to do craft. He spends all his time running around with the boys outside. He doesn't seem interested in the pre-reading and writing activities yet. But boys are often slower in that part of their development.' The teacher waved goodbye to one of the other children and returned to tidying up the collage pieces strewn on the floor.

Anya bent down to help.

'Maybe he prefers to read at home.'

By the look on her face, this was news to Miss Celeste. She brushed some hair off her forehead with the back of her hand. 'Do you sit and read with him?'

Anya nodded.

'Little boys always want to please their mothers and will go to great lengths to get one-on-one time with them. You are not living with your husband, I gather.'

'No, but—'

Miss Celeste smiled. 'All parents have great hopes for their children. Here we let them learn at their own pace. Ben is behaving as we'd expect any four-year-old to, except for his craft skills.'

Suddenly, Ben appeared from his game, short of breath, and pulled at Anya's shirt.

'Come on, Mum, let's go!'

From someone who wanted to stay, he had fast developed an urgent need to leave. Miss Celeste said goodbye to him by name, and Anya began to get the message. Ben didn't want her speaking to the teachers.

On the way home, they stopped at a park and the two climbed out. Ben ran towards the swings and clambered onto one. Anya pushed him from behind.

'Hey, Speedie, how do you like preschool?'

'It's okay; good.'

'What are the other kids like?'

'Good.'

'How do you like the work they want you to do?'

He swung higher. 'It's okay.'

Great. Benjamin had skipped childhood and gone straight for teenage monosyllables.

'You like fitting in, don't you?' She pushed his back.

He kicked both legs in the air and leant back. 'I really like having friends. There's a kid at pre-school who's different. No one likes him 'cause he's got Hamburgers disease.'

'What does that mean?'

'Miss Celeste said his brain makes it hard to make friends.'

Anya understood. 'You mean he has Asperger's Syndrome?'

'I think that's it. The other kids made fun of me after I talked about going to the ballet for news. They said ballet was for girls and kept picking on me.'

Anya hadn't forgotten how it felt to seem different, standing out from everyone else. It made her spend more time alone. Worse than that, it made her lonely. 'I didn't know you had a hard time to start with. You didn't tell me.'

129

'I know.' He used his feet as a brake and stopped himself mid-swing. 'Then Brandon, this boy with that problem, came along, and now I don't seem so different. No one picks on me any more.'

'Do they pick on Brandon?'

Ben shuffled his feet and nodded.

'Do you?'

'No . . . But if we let him play, he gets really rough and hurts us.' Ben wouldn't meet Anya's gaze. 'Everyone's scared of him.'

'Is he the one you didn't want to play with?'

'Uh-huh.' He stared at his lap.

Anya tried to swing him around to face her but he resisted.

'What do the teachers say?'

'That he has trouble learning and we should be nice to him. But Mum, he does naughty stuff on purpose. He waits until the teachers aren't looking then he hits someone or ruins our game.'

Anya moved around to face her son and knelt on the ground.

'Were you scared just then when you told him he couldn't play?'

'Uh-huh.' He looked up. 'No one else would do it.'

Being an adult wasn't all that different from being a child, she thought, only grown-ups had no excuse. The problem was, adult bullies got away with a lot more. People like Veronica Slater, Lyndsay Gatlow and every rapist used power to play on victims' vulnerability. It didn't take great social skills, either.

She bent forwards and held her son. 'Let's both agree to stop bullies, no matter why they hurt people, whenever we can. How's that for a deal?'

'That's a good deal.'

'Hey, how about having a silly day? Who can do the silliest walk back to the car?'

'Me!'

Ben leapt out of the swing and began zig-zagging his way through the park. Anya did her penguin walk, only backwards, much to his delight.

As she watched him giggle, she worried about her child growing up too fast, even if his empathy made her proud. Children were supposed to have fun, be carefree. They weren't meant to worry themselves about society's ills. Ben was never meant to feel responsible for what happened to other people or take it on himself to protect them. It was a lesson she could equally apply to herself.

18

At seven thirty on Monday morning, Anya parked behind the unmarked detective's car on Hastings Road. Still glowing from a full weekend with her son, she unclipped her seatbelt and admired the Castle Hill home. Immaculate lawns and box-hedges gave the Federation-style house an almost fairytale appeal. Anya retrieved her doctor's bag and a forensic-collection briefcase from the boot. In the quiet, leafy area, tall gum trees protruded from behind two-storey mansions, most with triple garages at ground level. The sound of a breeze rustling leaves gave it a homely feel.

The area reeked of affluence, the kind synonymous with 'new money'. Old money would have invested in acreage or land with water views. People here obviously put their resources into large homes and landscaped backyards in the hope of a better quality of life – a safe environment for children to grow up in.

Now that safety had been shattered.

Walking on the driveway to the path, Anya noticed white powder on the lid and handles of two large wheeled bins by the road.

Detective Sergeant Meira Sorrenti, from the sexual-assault taskforce, greeted Anya on the front lawn. The olive-skinned detective had short black hair that complemented large round brown eyes. She could have fitted in with any number of ethnic groups. The pair had never met before, but Anya knew that Meira's recent promotion to the unit had created some disquiet amongst the forensic physicians. Rumour had it Meira Sorrenti believed doctors were largely incompetent and hindered rather than helped investigations.

'We've secured the crime scene. The victim's inside. Name is Jodie Davis. She didn't get a look at the offender's face, so we're relying on you to get something.'

Anya didn't detect any animosity. 'Is she badly injured?'

The detective led her across the lawn towards a side gate, the entrance blocked by blue and white crime-scene tape.

'Took a beating. The guy attacked her here while she was putting out the rubbish bins.'

She pointed through the gate at a crime-scene officer in gloves and blue overalls who was photographing the area. 'He dragged her back here. Sounds like he wore a dark cap and gloves. He had a knife and threatened to kill her if she made a sound. He raped her once that she remembers. After that, she says she blacked out.'

Anya could almost picture the assault. Next-door neighbours, separated by a treated-pine fence, probably had no idea what had occurred so close.

'So, he didn't enter the house?'

'We don't think so. Nothing's missing and two small kids were in bed upstairs. It doesn't look like they were touched. Thank God.'

'Is there a husband?'

'Inside. Seems genuine. Poor bastard found her after he got home from a work function. Back door was unlocked and no wife in sight. That was about eleven. When he found her, he saw the bruises, panicked and called the local doctor, who's apparently an old friend. That's who first called the local Ds, who then notified us.'

Meira shoved a hand in the pocket of her grey jacket. 'The smart bastard even went back to finish putting out the bins afterwards.'

Probably to maintain the impression of normality, Anya thought. 'Don't suppose you found the condom if he used one?'

'If he put anything in the bin, he either planned it or got lucky. Garbage truck had already been by the time uniforms got here. Some SOCO is still chasing down the truck.'

'Even if you do find a used condom, it's a big leap to pin it to this place last night.'

'I know. But it may be all we've got,' Meira conceded.

'Did he say anything unusual to her during the assault?'

'Yeah, the sicko basically said he loved her, and that's why it hurt.'

Anya felt her stomach lurch. It had to be the same offender.

Across the road, a white delivery van pulled up to a green metal box sitting on top of a pole. The driver pulled a sack from the side door and placed it in the storage container.

Even a routine mail delivery would be treated with suspicion after last night. Detective Sorrenti took out a black notebook and documented the time and registration number of the van. Birds cooed in the warm breeze.

'I'll take you in. At least she hasn't showered yet.'

They entered through one of two wooden doors with intact stained-glass panels. A curved staircase led off the tiled foyer. A bunch of fresh yellow tulips sat in a glass vase on a round table under the steps, amidst wedding photos and framed shots of smiling babies and young children.

Further inside, a large kitchen/family room with a glassed observatory area had views to an expansive backyard and pool. Tastefully decorated rather than a show-home, this place had furniture and fittings especially for a young family. Colouring pencils and paper were strewn across a small wooden table in the centre of the living space.

The kitchen benches gave off the unmistakable odour of lemon-scented cleaner.

Detective Constable Abbott met them and

spoke quietly. 'The family only moved here a couple of months ago from the US and have had numerous tradesmen come and go, to replace taps, fit water-saving devices, not to mention gas outlets, pay-TV, curtains. There's a new pool man, delivery men, removalists. It's a long list.'

'Well, that's where you start,' Meira snapped.

The male detective headed for the front door.

Jodie Davis sat on a leather lounge in the rumpus room off the main living area. The petite blonde, enveloped in a white towelling gown, held her husband's hand. Her small knuckles blanched with the tight grip.

Anya introduced herself. James Davis stood and limply shook hands, exposing a brown towel placed underneath his wife. Jodie was probably bleeding. The towel would be an important piece of evidence.

'Did the police explain my role?' she asked.

The pair nodded.

'I'm here because you asked for me. Is that true?'

'Yes,' Jodie answered through a swollen jaw.

'I'm a lawyer,' the husband said. 'Jode was my receptionist before we had the kids.' He pushed small oval glasses to the bridge of his nose with the middle finger of his spare hand. 'We both understand what she's consenting to.'

The subject of the conversation silently nodded. She was letting James speak for her, but she had to give the consent herself.

Anya wanted to engage her one-to-one, but Jodie spoke first. 'I want to do what James says is right. What do I have to sign?'

Anya tried to explain that Jodie had to be exact in what she consented to, but the small blonde woman seemed adamant. Her husband spoke for her.

'I want the police to protect our children in case he comes back,' James said.

'How old are they?' Anya asked, noticing a large wooden cubby house through the windows.

'Our daughter's four and our son has just turned two.'

'I couldn't help noticing the photos on the table inside. They are gorgeous. Bet they love the cubby,' Anya said, trying to relax Jodie as she removed the large yellow SAI kit from her bag. Talking about children might help make the examination a little less difficult, for both of them.

Jodie spoke. 'They'd spend half their lives in it if I let them.'

'I don't blame them! My little boy would love it.'

Anya excused herself, stepped past the husband and asked if she could take Jodie's blood pressure. It wasn't a necessary part of the examination, but it would help make the whole process a little less foreign to a victim. And the initial touch helped ease into the forensic examination.

'110 over 70. Normal.'

Jodie released her husband's hand. 'How old is he – your child?'

'Four going on fifty-five, sometimes.'

'They're all a bit like that these days.' The woman half-smiled.

'Jode, would you like me to stay?' James offered.

She patted his hand. 'Maybe you could ring your mum and see if the kids are okay.'

Anya found the light switch and closed the curtains, noticing a small gap between the roman blinds and windowsills.

During the examination, Jodie disclosed that the man had pulled her jumper over her face so she couldn't see him. He then removed his gloves and dug his fingers hard into her flesh. Bruises on her breasts were consistent with the story. A linear bruise on the left side extending towards the collarbone was almost identical to the ones Anya had seen before. Her heart sank. The attacks were getting closer. There would be more women before he was caught.

She pulled the digital camera from her bag. Admittedly, a picture of the injury might help track down the weapon.

'The mark left by the knife is very distinctive. I've seen it twice before.'

'Is it legal to do this in the house? I mean, not in your surgery or the hospital?'

Anya smiled. 'Absolutely, I just need to follow the same protocol.'

Jodie pulled a rug up to cover herself. 'So this isn't his first attack?'

'I'm afraid it looks like it. If the police are going

to catch him, they have to try and find the knife. That'll help narrow down the search.'

'My husband does negligence cases for one of the biggest firms in the country. Sometimes he has to look at hideous pictures of surgery scars and bruises.' She clung to the rug. 'Do what you have to.'

'The knife mark is probably the most important, and we can cover your breasts, for more privacy.'

Anya took the digital photos as quickly as possible, placing a tape-measure guide adjacent to the bruise, then pulled the rug back up to the woman's neck before continuing the examination.

She followed the protocol for specimen collections and carefully sealed each tube, making sure she secured the chain of evidence.

'Did you build the cubby house? It's a great idea having a barn door the kids can open half of.' Anya made small talk as best she could as she performed an internal examination.

'It was here when we moved in, but the cats keep getting in. The latch is broken and I can't lock it.' Jodie winced and tightened her legs, but then relaxed again, staring at the ceiling. 'Can't tell you how many times I've scrubbed the smell of cat pee out of that place.'

Anya located the source of the bleeding. Again, it was consistent with the other assaults. 'The bleeding should settle in a day or two. It's like a scratch inside the vagina.'

'Please don't take any more pictures.' Jodie's eyes welled with tears.

'Don't worry, I won't. That's about it for the examination,' Anya said, careful to cover all of Jodie with the rug after giving her a sanitary pad from her doctor's case. 'I'll need to dry the towel you've been sitting on and put it in a bag to take with me.'

Jodie nodded. 'Can James come back in?'

'Of course.'

Anya headed for the door and let the nervous husband back in. 'I'll be back in a minute,' she said, looking for Detective Sorrenti, whom she found standing in the front hall, giving orders to crime-scene officers.

'Just heard you had a chat to Hayden Richards.' Sorrenti put both hands on her hips. 'I don't appreciate you going behind my back. If you've got relevant information, you come to me, especially with something as solid as the phrase he keeps coming out with.'

Anya bristled. 'I don't work for you, and I spoke to Hayden off the record because I had little to go on, with one victim refusing to speak to police. You know how it works. I was suggesting there might be a serial offender, and rather than waste your time it seemed sensible to have a talk to him first.'

'Thanks to you, he's now consulting on the taskforce.'

'So this is about rivalry?' Anya could barely

control her annoyance. 'Don't you think that's a little petty when it isn't even safe to put the rubbish out any more? With more than thirty unsolved rapes in this area, I'd have thought you'd be grateful for the extra manpower and experience.'

Hayden Richards appeared in the doorway, wiped his feet and entered.

'Ladies,' he said, hitching up his trousers. 'What have you got?'

'Detective Sorrenti can fill you in,' Anya replied, and wandered out the open back door. She headed for the cubby, about fifteen metres from the house. Built on stilts, it gave enough elevation for a great slide. Ben would definitely love it. Pity there was no real yard in her inner-city terrace.

Climbing the ladder, she stood on the small verandah and took in the view of the lounge room and kitchen. Opening the bolted door, she entered and saw the plastic table just inside. With the top half of the stable door open, she could see the police inside the house, wandering between rooms at the back. She closed the door and immediately noticed the stale smell of body odour. In one corner, she noticed a faint, pale stain, long since washed.

She called for the taskforce detectives.

Meira stood, hand on hip, shielding her eyes from the sun. 'What is it? Jodie said cats get in there all the time.'

'Well, the bolt works perfectly and from inside there's a great view of the rooms in the back. My guess is it isn't cat urine she's been cleaning up.'

19

The slide switched to that of Jodie Davis's bruised chest. Magnified, two additional perpendicular marks were visible midway along the bruise.

Meira Sorrenti sat forwards. 'What sort of knife are we looking at?'

'Melanie Havelock described a narrow blade, but can't remember anything else.' With the laser-pointer, Anya directed attention to a small mark at the edge of the bruise, just above the covered nipple line. Even higher was a fainter impression that could easily have been missed. 'This is made by part of the handle. My guess is the attacker put pressure on the woman's chest with the knife held flat, but moved the handle during that time, which left the two marks you can see.'

Hayden Richards stopped taking notes. 'It doesn't fit with a kitchen knife. The handle's too wide.'

'I agree. What's interesting is that the blade itself isn't very long, only about three inches.'

Meira stood and looked closer at the screen. 'Could be a switchblade.'

Detective Constable Abbott put his hands

behind his head. 'If it is, tracking it'll be almost impossible. There's a huge black market and chasing Internet sellers takes a lot more manpower and computer expertise than we've got.'

He looked across the briefing room at the analyst, who shook her head at the thought.

A gentle knock on the door caught their attention.

Hayden stood and shook hands with the adult Harry Potter lookalike. 'This is Doctor Quentin Lagardia. He's a profiler. Some of you already know him. For those who don't, he's got a PhD in abnormal psychology and has put together some profiles for SA units around the country.'

Meira remained standing and folded her arms. 'We have a detective in this building who is trained in profiling.'

'Yes, but Doctor Lagardia is here at the request of the Local Area Commander due to the media's propensity to jump on serial cases.'

Quentin repositioned his glasses and cleared his throat. A mild hand tremor disappeared when he unzipped his jacket and opened his briefcase at the table.

Hayden quickly introduced the profiler to everyone in the room.

'Doctor Crichton was about to discuss the pattern of injuries the two victims sustained.'

Anya drew two body outlines on the whiteboard and marked the areas in which each of the three women suffered injuries. Melanie Havelock and Jodie Davis were named, but Louise Richardson was labelled Victim One to protect her privacy.

'A fourth woman, Gloria Havelock – Melanie's mother – was raped by two men a year ago, but only one of the injuries matched, so we'll leave her out for now. The others all had trauma to the left sides of their faces from a hit. With the knife mark on the left side of the chests, he holds the knife in his right hand but must swap it to punch with that hand when he thinks they've looked at him. Jodie Davies had a swollen jaw even though he pulled her jumper over her face early in the assault. She didn't see him at all.'

'He's right-handed. Was her bra pushed up or cut?' Quentin Lagardia enquired.

'Intact and pushed up.'

The profiler nodded and scribbled on his papers. 'What about the others?'

'Havelock and Davis reported the same thing. I can't be sure about Victim One.'

'Can you tell me anything about Victim One and her assault?'

'She's a professional who works later than normal business hours, and who worked in the same area the other attacks have taken place. She's my height, a bit heavier and has brown shoulder-length hair.' Anya referred to the intelligence statement she'd written. 'She had on blue trousers and a white shirt, nothing revealing. She's a little hunched due to a scoliosis – curvature of the spine – so doesn't look her full height, I suppose.'

Meira sounded impatient. 'Did she see anything that can identify the man? Do we know if he looked familiar, did he have a car? Anything you can give us that will actually help?'

'This is helping. The detail is crucial,' Hayden said. 'May I suggest we make the most of the resources we have with us today.'

Meira shot him an angry stare. 'Then let's ask the locals. Did you find anyone last night? Any information from the canvass?'

DC Abbott cleared his throat. 'The doorknock of the area didn't yield much. No one even knew the family, and had no idea what cars they drove. It's a problem with automatic garages. No one knows the regular comings and goings of the neighbours. They did manage to remember who owned the most expensive house in the area.'

'Who lived there before?' Quentin asked. 'Maybe Jodie wasn't the original target.'

'A widower and his four sons.'

Hayden stood and paced. 'I want to go over all offences within a ten-kilometre radius that might have been misrecorded: bag snatches, robberies, muggings. It's possible he was interrupted and the incidents were never reported as an assault. We may have to reinterview the complainants, to see if he threatened them with sexual assault, or if he fits the description we've already got.'

The analyst took copious notes. 'I'll get right on it.'

'I've asked Anya to fill in any details she can on Victim One. Given the fact that she won't come forward and speak to us, we need to know as much as possible about her.'

'What about the rape kit she had done? Can that be tested anonymously?' Abbott asked.

'No,' Meira snapped. 'Not unless she gives us permission, and that means making a statement.'

'Yeah, but if it's anonymous, even if the evidence links the same offender with the other victims, it gives us a pattern and strengthens the brief we'll give to the prosecutors.'

Anya understood his logic, but it wasn't that simple. 'The Office of the Director of Public Prosecutions has made it very clear that it can't use anonymous samples in evidence. I've been trying to get them to accept coded samples, but there's debate as to whether that still betrays a victim's confidence. Especially since a code has to be able to be traced back to the victim. It's a chain-of-evidence concern that opens up a legal can of worms.'

Abbott thought for a moment. 'Then why don't you just encourage the women to give false names? Who are we to know if the woman isn't who she says? That way she might feel safe enough to give a statement.'

'I didn't hear that,' Meira said with a wry smile.

For the first time, Anya felt she was on the same wavelength as the taskforce leader.

'Victim One wanted her kit destroyed and we had to comply with that request. There's no evidence left.'

Meira threw a pen across the desk in front of her.

Hayden scratched his moustache. 'Any suspects so far?'

Abbott spoke with less confidence. 'The local boys pulled over a guy last night. Twenty-eight-year-old Caucasian. Five foot nine, solid. Had a porno mag in the car and had a dark cap, sunglasses. He was abusive, uncooperative and lives near the station.'

Hayden walked to the whiteboard and wrote down the details. 'Put him down as a person of interest. Anyone else?'

'Geoffrey Willard,' Meira announced. 'Released three weeks ago from Long Bay. Did twenty years for the rape and stabbing murder of a fourteen-year-old girl. He's 1.7 metres, weighs about 80 kilograms.'

'He did a runner a few nights ago when the locals found out where he lived and threw rocks at his mother,' Hayden said. 'We want him under surveillance when we find him.'

'Haven't the women described their attacker as taller and heavier than that?' Abbott ventured.

Quentin shifted in his seat. 'Often people overestimate the size of their assailant. It's understandable given they've been overpowered and don't have the normal perspective.'

148

But eye-witnesses still swayed courts. Anya had been to one of Hayden's talks in which a man in sports gear ran into the lecture theatre, held a prop gun to Hayden's head and took his wallet before fleeing. From the theatre full of detectives, descriptions varied from a five-foot-tall white man to a six-foot-tall dark, swarthy-looking man of Middle Eastern appearance. An hour later, the supposed thief returned to the theatre and took his place in the front row. No one recognised him in a suit. That proved a great lesson to Anya. Eye-witnesses were notoriously unreliable.

'But bear in mind,' Anya said, 'that women being assaulted often notice tiny details about their attacker. They are close to them for a relatively long period of time. Their senses also seemed to be heightened, they notice smells, sounds, things that other victims don't.'

'Exactly,' Hayden said. 'That's why I'd like to reinterview the two victims who've already made statements. The statements are in no way detailed enough.'

Meira seemed to take that personally, but it probably wasn't intended that way. Hayden was a perfectionist and asked far more questions than any other investigator. It meant he also got more answers.

'Let's talk about the profile,' he added, sitting down.

Quentin handed out some typed pages.

'From the statements, and especially his saying

149

about hurt and love, this guy sounds like a classic power-reassurance rapist. He commits sexual assaults to assert power over victims, which reassures him of his masculinity. He often doesn't do well socially and lacks confidence sexually, especially with women. Generally, he'll use minimal force to subdue his victims, although this guy lashes out when he thinks he's been seen. If he carries a knife, he doesn't intend to use it. It's more for the power and effect it has. He also uses surprise as a weapon.'

'Which is why he lurks around stations and car parks,' Meira said.

'Actually, no. I believe this man carefully chooses his victims. Often this kind of rapist stalks the women in advance. He knows their routine and pounces when the best opportunity arises.'

'If you rule out Gloria Havelock's attackers, the rapes may still be opportunistic,' Meira argued. 'The one in the car park and the Havelock girl coming home from the station. Even the woman putting out her garbage could have been bad timing on her part.'

'Not necessarily. I think you have to consider the fact that this man knew the victims' movements in advance.'

'What about the saying he comes out with?' Hayden seemed even more interested than the others.

'That's quite predictable,' answered Quentin. 'What we call pseudo-unselfish behaviour.' He thinks that if he shows some kind of concern, he isn't such a bad guy. He's telling himself that he's actually doing something good for these women. In the past he would have been called the "gentleman rapist".'

'Don't reckon that's in the Queensberry Rules,' Abbott quipped.

'He's a gentleman in the sense that he doesn't go out of his way to humiliate and denigrate his victims.'

'Any more than raping them at knife-point does,' Meira responded.

Quentin didn't react this time. 'He also fantasises that the woman is a willing participant and will try to act out his fantasies, especially if she doesn't resist. Like the Havelock girl; he'll spend a fair amount of time, even taking a break to go and eat a meal before assaulting her again. He's playing the role of the partner.'

Hayden drew a timeline on the whiteboard. 'How much time do we have before he attacks again?'

'Not long. This guy is all about ego and self-esteem. He needs to keep raping because his ego can't handle not being boosted. I'd suggest monitoring his victims for a couple of weeks after the assaults, because he may like to have some sort of contact with them. Either bump into them in the shops, phone them, or watch them. He won't stop until he's arrested.'

'And that's the good news?'

'Kind of. Bad news is that if his assaults don't live up to the fantasies he's built up, he could get frustrated. In that case, the violence in the attacks will escalate, particularly if someone resists. He could easily end up killing future victims.'

The room went quiet. A knock on the door interrupted the silence. A woman in plain clothes entered the room with a pile of handouts.

Hayden thanked her and handed out questionnaires that each victim needed to answer. The detectives groaned.

'Do you know how much time this is going to take? Couldn't a psychologist do this instead?' Abbott complained. 'We could be chasing up leads like the one the local boys pulled over.'

Hayden disagreed. 'If he's not our man, we'll have wasted a lot of time. The more we know about the victims, the better. We need to put out a general press release. Anya, I'll leave it to you to contact the mystery woman – Victim One. It'll be less worrying coming from you, and it'll give you a chance to interview your mystery victim.'

Anya looked at the list. The woman who had brought the questionnaires said that she had driven past the Davis home this morning. The place was for sale, and there was no sign of the family. Through the window she noticed the furniture had gone. When questioned, neighbours didn't know where they were, though someone thought they might have left for an overseas holiday.

It was common for assault victims to move

within months of the attack and not to let the police know where they'd gone. If the family had disappeared that quickly, it didn't sound as though Jodie Davis really wanted to be found. She must have panicked about staying in the house. And who could blame her after moving so recently? Physical evidence did not mean much if the victim refused to testify.

'If we can't find her, all we've got now is Melanie Havelock,' Meira said. 'Let's get to work. From the sounds of it, we need to move her to a safe place as soon as possible.'

Abbott stood. 'I'll pay her a visit and arrange for uniforms to keep an eye on her as well.'

As they left the meeting, Hayden spoke quietly to Anya.

'You need to be careful when you interview Victim One. Anything you say can be cross-examined in court. Tread carefully; don't give a defence lawyer anything that'll weaken the victim's evidence. Don't coach her, ask leading questions or put words in her mouth. If you do, the case could go belly up in court and this bastard will have got away with it.'

Great, no pressure, Anya thought. She looked down the list of points to cover. Most made sense, like the physical characteristics, friends, enemies, work history. Then there was 'marital reputation'? What the hell did that mean? Personal demographics were straightforward: education level, intelligence, previous residences. Touching on psychosexual history was understandable, but Anya wished someone else would do it. Any information could be used as a weapon in character assassination of the victim. A victim's arrest record had little to do with the assault, in her experience. Again, it made a jury see the victim as some kind of evil being, and somehow deserving of assault.

Outside the building, on the steps, Hayden explained, 'Things are pretty tense in there. Sorrenti's new to the job and feels undermined by my presence. Don't take it personally.'

'I didn't.'

They descended the stairs, Hayden a little short of breath. 'I need you to ask the pharmacist some more specific questions. About the assault.'

The pair waited for a marked car to exit the underground police car park.

'Even if I track her down, we don't even know if this woman will agree to see me, let alone be quizzed on every aspect of her attack.'

'I know. An unofficial statement is the best chance we have right now. The more we have on how this guy behaves during the attacks, the better the chance of catching him sooner. He may have given something important away, in the way he spoke, what he said, what he didn't say. If he changed attitude during the assault, and what, if anything, provoked him. Did he oblige when she begged him to stop, or did it make him more aggressive?'

'You're asking a lot. This could compromise the sexual assault service if the Department of Health finds out. I'm crossing the line from patient advocate to police interrogator.'

'Every doctor has a duty of care regarding public health. Any information you collect is as important as tracing sources for transmissible diseases. This guy is a disease, and he's spreading sickness fast.'

They crossed the road at the next corner, careful to avoid a grease patch.

'There's no way I'll push her. She's fragile enough. If she says no, that's it.'

'Agreed.' The detective began to puff again as they picked up pace. 'I also need to know whether he took anything belonging to her. Anything at all, or could he have taken it before the assault?'

Anya stopped and waited. Hayden pulled a folded sheet from his jacket with another list of questions. Catching his breath, he said, 'I'm counting on you. Anything that seems insignificant could turn out to be vital.'

20

Back in the SA unit, Anya prepared for the weekly staff meeting. It was mostly a progress report on the week's cases, and an opportunity to discuss issues or rosters.

Each meeting normally began with afternoon tea and a discussion of any clients who concerned the counsellors. Mary Singer chose instead to raise the question of funds for another fridge for storing forensic samples.

As she spoke, the women took their seats in the staffroom.

'Doctor Sinclair had to phone sixteen women this week to make room for new samples. Fourteen women and two men refused to make formal statements. As a result, those specimens have been destroyed. We all know that victims often change their minds and agree to go to the police down the track. We're no good to anyone if the evidence is thrown out because we don't have enough room to keep it.'

One of the other counsellors dunked her teabag in a Garfield cup and grabbed a biscuit before sitting. 'I often have to phone around when space becomes a problem. A bar-fridge just isn't big enough for the amount of work we do.'

Anya and another forensic physician, Pauline Sinclair, shared the full-time job and had the help of four general practitioners for the after-hours roster. The meetings were the best way to find out what had happened on anyone's days off. Anya had not realised space was such a premium in the unit.

'What about the bagged samples – the underwear, towels, sheets that need to dry out?' she asked.

'They're kept in the top cupboards and given to police as requested. The remainder are not a problem. I suppose we've never really thought to throw any of them out because there's always been room for them. It's the refrigerated samples we need to do something with.'

'I'll let Pauline know when she comes in tomorrow.' Mary took notes. 'She apologised for not making it today, but her daughter was getting a music prize at school.'

The women in the group raised their cups and smiled. With all the staff, the achievement of someone's family member was cause for celebration, and something normal and positive to focus on, even for a moment. Everyone spoke amongst themselves for a couple of minutes.

Anya wanted the day to end. 'So, anyone have a case they'd like to discuss?'

Mary chimed in again. 'Melanie Havelock. She

appears stoic and as though she's coping, but her mother tells me she is showering in a swimsuit. She won't be naked. And she'll only shower if her mother is in the next room.'

For the others' benefit, Anya explained. 'We're concerned this might be a serial rapist in the area. We have three cases now, but there could be others. This time, he made Melanie shower after the assault and watched her. That's also where he threatened he'd be back. He carries a knife and leaves a bruise on the left upper chest in the shape of the blade.'

The staff uniformly nodded. Almost every rape victim experienced post-traumatic stress. The scenario was not uncommon.

'Melanie's attacker tells the women that if they can't be hurt, they can't be loved.'

The mood in the room felt flat. Most of the staff had been called out at least once overnight during the week, and looked exhausted.

'Does that sound familiar to anyone?' Anya checked. 'Even de-identified information could help the investigation, so you don't have to worry about breaching confidentiality.'

The ten staff shook their heads. It didn't sound familiar.

'How is Melanie doing otherwise?' Anya asked Mary.

'She's started a new job as planned, but her mother is picking her up from town. It's going to take a lot of time and support.'

One of the newer counsellors apologised for interrupting, but thought it a good time to raise the issue of overtime payments. Anya excused herself and ushered Mary into the corridor.

'Where exactly are the bagged samples kept?'

Mary took a wooden chair from the office into the second counselling room. The chair unfolded into a small stepladder.

'Top cupboard,' she suggested. 'You can pass them down if you like.'

'I'm looking for one in particular,' Anya opened the top cupboard and felt around. Dust covered everything, including what felt like a dead cockroach. She pulled out some large paper bags and examined the names before handing them down to Mary.

'Why the sudden urgency?'

'There's another one right at the back.' Anya stretched her arm and fingers, making contact with the dusty paper. She could just tease the bag closer until it was in reach. Pulling it out, she coughed, then sneezed. Relief filled her as she recognised her own handwriting. Written in large bold print was the name GLORIA HAVELOCK.

21

Peter Latham spoke into his dictaphone. He could have been reciting poetry as he rhythmically outlined the findings in each system of the body.

Having worked at the Sydney Institute for so many years, Peter was leader of the morgue 'subculture', a mini-society in which every member performed tasks that few people understood or really appreciated.

Anya Crichton had gladly accepted an invitation to lunch with her mentor. Even the formalin smell provided familiar comfort. Today, no music played, which meant either the day's post-mortems were finished, or relatives were due to view a body.

'Ah, my favourite interloper,' Peter declared as he clicked off his recorder. 'Just finishing up.' He referred to something in his notes. 'Third hit-and-run this month. The police and coroner want the report ASAP.'

On the steel table lay the body of a young female with severe head injuries and bruising to her abdomen. Her right leg had almost been severed, with a large section of bone protruding through the front of the thigh.

Anya studied the X-ray attached to the viewing box on the wall. The young pelvis had been fractured, along with the femur. The trauma had to be substantial. Other X-rays showed the growth plates on the bones open, so the child was still growing.

'How old?' Anya asked, examining the skull film.

'Eleven. Witnesses say she was riding her bike when a speeding car hit.'

Judging by the extent of the injuries, the vehicle would have had some damage.

'Helmet?'

Peter shook his head and adjusted his glasses. 'If she had, she wouldn't be here.'

Despite the leg and pelvis fractures, the massive head injury was what had killed the child. Anya could only imagine the parents' grief, for the sake of a twenty-dollar helmet.

One of the other staff members pushed through the room's plastic doors. 'Family's in the viewing room, whenever you're ready.'

The technician covered the body with a fresh white sheet and draped another around the head wound, trying to expose only the undamaged part of the face. Regardless of the cause of death or state of the body, staff went to great lengths to protect the relatives from any further distress at the viewing. Again, it was a task that no one really appreciated, but would cause more unnecessary suffering if they didn't bother. The final image of a loved one was often the one that lasted the longest.

Once satisfied, the technician wheeled the metal table up to a window. Peter and Anya left the room before he opened the curtain.

'You okay?' she asked as he washed his hands in the corridor sink.

'With the gang shootings, we've been swamped, but we'll have caught up by this afternoon.'

'That's not what I meant.'

'I can switch off when we get children, which is why I do them myself,' he said, drying his hands on a paper towel. 'That hit-and-run didn't bother me. I feel sorry for the young constable who had to go and tell the parents.'

Anya had always been amazed by Peter's clinical detachment. As a mother, she found autopsies on children very difficult. Out of all the pathologists, Peter seemed most skilled at suspending his emotions when work demanded.

He clapped his hands together. 'How about some tea?'

'Love one. I'll meet you in your office.'

Peter arrived shortly after Anya wearing a lime-green shirt and yellow tie. Brown corduroy trousers complemented the look. He put two teas on the desk and closed the door, something he rarely did.

He moved a pile of papers from the spare chair next to Anya's and sat.

162

'What happened to your med student researcher?' Anya asked.

'Ah, Zara Chambers. Did an outstanding thesis. She's completing her medical degree but something tells me she'll be back again.'

As they began to sip, Peter seemed sombre.

'Rumours are circulating that you're investigating Alf Carney.'

Anya almost spilt her drink. *How many people know?*

'I'm not investigating anyone. Morgan Tully asked for a second opinion on some cases and that's all. It's nothing unusual. We've all been asked to review each other's work.'

'I suspect there's more to it than that,' he said, looking up.

'Then you must know something I don't.' Anya disliked playing word games, especially with her friends.

Peter sat back and put his glasses on top of his head. 'Morgan's placed you in a very difficult position. I've known Alf for years, but there have been whispers about him from police for a while now.'

'And you knew his findings were dubious?'

'I just wanted any examination of his conduct to be fair and objective. That's why I suggested you to Morgan.'

Anya sat back against the desk. 'You knew, and you *wanted* me to review his cases?'

Peter rubbed his salt-and-pepper beard. 'It's

not easy to scrutinise a colleague when the consequences could destroy a career. It'll put you under pressure, but you can definitely handle it, and your expertise is without question.'

'What are you really saying?'

'Alf's had a long career and has made enemies in the process. We all have, whenever there's been a controversial decision. He hasn't had an easy time of it. I'm a little concerned there is a political motive within the College of Pathologists to stop him working, and you could be part of the fallout.'

Anya didn't like where this conversation was heading. She suddenly felt uncomfortable and disappointed in her former teacher. Putting down the cup, she said, 'Sorry, but I can't stay for lunch.'

Peter Latham stood. 'I'm not trying to influence you, Anya. I'm afraid you misunderstood. If Alf is incompetent, things could become difficult and the implications are enormous, for all of us, and God knows how many convicted prisoners. I'm saying that if you need some support or help, I'm available.'

22

Mary Singer came into the room, uncharacteristically flustered. In her hands, she held the newspaper. 'Have you seen this?'

Anya studied the front page of the *Daily Telegraph*. A large photo of a woman with short-cropped hair and dangling earrings smiled back.

The headline read, '*Teacher slain in horror bloodbath.*'

As she scanned the first few paragraphs, she felt a chill. Elizabeth Dorman had been found brutally stabbed to death in her Kellyville home.

'*The popular high-school teacher . . .*'

Anya stopped reading. It was the woman from last week. The one who'd given the false phone number. 'Just Elizabeth' had been mutilated.

Mary said, 'Do you think it could be related to the sexual assault?'

Anya felt numb. 'You'd have to wonder.'

Attacked a week ago, and murdered – with a knife – last night.

She read the rest of the article. Liz Dorman's boyfriend, a band member, was performing at a local pub and returned home at two a.m. to find the body in a pool of blood on the lounge-room floor. Parts of the room were damaged, suggesting that Ms Dorman had fought her attacker.

'The poor woman.' Mary had tears in her eyes. 'I didn't push her to stay, she kept saying she had to go.'

Anya thought for a moment. It was too much of a coincidence, to have been raped a week earlier and then murdered. From the way she'd behaved, it was possible that Elizabeth had known her attacker, which is perhaps why he'd returned.

'I've got to let the police know that she came here.'

'What about confidentiality?' Mary wiped her eyes.

Drumming her fingers on the desk, Anya said, 'Our duty to Elizabeth doesn't end with her death, but we have a duty to the community as well. The police need to know about the assault. Without it, they're probably suspecting the boyfriend. And it may help prevent someone else getting killed.'

'Or maybe the boyfriend did do it. We should have paid more attention to the signs – too afraid to talk about her attack, the inappropriate clothing that covered her. Domestic violence was a definite possibility.'

Mary closed her eyes and said a prayer, something she hadn't done in front of coll-eagues before. Anya understood that Mary felt somehow responsible for not looking after Liz

Dorman better, even though she had done all she could at the time.

She dialled homicide.

Hayden Richards, Meira Sorrenti and two homicide detectives stood outside the Kellyville house. Though this was essentially a homicide investigation, any possible link to a sexual assault needed to be thoroughly investigated.

Local newspapers lay on the front lawn, and the letterbox was stuffed with catalogues and junk mail. It appeared like any other suburban home, except for the crime-scene tape surrounding the perimeter.

The area was filled with 'McMansions', as they were known in the press. Rows of similar homes, designed to fill almost every inch of the small blocks of land. Gone were the backyards, replaced with two storeys, four bedrooms, a rumpus room and double garage. In an area where heat could be searing, every home had an air-conditioner, which attracted the ire of environmentalists and beach-dwellers who were lucky enough to enjoy an ocean breeze. Their criticisms filled the letters pages of the local newspapers.

As a mother, Anya could understand the trend towards a bigger home with more space, even without children. With the burden of mortgages, people couldn't afford to go out that much, so home became the entertainment centre of their world. Time otherwise spent on a garden went towards enjoying movies on home cinemas. Or so the theory went. The irony was that families felt safer closed off from their neighbours, but these areas led the state's crime figures for break-and-enters.

Anya hesitated before getting out of the car. Like Mary, she couldn't help but feel guilty about a death that might have been prevented. Even if she had no idea what more could have been done.

'What are you doing here?' Meira glared.

'She's the only one of us who saw the victim alive and she's still a pathologist. At this stage,' Hayden said, 'we need all the help we can get.'

Cars slowed to a crawl as they passed by, some passengers straining to take photos of the site of a tragedy. Anya wondered where those photos ended up. Not the sort of thing you'd scrapbook for future generations, surely.

'Crime scene's done. You can go in,' said one of the uniformed police manning the barricade.

Out of habit, all the police wiped their feet on the doormat, although it seemed unnecessary given the amount of blood on the carpet in the hallway. They followed the red trail to the lounge room. The smell of death was all around them. A combination of perspiration, fear and the metallic odour of dried blood filled Anya's nostrils. She preferred the more sterile formalin.

A lamp lay on the floor in the entrance, with small markers indicating its position.

Inside the room, the darkness hit them. For the

middle of the day, no light came in from outside. Someone switched on the light. The curtains were all drawn.

'Nice kitty,' Meira said, pointing to a mounted cat on the mantelpiece.

The once-living feline had been preserved in an attack pose and looked extremely unlovable. A small streak of blood had landed across its face.

A plasma television hung on the wall, with surround-sound speakers in the corners. They were all splattered with blood. In the centre of the floor lay the largest pool. It was where the body had been found.

'The boyfriend said he tried to drag her into the street to get help. The phone wasn't working and his mobile was missing,' the taller junior homicide detective explained. 'We thought he was bullshitting until we got your call.'

Anya explained, 'Elizabeth said she was asleep on the lounge and woke up with her attacker on top of her.'

'Why don't you think she stayed for a medical examination?' Hayden asked.

'I can't be sure, but she implied she was partly responsible because she'd left a window open.' Glancing about the room, she said, 'The attack was very violent and frenzied, judging by the blood distribution. There has to have been a lot of movement during the stabbings.'

'Can't have been that much. The body had over forty stab wounds, mostly in the upper chest and neck.' The second female homicide detective checked the windows in the room. 'She can't have fought through that many.'

'It depends on the depth and location of the wounds. Although, by the volume of blood loss and the way it spurted across the room, some have to have hit superficial arteries.'

Hayden had remained surprisingly quiet until now. 'Some of the blood could belong to the attacker.'

'It'll be a few days before we know.' The female detective couldn't open the window. It had been boarded up with wooden planks. 'No one's going to be peeping through these again.'

The group walked slowly around the house. Each room had suffered the same window treatments.

'Did Crime Scene check the fridge? If he's anything like our rapist, he might have stopped to eat something,' Meira offered.

'Good point,' said Hayden. 'Make sure we've checked that and the bins as well, in case he threw out any leftovers.'

Anya looked around the kitchen, with its laminated benchtops and photographs on the fridge door. Two of the photos were of Liz Dorman cuddling a man, and another with a large group of people at dinner, raising their glasses.

'The way Elizabeth acted and spoke at the unit was the way victims often behave when they know their rapist,' she said.

Meira sounded impatient, again. 'Maybe he realised and that's why he came back.'

Hayden studied something on the floor. 'Or maybe he's one of those gentlemen rapists and he came back as part of his fantasy, like Quentin's profile suggested. Only this time the fantasy got more violent.'

The other female detective continued to check the windows.

'The back windows all have keyed locks on them. This woman was suddenly very security obsessed. It's the same in every room.'

'So how did he get in?' Hayden almost muttered.

'Looks like she opened the door and got stabbed in the back, then again as she ran into the lounge room,' the tall detective explained.

Anya studied the photos on the fridge. They were all placed symmetrically, with one space left. She wondered if that had been the spot where a photo had previously been.

A male voice called from the doorway, 'Who's here? I need to come in.'

They turned to see an unshaven man with a V-necked T-shirt and shorts. His visible chest hair was matted with dried blood, hands and face were smeared as well. He had to be the boyfriend.

'You can come in. It's all right,' said the tall detective.

The man carefully avoided treading on the carpet stains and turned his head away from the lounge room as he passed.

'Greg found the body. He's Elizabeth's boy-friend. They lived here together,' the junior de-tective explained.

Greg looked like a broken man, stooped and unkempt. 'I don't have any clothes, not even my wallet,' he mumbled.

Anya assumed that, after moving the body, he had been covered in blood and the police had taken his clothes for forensic testing at the station. He was, after all, their prime suspect. He was still 'a person of interest' until proven otherwise.

She stepped forwards. 'I'm Doctor Crichton. I met Liz last week when she came in briefly to the clinic, the day she went on the school excursion.'

He looked embarrassed and wouldn't make eye-contact.

'Were you the one in the car that morning, waiting?'

Greg ran a dirty hand over his face, leant on the bench and began to cry. 'I didn't know what to do.' He sobbed for a few minutes before catching his breath. 'She almost didn't go to see you, but I pushed her. I thought she should go to the police.'

The detectives each moved closer to the door-way, giving them some sense of privacy.

'Do you know why she was so scared about that?'

'I shouldn't say. It'll get her into trouble.'

'Greg, we need to know. It might help the police work out who did this to her.'

'She said it could ruin her career. The night she was . . .' he paused and gritted his teeth, 'raped by

172

that bastard, I was at a gig. She sat up late with a girlfriend and they smoked a couple of joints and had a few wines. Then she fell asleep on the lounge.' He seemed to steady himself. 'She was scared that if the school found out, she'd be sacked, and no one would believe her anyway.'

Anya suddenly understood Liz Dorman's reluctance to be examined. With alcohol and marijuana in her system, giving a statement would allow for that to come out in an investigation, and would have left her open to prosecution. She must have known that her credibility as a rape victim would be questioned. Staying silent probably seemed like her only option.

'Did she tell you anything about the attack?' Anya kept the thought in her mind that Greg could be Elizabeth's rapist, and her killer. The scenario was all too common. But why would she board up the windows if he still lived there? Unless she'd thrown him out . . .

He shook his head. 'She was ashamed. It didn't change the way I loved her, she didn't ask for it to happen.'

'You're right. It wasn't her fault.' Anya reached for a tissue from the box on the bench and handed it to him. 'How was she afterwards?'

'A bloody mess. She should have gone back to see you but she kept saying she was taking control. She said every time she hammered a nail, she felt more in control of her life. Look at the windows – that's not control, it's a bloody prison she made.'

173

Anya wanted to ask about the emergency contraception. 'I know this is a personal question, but did you use condoms as a form of contraception?'

'No. We didn't have to. I had a vasectomy years ago. We were talking about having it reversed.'

Anya wanted him to stay calm. If what he said was true, then Greg wasn't the rapist. 'Is that why she wanted the morning-after pill? Because the man who raped her didn't use a condom?'

'She was so upset, she didn't remember. All she knew was that she didn't want to have his child.'

Meira moved closer. 'After the attack, did she stay in the house?'

'We went to her sister's on the weekend. In the Blue Mountains.' He began to cry again. 'Jesus, I haven't told her yet. It's all over the papers.'

'Local constables will have told her,' Anya said. She didn't think it appropriate to push any more. Not now. 'One last thing. Did the man who raped her take anything?'

'Some cash, credit cards, and a photo of her from the fridge.'

'Is this the one?' The female detective entered the room with a torn, blood-stained photo on a paper plate, careful not to touch it. 'We just pulled it from the bin outside.'

Greg glanced at it, then ran to the sink and gagged.

Anya wondered why the perpetrator would take the photo as a trophy after the rape, then return to the scene and destroy it a week later. Moreover, if

174

the same person had committed both the rape and murder, why hadn't he killed Liz at the time of the rape?

She watched Greg for a moment, unsure what to think. He may not have been the rapist, but he was still the lead suspect in his girlfriend's murder.

As they left the house, Meira Sorrenti offered her opinion. 'If you ask me, Liz Dorman was having it off with someone, the boyfriend found out and she cried rape to cover herself. That's why she needed the contraception and didn't want to be examined. There were no injuries to find.'

'What about the photo?' Hayden sounded sceptical.

'She gave it to the new love interest, the boyfriend got it back and killed her. He has to know who she's been sleeping with.'

Hayden cleared his throat. 'That doesn't explain why Elizabeth boarded up the windows yet stayed with the boyfriend.'

The only reason for doing that, Anya thought, was to prevent the windows from being opened, and to make sure no one ever looked in and watched her again.

23

Quentin Lagardia placed his silver briefcase on the floor in the foyer of the SA unit.

'I've brought the results of the PM report on Elizabeth Dorman. There are some things I'd like to ask you about, given your knowledge of the other assault victims.'

Hayden Richards hitched up a pair of even baggier trousers. 'Hope you don't mind me eaves-dropping. Thought I could learn something.'

'No problem.' Anya showed them into her office. The room was more the size of a large cupboard. Not wide enough to fit a bed, but adequate for paperwork. Besides that, no one wanted to spend time in there, so Anya managed to catch up on the endless stream of red tape with minimal distraction.

'Hope you're not claustrophobic,' she half-joked.

'No problem. I know what it's like. I had to write my doctoral thesis in a room this size with three other researchers.'

Quentin unzipped his jacket and sat in the only spare chair. Anya left to find another, which had to be positioned next to hers to allow room to close the door. Inside, the desk comprised a shallow shelf, wide enough for a computer screen and keyboard. Not exactly ergonomically sound, but the staff did their best with what they had. It wasn't in anyone's interest to complain or start making demands. Funds to stay operating were scarce enough.

'This is one of the few places we can talk in private. The examination room's got to be empty in case anyone comes in.' She sat and crossed her legs. 'What can I do for you?'

Quentin cleared his throat. 'The police appear to be focusing on one offender, but I'm a little concerned that this homicide could be the work of two different people.'

He pulled a file from his case and placed it in front of Anya. It contained crime-scene photos of Liz Dorman's body and pictures taken during the post-mortem. Once the blood had been cleaned off her naked skin, the number of stab wounds became evident. Anya scanned the PM report, which outlined forty-eight discrete incisions. Some penetrated organs, while others were superficial. A few wounds on the shoulders and upper arms were inflicted after death.

'That's interesting. In addition to multiple deep wounds, there are some shallow, peripheral ones. Given that they appear to have been made post-mortem, it suggests the killer was experimenting, exploring what damage the knife could do, if you like.'

Quentin listened with the intensity of a student being taught by a master. Anya wasn't sure she deserved the kudos. Maybe that's why he was so good at profiling. His listening skills encouraged subjects to blabber on and give him everything he needed to make a judgement.

Anya continued. 'The distribution and high number of stab wounds are usually associated with sex-type crimes. Like a jealous lover, or an ex-partner. You sometimes see this in homosexual murders. Stabbing the chest and neck is pretty angry and directed. The attacker hasn't lunged indiscriminately, each wound is targeted.'

Quentin nodded. 'So the perpetrator was filled with hate and anger. We might be dealing with a crime of passion.'

'Which would mean Liz Dorman possibly knew her killer,' Hayden said. 'Like the doc here suggested. What about the wound in the back, the one we think got her first? There were blood splatters in the corridor.'

'That may well have been the first wound, but again, it's shallow and didn't hit any arteries. Enough to cause pain, but not be fatal. The blood splattering on the walls could have happened when blood was thrown off as she struggled or tried to get away. It also could have been flicked off the knife as it came out of her back.'

Anya double-checked the photos. 'There isn't one wound on the abdomen or legs.'

Quentin barely blinked. 'Is it possible that the pre-mortem stabbings were done by someone angry, whereas the exploratory wounds, the ones inflicted after she had died, were actually done by someone else? Someone calmer?'

'It's possible. The body had been there at least a couple of hours when the boyfriend found it, judging by the lividity.' She chose a picture of the body at the scene. 'You see, she died flat on her back because the blood settled with gravity. That's why you see the pattern on her back and down the backs of her legs.'

Hayden sat forwards. 'The boyfriend dragged her away then picked her up. She weighed about ninety kilograms, so he struggled. When the ambulance came he was cradling her semi-upright in his lap.'

Quentin added, 'From what I read about the boyfriend's statement, I have doubts that he is the actual killer.'

'Why?' Anya was curious.

'He described his girlfriend in the present tense. That's unusual for a killer. Unless, of course, he's in denial or was in a fugue state at the time and had no idea that he was stabbing her to death. But there was nothing to suggest that.'

'From the way he cried, he can't have been in denial,' Anya said, surprising herself. She didn't place much credence on profiling, given it was in no way an exact science, or even science at all. It was merely conjecture based on pattern

179

recognition and subjective judgements. Even so, hearing new theories was always interesting.

'He could just be clever and manipulative,' Quentin said.

'What can the wounds tell us about the knife?' Hayden concentrated on the facts. 'So far we haven't found it.'

'The depth of the wounds doesn't help much, because depth depends on a number of things like how much pressure was applied. A short knife can go in a long way if enough force is applied. It also depends on movement of the victim. If the victim is running at the attacker who's applying force, the impact is greater. And the sharpness of the knife plays a big part, too.' Anya hoped she wasn't boring them, but they still appeared interested. 'Just to make it more difficult, clothes, bone and cartilage offer more resistance than skin and can affect how deeply the weapon penetrates.'

'What about the size of the entry wounds?' Hayden tried. 'Can you tell anything about the blade's width?'

'Not really. Skin is elastic and the wound often distorts after the weapon is removed. Stab wounds are rarely the same size as the knife. The size of the entry can vary by at least plus or minus a centimetre.'

'That's a pretty big margin of error in estimating the weapon size. You could be talking about anything from an ice-pick to a bloody Bowie knife.'

180

'It gets worse. The size of the wound is also affected if the attacker "rocks" the knife, or the victim moves while the knife's still in place.' Anya demonstrated with a bread-and-butter knife left over from lunch. She made a circle with her index finger and thumb and twisted the knife. 'That makes a much bigger entry wound.' She chose one of the wounds on the chest. 'It's happened here. See, this one is triangular for that reason.'

'What about serrated edges?' Hayden asked. 'Can you give us a bit more of an idea?'

'The ribs were nicked, but it doesn't look like a serration. You'd have to check with a forensic anthropologist to be sure.'

'Is there anything else that could have caused the injuries?' Quentin stroked his chin. 'We're assuming it's a knife.'

'Blunt objects like screwdrivers leave different patterns of injury. They'd split the skin. Scissors tend to leave a Z-shape.' She studied the wounds again, this time with a magnifying glass. 'I'd say your killer, or killers, used a knife. A very sharp one.'

She scanned the reports of genital injuries. Faint bruises were visible on the inner thighs. 'The bruises on her thighs are old. Normally people bruise on the outside of the thighs by bumping into things. It's hard to bruise the inside unless there has been some kind of force used.'

Hayden sighed. 'You mean like fists trying to open the legs in a rape?'

'Exactly.'

Quentin added, 'There was no evidence of sexual intercourse at the crime scene, either, which I find intriguing. If this woman was killed by a rapist, he is most likely a fantasy rapist. He must be assuming he's the real partner. If he was still watching Elizabeth Dorman, he could have become incensed that she still had her boyfriend. Although, from the different types of stab wounds, I still can't discount two perpetrators at the murder scene.'

'We still haven't excluded the boyfriend, either.' Hayden stood up and stretched, hands on his belt. 'From what you two are saying, our killer, or pair of killers, wasn't there to rape Elizabeth. She knew him or them, then something happened and he, or they, went crazy, hacking her to death. So we're looking for one or two guys who may or may not rape women, but stab them to death in a fit of rage, and may even be friends.' He scratched his moustache. 'Glad we've got that sorted. Can't wait to see Sorrenti's expression when I bring her the good news.'

'Wait a minute.' Anya pulled out one of the photos of stab wounds around the left collarbone and stared at it closely. 'Could you please pass me the other magnifying glass?'

Hayden handed it across. 'What is it?'

She collected more photos from the same part of the body and laid them in a row, scanning each one slowly.

'There are a series of faint bruise marks around the left clavicle. If you weren't actually looking for them, you could miss them. But in context, they fit with the markings of a knife.'

Hayden leant forwards. 'How do you mean?'

'I mean like the marks caused by a knife pressed against the chest. You need to use a bit of imagination, but I'm sure that's what the bruising pattern is.'

The three bent over the pictures, squashed together in the lack of space.

Hayden squinted. 'It doesn't take imagination. It is faint, but I reckon it looks like the bruise you showed us on Jodie Davis.'

'As well as Melanie Havelock and the first victim,' Anya agreed.

The detective took a moment to digest the implications.

'So she was attacked. And probably by our serial rapist. Only this time, he came back to finish the job.'

24

Hayden stood and lingered over the photos after Quentin had excused himself for another appointment.

'The outline of the knife is definitely there. Can't believe it got missed in the morgue.'

Anya measured the lengths for comparison. 'It wasn't missed, the bruises were just recorded separately.'

'If our guy is escalating the violence, we are running out of time before he does this again. Interviewed her yet?'

Anya had almost forgotten. 'This morning she finally returned my call. At least her mobile-phone number hasn't changed. She was pretty distraught about the other victims, but wants to put it all behind her. She reluctantly agreed to meet later this afternoon for a conversation, but that was all.'

Hayden sounded relieved. 'What are the chances that I can come along?'

'Zero. I'm not violating confidentiality.'

'I'm not suggesting you do. At least phone and give her the option of having someone from the police listen in. You can even call her by a false name. If she hasn't signed a statement, no one can hold her to it.'

Anya tried to hide her frustration. 'What if you subpoena her?'

'I can't if I don't know her name or address. Blindfold me on the way, if you want.' He stood, looking like a starving puppy. 'I wouldn't ask if I didn't think she could make a difference. She could hold the piece of info we need to track this guy down.'

Anya relented and made the call. To her surprise, Louise Richardson agreed to let the detective sit in on their discussion.

An hour later, they were sitting in a café at a local bowling alley. They chose a table against the back wall, furthest away from the serving area. 1970s disco revivals blared out of the sound system. The cacophony put Anya on edge as they waited for Louise.

'I don't think she's coming,' Hayden said, checking his watch. 'Did she say why she chose this place?'

'I didn't ask. Let's give her a few more minutes.' Anya watched through the glass window. A group of disabled children cheered as one pushed a bright pink bowling ball down the metal ramp. The next player had her wheelchair rammed by an opponent, just as she released the ball. She swore at the offender, but then the group laughed.

Even a friendly game of bowling was competitive these days, she thought, feeling old.

The smell of chicken salt and fried food seemed to catch Hayden's attention.

'Damn, that makes me hungry. Don't suppose they serve salads here.'

'I doubt it, but they probably do reasonable coffee.'

Hayden tapped Anya on the elbow as he looked towards the café entrance.

A woman dressed in loose jeans and a baggy jumper stood, fingers twisting the shoulder strap on her bag.

Anya stood and walked over to Louise.

'Thank you for coming.'

'I almost didn't,' Louise said. 'I've been sitting outside in the car trying to decide what to do.'

'You're here now, but you can leave or end this conversation at any time. All right?'

Louise grimaced. 'I need to know. Do you trust this policeman?'

'With my life,' Anya said, surprising herself.

Hayden stood as Louise joined them, and asked if she minded if he took notes.

She sat with one hand pulling hair behind her ear. 'I wanted to meet somewhere no one would notice us.'

Three people at a corner table in a bowling alley taking notes and speaking in hushed tones would make anyone notice, Anya thought.

'I figured kids and teenagers would be more interested in themselves,' Louise said.

She had a good point.

Hayden explained that he was there to gather information and not to identify her to colleagues. Anya studied Louise as she listened. Since they had met, the woman had developed a facial tic in the left eye. She probably had not slept much and was having nightmares about her attack. The combination of anxiety and fatigue could bring on the involuntary twitch.

She'd also lost weight. Her face and wrists seemed thinner.

'How are you getting on?'

Louise twisted her wedding ring. 'I'm scared to stay awake and too scared to sleep. I can't keep any food down. It just comes straight back up.'

'You need to give yourself time,' Anya offered. 'And so does your husband.'

Louise didn't respond, but continued fiddling with her ring.

'I've moved in with a friend for a couple of weeks. I can't go back to the pharmacy again. Not after—'

She stopped herself.

Anya spoke first. 'We'd like to talk about what you remember from that night. Things you might not realise you noticed. Smells; what you heard; the way he spoke to you. Anything could be helpful.'

'I know this is going to be difficult,' Hayden

said softly, 'but we need to talk about what happened. Anything you can think of, even if you don't think it's important.'

She took a deep breath. 'When he grabbed me from behind – around the neck with his arm – he said he wouldn't hurt me, just wanted my handbag. And then he loosened his grip around my neck.' Louise rubbed her neck, as though she were reliving the moment. 'I stood up and went to turn around, to give him my bag. That's when he hit me hard in the side of the face, as I was turning.'

Hayden began scribing on a large pad. 'Did you see any part of his face? A nose, chin, ears?'

'The tip of his black cap. It covered his face. Then I saw his hand and it felt like my face was on fire.'

'What happened next?' Anya was impressed by the sympathetic tone the detective showed.

'He said he had a knife and would kill me if I didn't do what he wanted or if I made any noise. Then he pushed me to the ground and raped me. I couldn't bear to look at him, but he seemed to have trouble and got angry.'

'Angry in what way?'

'Frustrated, as though it was my fault he couldn't climax.'

Hayden took copious notes. It was either shorthand, or atrocious handwriting.

'Did he say anything?'

'Called me a bitch. And told me not to look at

him. That's when he stopped and dragged me across the car park, on to the grass near one of the trees. Before that we were on gravel. When a car started up nearby, I thought he would kill me.'

Her voice trailed off.

'But he didn't kill you,' Anya said. 'You stayed alive.'

Louise fiddled with her hair again. 'When the car drove off, away from us, he whispered in my ear, "If you can't be hurt, you can't be loved". I remember because he said it like he was helping me understand what he was doing.' Her eyes glassed over. 'That's when he took off his gloves and dug his fingers into my chest. Then he raped me again, under the tree.'

'You're doing really well,' Hayden said. 'What did he do next?'

'This time, I think he came because he got off me. He grabbed my bag and said he knew where I lived. If I went to the police, he'd come back and finish me off. Then he was gone.'

'Can you describe the knife at all?'

Louise thought for a moment. 'Sharp, small. I don't know what happened to it. One second it was on my chest, then it was gone.'

'Was there a click sound?'

Louise hesitated. 'Maybe. There was a noise.'

'Could have been a switchblade.' Hayden scribbled fast. 'Do you remember what the gloves looked like?'

189

'They had to be surgical gloves. I could smell the latex.'

Anya said, 'That's why there was a trace of talcum powder on your leg. It's used to stop the gloves from sticking to themselves.'

'That's really, really helpful,' Hayden urged. 'Did you notice anything about his hand? Like, whether he had a tattoo?'

'No, I don't think so. It was a white hand.'

Suddenly distracted, Louise looked around the café. A group of bowlers ordered and collected their fast-food from the service counter.

Hayden moved closer, locking eyes with Louise Richardson.

'How do you mean, white? Like a Caucasian?'

Louise avoided the detective's gaze, as if losing confidence. 'It was pretty dark, but I remember this flash of white skin when he moved.'

'Could you see his wrist, or any other part of him?'

Louise closed her eyes again and paused. 'I didn't think of it before. I did see his wrist and it looked normal.' She faltered. 'This is going to sound crazy, but he must have had some kind of white stripe on his hand. I remember a flash of skin. I'm sorry, this isn't helping. It doesn't make any sense.'

Hayden looked enthusiastically at Anya. 'There's nothing to be sorry about. You are help-ing – a lot. Do you think there could have been a mark on his hand?'

'I suppose so. That makes more sense – like a streak of faint white paint.'

Anya admired Louise's strength. She had just given them the most helpful lead yet.

25

Geoff Willard lay in the dim light, body aching. He wasn't sure what hurt more – his back from where he had taken the boot, or his hand from where he had punched the bastard who did it. His right hand felt broken but he could just make a fist. All he'd wanted to do last night was sleep where he lay on the floor in the rotunda. In the park, he'd been out of sight but could see the main road and police patrols. He hadn't bargained on being beaten up by a couple of drunk teenagers with dutch courage. At least one of them had scored a broken jaw for his trouble. He suppressed a grin at the way the boy had whimpered as he slunk away.

Now, Geoff sat up and propped himself against the laundry wall. He heard the back door open and slam shut, followed by heavy footsteps down the back steps. The owner wheezed in between each step. Having taken the light globe out as a precaution, Geoff pulled himself behind the door and waited.

The door creaked open and the light switch clicked on and off. He inhaled the second-hand cigarette smoke from the other side.

'Marge, the globe's blown,' bellowed the elderly voice. The owner coughed a few times and then managed, 'I'll fix it later.'

The footsteps back to the house were slower. The old man struggled up the flight, and after what seemed like ages, the back door slammed again.

Geoff breathed out. Since the door had been left ajar, he could make out men's clothes hanging on a rail. He quickly stripped, grabbed a flannel shirt, a pair of pants and a large jumper. A woollen cardigan tied around his waist would be good for extra warmth tonight. A large pair of women's knickers lay on a pile on the washing machine. He picked up the pair and took a moment to sniff the crotch area before throwing them back. The coins in the pockets of the other trousers would feed him today.

Hearing nothing but the sound of a distant lawnmower, he slipped out of the door and down the side of the house.

A few streets away, he found a huge fast-food takeaway place on the corner. After a hamburger meal, he felt a lot better. Four cups of coffee later, and two trips to the toilet, Geoffrey Willard decided to find Nick's friend Luke. At least he had tried to help the other night. Finding someone wasn't hard. The guys in prison had taught him how to do lots of stuff. All he had to do was remember things, like he did with movies and TV shows.

Nick had written the phone number down on a pad next to the phone, and Geoff remembered it really easily. Everyone thought he was dumb, but they would be surprised to find out how much he really could do. He could say Nick's credit-card numbers off by heart after going through his wallet.

At the takeaway, Geoff dialled Luke's number on the public phone. A woman answered.

'Hello, is that the home of Desiree Platt?' He felt like 'Sunny' again and made his voice sound deep, so she wouldn't recognise him.

'Who's asking?'

Geoff cleared his throat. 'I'm just checking the address on a package going to your house. The street number got smudged and it looks like eighty-seven.'

'What's in the package?' The woman sounded bored.

'It's a steam mop and a box of cleaning products worth over a thousand dollars from the Spring Clean Your House promotion.' He tried to make his voice sound like a TV announcer, like the fellows in jail had taught him.

'I don't remember entering that competition.'

'If you don't want the prize, I'll let them know. Sorry to have bothered you.'

'Wait,' she said. 'Now I remember. I enter so many competitions, sometimes I forget. I'm at thirty-eight Fitzwilliam Street.'

'You need to sign for it, so will you be home in the next hour?'

'I've got a check-up at the clinic, but I should be back by two.'

'Thank you, madam, and congratulations on your prize.' Geoff hung up, pleased with himself. Stupid bitch, he thought. People'd tell you anything if they think it will get them something.

Geoff had been inside the house for over two hours and helped himself to crisps, biscuits, black coffee and some cash from a jar in the kitchen. He'd also ordered pizza using one of Nick's credit cards and flowers for the girl at the op shop on another. One more thing he'd learnt was how to get away with using other people's accounts. The trick was to take small amounts at a time. Most people were too dumb to check their statements and had cards lying around the house that they didn't carry with them.

No sleeping outside for him tonight, he decided, as the bossy cow waddled through the front door.

She froze as she saw him on the lounge. He recognised fear in her eyes.

'What do you want?'

Geoff sat still, enjoying the power.

'Please don't hurt me or my baby.'

She looked more like a Teletubby than a person. He wondered what Luke saw in her. 'Sit down and shut up!'

Desiree put down her bag, slowly walked into the room and lowered herself into a single lounge nearest the door. 'Luke said the police are after you. You should go, they're probably watching the place.'

'Bullshit.' He knew she was scared. Her eyes were so wide they could have popped out.

'No. They searched your house and took stuff. Nick reckons they're following him, too.'

Geoff tried to think. It was like before, with Eileen Randall. His heart started to race. They weren't happy hounding him. They wanted him back in prison.

They sat in silence, with a clock on the mantelpiece ticking away. Geoff wanted to smash the fucking thing. He stood up as they heard voices at the door. One of them was Nick's.

Luke and Nick were laughing as they came through the door, but Luke went pale when he saw his visitor. 'Are you all right?' he said, putting his arm around his wife.

She clutched her bag and ran to the bedroom.

'Jesus, what are you doing *here*?' Nick asked.

Geoff stood up, almost collapsed with the pain in his back. 'I got bashed. I think my hand's broken and I'm pissing blood as well.'

'Jesus, mate.' Nick's eyes darted around the room. 'You're in deep shit this time. Where did you disappear to?'

'I want him out of my house.' Luke stood, fists clenched. 'He fucking killed that schoolteacher.'

'Bull-fucking-shit.' Geoff stepped towards Luke. 'You're a fucking liar.'

Nick stepped between them. 'Back off. He's right. The cops came around and took a whole heap of your stuff. There's a warrant out for your arrest.'

Desiree came back and went straight to Luke's side. 'The police are on their way.'

Sirens sounded in the distance, then went quiet. Car doors slammed outside. Luke looked through the window. 'Christ! The place is full of cops and they've got guns. Get down!' He took a couple of steps and pulled his wife and unborn child to the floor.

Sweat dripped off Nick's face.

Geoff had never seen his cousin so afraid. He looked around the room and fell to his knees in pain. Sunny was going back to prison.

26

Veronica Slater sat cross-legged, short skirt revealing the upper part of her thighs. 'Dan's talked about this place. I had to come and see for myself. It's quaint, and in good condition considering the area.'

Elaine delivered the water. Not the bottled variety, as Veronica had requested, but affordable, fluoridated tap-water.

Anya drummed her fingers on the arm of her chair. If this lawyer were offering work, she would be insane not to take it, no matter how annoying the woman could be. Her private practice needed to expand, and alienating Dan Brody via Veronica wouldn't help.

Elaine glanced upwards and left the room.

'As part of my pro bono work, I represent a man named Geoffrey Willard.'

Anya understood that meant Legal Aid was paying for the defence and could only pay around one-third of her normal fee. She let out a breath as Veronica continued.

'He's been charged with the rape and murder of Elizabeth Dorman, and I gather the police might be looking at him for a series of rapes as well, based on similar pattern evidence. He surrendered to police after allegedly breaking into some woman's home. Have you read about the case?'

'I don't put much credence on what I read in newspapers.'

'Oh yes,' she said. 'That exposé on you last year was quite a piece of work.'

Anya detected a hint of sarcasm and wanted the meeting to end before she said something on impulse she'd later regret. 'What would you like me to consult on?'

'Well, I wanted to go through some of the evidence with you. If the police argue the crimes are inextricably linked in terms of the pattern of evidence, I want to know whether or not that's true.'

'The information on the sexual assaults has to come from the police. I'm not in a position to discuss that at this stage.'

'Even though I hear you examined the victims and are involved in the police investigation? Of course, I wouldn't ask you to do anything unethical.' Veronica smirked. 'I'd like you to go over the pathological findings in the murder of Eileen Randall, from twenty years ago. She's the fourteen-year-old girl Willard was convicted of raping and killing.' She paused, then added, 'I also wanted to ask you what you know about Asperger's syndrome.'

Anya thought of her recent conversation with

Ben about the preschool boy he would not play with. 'It's considered a variant of autism.'

'Excellent. There's been a question as to whether or not Willard has the syndrome and was never previously diagnosed. It could be a valid defence if necessary. He may not have been responsible enough to commit any crime, let alone premeditated rape and murder.' Her mobile phone rang and she excused herself to argue with someone on the other end.

Anya studied her. She guessed Veronica was the sort of woman who didn't have female friends. She probably justified it by saying that her success intimidated and threatened other women. The reality was, she was just one of those ambitious people who used anyone she could to get what she wanted. Only women saw right through the act because they weren't distracted by the package. Medicine had its share of 'Veronicas'. The sad thing was that they were bright enough to do well without being prize bitches and put-down queens.

The powerpaths and sociopaths who pursued their own agendas without a conscience weren't all in prison, she thought, as Veronica kept her waiting even longer.

Veronica returned to her seat and checked her watch. 'Where were we?'

'A diagnosis of Asperger's doesn't preclude responsibility, and it's not a form of mental illness. Half of the professors at universities are thought to have it. It's associated with high IQ, sometimes what we call "pencil intelligence", where someone has a lot of knowledge in one area but low emotional intelligence.'

'Emotional intelligence sounds like an oxymoron,' she quipped.

'Surely you've met brilliant legal minds who have very few social skills.' Anya wondered whether Veronica could in fact be a sufferer. The thought was almost reassuring. 'People with the syndrome are capable of telling right from wrong. Using that as a defence tactic might go against your client in court.'

Clearly, that didn't impress Veronica Slater. The forced smile disappeared. She unwrapped the pink ribbon from a large stack of paper and instead of extracting a sample, handed over the lot. 'Here are copies of the original court transcripts and expert reports. I'd like you to review the PM and reports on Eileen Randall and compare her wounds with the ones inflicted on the Dorman woman. Any differences, I want highlighted.'

'And similarities?'

The false smile returned.

'We'll deal with that if the time comes. I don't know why the police are so keen to stitch up my client for the rapes, but I want to know if there are inconsistencies in the victims' statements.'

Anya said, 'I guess you'll see the police brief if charges are laid.'

Veronica stood and pulled her miniskirt down a

mini amount. 'Can you have the report done by Monday morning? My client's on remand and he should be out on bail.'

The last thing Anya wanted was to spend the whole weekend working for Veronica. 'I'll do what I can,' she managed, feeling her face redden.

'Excellent.' Veronica checked her watch and collected an immaculate leather briefcase. 'Don't want to keep Dan waiting,' she said, and tottered off.

Elaine came back in. 'She's a piece of work, don't you think?'

Anya didn't answer. A signature on the PM report caught her attention. 'Oh hell,' she muttered. 'Things just got more complicated.'

'Why? What does she want?' Elaine bent over to look at the papers.

'The pathologist and expert witness in Willard's original trial was Alf Carney.'

27

Anya arrived at the cabin by the beach and unpacked the car. She'd booked the weekend away at the last minute, to examine first-hand the site at which Eileen Randall had been murdered, and was grateful for cheap, decent accommodation. The drive to Fisherman's Bay had the normal Friday night exodus crawling along the freeway. So much for getting away, she thought, but as the traffic thinned along the coast road, the drive became more relaxing – and liberating. Even in the moonlight, the scenery was impressive.

She placed a box of groceries and wine on the kitchen bench and opened the sliding door. The fresh sea breeze cooled the cabin almost immediately.

The best part was no interruptions, just privacy, sea air and the sound of the ocean. And the pile of papers to review. The clock on the wall chimed eight. She decided to go for a walk to buy milk and other perishables. And maybe even fish and chips followed by some decadent, fat-filled ice-cream.

The Bay was smaller than the Internet pictures

suggested, but there were a number of takeaway shops, equipment-hire sheds and a discount supermarket on the way into town. Two cafés, a restaurant and all but one of the takeaways were closed.

Over the jazz band, Anya asked at the pub why almost everything was shut on a Friday night. The woman at the bar just laughed.

'Darl, people moved here to get away from the city. None of the locals wants to work twenty-four hours, seven days a week.' She poured a beer. 'Here's a tip. If you want a hot chicken tomorrow, you'd better pick it up in the morning or they'll be sold out. They only cook once a day.'

Anya had to smile. Tourists wanted it all – the nature and unspoilt atmosphere of a coastal town; with round-the-clock conveniences.

'We never asked for tourists,' she said, not hesitating to take a hundred-dollar note from a group who looked anything but local.

On the way back to the beach cabin, kids hovered on the corner, some riding bikes, others egging drinkers on; all of them smoking. Friday nights and boredom in a country town hadn't changed since she was a child.

With an increased appetite, she opened the wine as soon as she reached the house, devoured the hamburger – beetroot included – and consumed half the calamari. Why was it that the smell inside takeaways always made her buy more than she could ever eat?

A cushioned wicker sofa proved much more comfortable than it suggested. Anya put her glass on the wooden floor and began to read the musty file.

The half-dressed body of Eileen Randall was found at two a.m. on Koonaka Beach. From the police report, a local teenage girl and friend of the deceased had seen a man with blood-stained clothing holding the dead girl's underpants. The witness identified the man as Geoffrey Willard.

At the time, Willard had been arrested for malicious damage to a car and had been cautioned about antisocial behaviour. One of his former teachers said that Willard had always been different from the other children and, as a result, was the victim of bullying. His temper got him into trouble, usually when people teased or made fun of his learning difficulties. He tried hard at school and had what appeared to be a photographic memory. The problems he had were in making friends and socialising. At times he behaved inappropriately, but the teacher suggested that was due to his need for attention.

His boss at the service station said Willard was a hard-worker, but became angry when a local woman called him a pervert and demanded another petrol attendant. The then eighteen-year-old responded by kicking in her car door.

On the night of the murder, Eileen Randall had been to the only cinema in town. Willard had shown interest in one of her friends, and Eileen told him to 'rack off'. Witnesses said he responded by swearing at Eileen and telling her she was a stuck-up bitch. They all walked home, and a girlfriend thought Eileen was meeting a new 'mystery' boy later that night, but didn't know his name.

The melodramatics of adolescence read like a soap opera, Anya thought, sipping the sparkling Pinot noir. The miniature bubbles danced in her glass. At times, being an adult definitely had its advantages. She could drink alcohol inside, not on a street corner. Then again, at times life still played like a soap opera.

So Eileen Randall sneaked out without her parents knowing and was murdered that night.

Anya began laying out piles of documents on the sofa and floor. The PM photos had faded a little, but were still reasonable images. The upper body was streaked with multiple stab wounds, some deep and others superficial. Most of the wounds were inflicted pre-mortem. Just like in the Dorman murder.

The police had collected her clothes, which they described as damp. The girl's jeans showed some blood splatters, but her feet were unmarked and clean.

Anya took mental note of that. Normally in a stabbing, unless the body is horizontal the whole time, blood drips onto the legs and feet.

There appeared to be little blood at the scene,

although some may have soaked into the sand and been difficult to identify on photographs. Some hairs had adhered to her shirt, found later to be canine, not human.

Anya grabbed a pad and pen. 'Wet clothes, clean feet', she wrote. With the pen between her teeth, she searched for a weather report. Twenty-two degrees Celsius, with high-level humidity, winds of twenty to thirty knots.

Beneath the weather report was a photograph of Geoffrey Willard on arrest, holding both arms out. The front of his shirt was smeared with blood. His arms appeared free of injuries. There were no 'stabber's wounds', left when the attacker's hand slid over the handle of the knife and on to the blade. His hands were free of scratches and bruises as well. Eileen Randall may not have had the time nor the strength to fight Willard.

She flicked back to the PM report. Alf Carney had listed time of death as between one and two a.m., the time Willard was found with the body. The conclusion was based on stomach contents and the time of the last meal. Anya scribbled 'time of death questionable', and underlined it twice.

Time of death was one of the most misunderstood aspects of pathology and one of Anya's pet annoyances. Former criteria such as analysis of stomach contents had long been proved inaccurate. Rates of digestion were so variable that it was a notoriously unreliable gauge.

Genital examination had found sperm in the

vagina. The only tests available at the time found that the ejaculator had the blood-group O negative

Anya took a closer look at some of the crime-scene photographs. Evidence on beaches could be difficult, thanks to the continuing tides. She'd occasionally thought that the best place to commit a murder was far out at sea, or, if on the beach, preferably during a storm.

She read through the organ systems on the PM report. Despite no saltwater in the larynx or lungs, Carney had found some in the pleural space between the lungs and ribs. He performed a Gettler test to determine chloride levels in the heart. The results showed there was no evidence of saltwater inhalation. Eileen Randall hadn't been drowned, despite her clothing being so wet. At least Carney was thorough enough to check, she thought. Maybe the clothes were damp because of the high humidity that night. She wrote a question mark on the pad.

Flicking through the histology results on the back page, Anya noticed something she'd never seen before. Some kind of infestation, deemed crayfish larvae, was found in the pleural cavity.

She paused and performed a web search on her laptop. Crayfish larvae only lived in water. They were not found in the sand. Anya felt herself shiver. The tiny creatures had crawled in through the stab wounds. It was the only probable explanation.

She would probably avoid eating crayfish from now on.

Tired, Anya wondered why the photo of a young Geoff Willard showed a relatively small blood smear on his shirt. If he'd stabbed Eileen Randall in excess of thirty times, why wasn't he covered in splashes and spurts consistent with her injuries? More importantly, why hadn't Carney's pathology report commented on that?

28

The following morning, Anya awoke to the sound of the ocean slapping the shore. Overnight drizzle had made the sleeping temperature ideal. After a lie-in, she cooked French toast and headed for a walk. Even in the off-season, Fisherman's Bay was active. Older couples walked hand-in-hand on the beach as anglers patiently waited for the next big catch. Toddlers squealed for the sake of it as they chased the waves, then ran away as fast as their chubby legs could manage.

At the end of the beach, she passed a playground opposite the newsagent. Stopping to buy a paper, she asked the man at the counter whether he remembered the Eileen Randall case. The owner seemed less than willing to talk.

'You're not from the bloody press, are you?'

'No. Definitely not. I was wondering if you know what happened to the policeman who was in charge at the time. I don't suppose he's still working?'

'No chance,' the man said. 'Charlie Boyd retired years ago.'

Not surprised, Anya paid for the paper,

thanked the man and wandered past the tempting smell of hot pastries from the bakery. Sea air definitely increased the appetite, she thought, as kids on bikes rode on the footpath, chomping on pies. The place had such a holiday atmosphere, it was impossible not to feel relaxed.

Just past the hairdresser's, she felt a tap on her back.

'Excuse me,' a middle-aged woman said. 'Were you asking about the Randall case?'

The woman had a broad-brimmed hat tied under her chin. And unlike the tourists, she had on a long-sleeved shirt and long cotton trousers. Her hands were coarse and tanned. She had to be a local used to hiding from the sun, not basking in it.

'Yes, I was hoping to speak to the former policeman, but he's retired. Do you know anything about the case?'

'You have to understand, people around here are careful about who they talk to. The murder pretty much killed business a while back. And the whole town suffered from the loss of that girl. We don't want it all dredged up again.'

'I understand, but I'm a pathologist and I just had some questions for Charlie Boyd.'

'A pathologist?' Her eyes widened. 'Like on those TV crime shows? Why didn't you say?'

It astounded Anya that a few years ago no one cared what she did for a living. Now it was flavour of the month.

'Charlie will probably talk to you, then.'

A teenager on a bike whizzed past them, almost clipping Anya. The woman called after him, 'I'll be telling your mother you've been riding on the footpath again, Jason Rogers.'

Anya smiled. People were pretty much the same everywhere.

'Do you know where I could find Charlie?'

'Oh yes, love, down on the wharf. He's usually there this time of day. You can't miss him. Looks like Santa Claus with a big silver beard.'

'Thanks so much,' she said, and headed towards the jetty.

Teenagers took turns jumping off the pylons into the water below. She stopped and looked over the side, checking the depth marker.

'It's deep down there. There's never been a problem,' a man reassured. He was with the jumpers and was probably used to strangers showing concern about the practice.

Towards the end of the wooden wharf, a man with grey hair sat in a plastic fold-up chair, large fishing rod and basket beside him. On his lap he had a fish clamped to a wooden board. A small radio played.

She approached and asked, 'Mr Boyd?'

'Shhhhhhh,' he said, straining to listen to the news headlines. He squinted up at his visitor. 'Who wants to know?'

Anya introduced herself and he repositioned himself in his seat.

She decided to ease into the topic and perched on a bollard nearby. 'What have you got there?'

'Bream. Good, pan-size, too. Only take what I can eat,' he said, admiring his prize.

'You're pretty well set up for it. We used to catch trout in the lakes where I grew up. In the midlands of Tasmania.'

His eyes glistened. 'Always wanted to fish there.' He studied Anya for a moment, as though assessing her.

'It's a long way to come to talk fishing.'

Relieved to have passed muster, she began by briefly explaining her involvement in the current rape cases and the importance of possible links with the Randall case. 'I'd like to get a feel for what happened the night Eileen Randall was found.' The wind picked up and blew her hair about her face. 'Were you there?'

'One of the worst nights of all my thirty-eight years in the job,' he said, scaling the fish from the tail end. 'To see a mate's daughter killed like that, and then have to go and break the news. But you didn't track me down to hear that.'

'Was there anything about the scene that seemed out of place?'

He frowned. 'In what way?'

'Is it possible she was killed somewhere else and brought to the beach?'

Charlie turned the fish over and removed the remaining scales. 'She was killed on the beach, all right. Willard was caught with the body. The bastard had just raped her and still had her panties in his hand.' He gave it one last scrape. 'Just like a fish on a hook.'

He stared at Anya with an unnerving intensity. 'Why do you want to go raking over this now? Willard's out and there's nothing anyone can do. Emily Randall didn't only lose her daughter that night. She lost her will to live.' He squinted in the distance at an overturned surf-ski. 'She died not long after the trial. Her husband passed away a couple of years later.'

The surf-ski rider surfaced and the old man seemed to relax. 'I'm just glad they're not here to see him released.'

'Was there other family?'

He shook his head and tapped the knife on the board. 'Don't think so. Why do you want to know?'

Anya glanced around the jetty. Fishermen packed up their morning's catches and headed back to town. Seagulls hovered and squawked for burley thrown back into the water after fish had been cleaned.

'I'm reviewing some old cases for comparison with new ones. Old methods versus new techniques.'

'You should be a bloody politician.'

Anya smiled and thought he gave a smirk beneath his beard. The old man swapped knives. This one was flexible and slit the fish from gills to the anal vent. He handled the blade as though it were second nature.

Anya preferred her fish already clean and cooked.

'Do you have any idea how many times Willard stabbed that girl?' he said, without looking up.

'I've read Alf Carney's report.'

'Ah.' Charlie pulled the guts of the fish out with his fingers. 'Alf Carney – one of the best.'

Another of Carney's fans, she thought. Only this time he was on the prosecution side, not the defence.

'It took a hell of a lot of strength to stab that deep that many times,' he said. 'Willard was one strong bastard. Nature's way of compensating, you could say.'

'Something the report didn't mention was whether Willard confessed to raping and murdering Eileen?'

'Sure did. Then he panicked and spun us some bullshit about watching TV. He was like a walking timetable. Could memorise the TV guide and all he could talk about were shows he'd watched. I didn't believe anything he said that night.

'Anyways, after something, what was it, *The Eleventh Hour*, I think, he said he took off on his push-bike for a midnight ride and saw something floating in the water. Then he claimed he realised it was a person and carried her up to the beach. He said he thought she was still alive, which was why he was getting her dressed when Eileen's young friend, Michele Harris, found them.'

Anya remembered the wet clothes. There was a

reasonable chance the body had been immersed. 'Was he arrested at the scene?'

'That chicken-shit? No. We found him in his bedroom, hiding in the cupboard. Still covered in Eileen's blood.'

A couple of boys ran up to Charlie and checked his bucket.

'Hey, mister, what'd you catch?'

'Two bream. Real beauties. Want to know my secret?'

Suddenly, Charlie did resemble Santa Claus. The boys nodded eagerly.

'Here,' he said, reaching down to pull a jar from his basket. 'I make up the liquid with sugar, water and salt and drop prawns in for bait.' He urged his audience closer with his grubby index finger. 'Then I add two drops of aniseed oil. The fish love it.'

'Wow! Thanks, mister. I'll go tell my dad.'

'So do the fish end up tasting like licorice?' Anya smiled.

'Not to my reckoning.'

Anya was sceptical of the secret but chose not to question it. 'You said that Willard later confessed?'

'Yeah, dopey bastard caved in after questioning. Confessed to everything. Reckons she pissed him off and deserved everything she got.'

He chopped off the fish's head and threw the scraps into the water.

'Willard was always trouble, real antisocial.

Used to peep at girls in the changing rooms, steal underwear from clotheslines, that kind of thing. If I'd had my way, we'd have locked him up long before he mutilated Eileen Randall.'

Old-fashioned policing, she thought. There seemed little point pursuing discrepancies in Carney's report with Charlie.

'Do you think he planned the murder?'

'Don't reckon he had the smarts to plan. My guess is she turned him down, said something he didn't like, and he went berserk.'

The wind gusted again and she shivered. 'Were there any reports of sexual assaults around that time?'

'You've got to understand that this is a small town and there's not much for young people to do. There's the football club, and all the girls treat the players like heroes. There were always whispers of gang-bangs and some of the girls would have participated willingly. Believe me. Occasionally, a girl would accuse someone who didn't return her affections, but none of them took it further. In retrospect, I guess there could have been some assaults that went unreported.'

Anya stared in disbelief at a man who had been entrusted with protecting the community. Some Santa Claus.

She couldn't understand the culture of protecting sportsmen, even non-elite ones. She suspected that things in this town had remained pretty much unchanged over the last twenty years.

Charlie thought back. 'There were a couple of serious assaults. A local woman identified Willard as her rapist, but he was never charged for it. She wouldn't testify. She was too afraid when she found out that he'd killed that girl.'

Anya knew that if Willard were a serial offender, there were likely to be other victims. She stood up and wiped sand off the back of her shorts.

'Is there a statement about her assault that I can see?'

'Not any more, but I'll see if she's prepared to talk to you, given you're a doctor and all.'

'Thanks for your time, Charlie. I'd better get back to work.' She walked a couple of feet and turned. 'There was one more thing. I was wondering whether anyone in town defended Willard, stuck up for him?'

Charlie wrapped the fillets in a piece of his newspaper and placed them on top of his basket.

'There's a local eccentric who carried on about how Willard had to be innocent. He's an amateur in town who's charted every tide for the last forty years. A bit of a hermit, but he badgered us day and night. Old Bill Lalor. Lives in the shack at the end of Koonaka Beach. Come to think of it, he used to have a thing for Willard's mother. He came out with some notion about the tides that night, which was discounted by the prosecution's expert. Just some crazy bastard trying to get attention. Old Bill still goes on about it to anyone who'll listen.'

He began to disassemble his fishing rod. 'So what are you really here for?'

'I need to know if there are any similarities between Eileen Randall's death and that of a teacher recently. This one was raped a week before.' Anya paused. 'Willard's under suspicion. If your victim wants to talk, I'm staying here until tomorrow.' She pulled a card from her wallet and wrote the number and address of the cabin on the back.

'Always said we oughta have the death penalty.' Charlie Boyd wiped his hand on his shirt and took the card. 'I'll see what I can do.'

Anya left the jetty and turned to see Santa Claus speaking quietly into his mobile phone. He bundled his belongings into the cane basket, collected his rod and fold-up chair and cut through the pub car park to the police station.

29

Bill Lalor lived in a dilapidated shack with his name scratched on the letterbox. The beach was a sheltered cove, and families played, oblivious to what had happened to Eileen Randall so long ago. Anya knocked on a bit of non-chipped paint on the door. She was about to leave when it creaked open.

A short, bald man stood there, bare-chested, in pyjama pants.

'I'm looking for Bill Lalor. The tides expert.'

'That's me.' He grinned, scratching a silver-haired chest.

'Charlie Boyd sent me.'

The man sighed. 'You can get stuffed if you're here to make fun of me. The town eccentric isn't playing today.' He began to close the door.

Anya held out her hand. 'Actually, I am in need of your expertise.' Looking at his attire, or lack of it, Anya offered, 'If it's a bad time, I could come back later?'

'Why would you think that?' he asked, scratching his unshaved stubble. 'Come in, come in.'

Anya wiped her feet on the straw mat. 'I hear

you've got records of every high and low tide in this area for over forty years.'

'Sure have.'

'You must really know your stuff.'

Bill Lalor grinned again. Three of his front teeth were missing.

'I specifically need to know about a date twenty years ago.'

The man's pale-grey eyes flared, revealing more of the white sclera. 'If it's about the night Eileen Randall died, I have nothing to say.'

Anya could understand the unwillingness to talk to strangers, but hoped this man might be upfront about his theories regarding that night.

'I understand that no one listened to you before. I want to know about the tides that night. Why you think the police got it wrong.'

The man scratched the back of his head. 'I got death threats after I went to the police. Someone even burnt me old house down.'

Anya said, 'I'm reviewing the case. If they come after anyone, it ought to be me.'

'I don't want my name mentioned. You under-stand?'

'Absolutely. I'll get experts from somewhere else to confirm the details if they agree.'

Inside she heard a twitter and the rattle of a bell. She followed the old man down a linoleum corridor into a back room filled with potted ferns. A white fluffy cat sat perched on a chair, clawing at the birdcage.

'Get down, Snowie,' Bill said, clearing the chair for his guest. Overweight Snowie's bell jingled as it begrudgingly moved.

Then her host vanished. Anya stood in the room, watching the bird, when Bill returned with a roll of maps. He laid them on top of piles of papers on the kitchen table and asked her to hold down one side. She obliged.

'I made copies after that night. Ones for the police, but they didn't want them. These weren't at my place when it went up.'

Anya wondered how many other people had been affected by Eileen Randall's death. The cat purred at her ankles and brushed against her legs.

'Geoff Willard couldn't have killed the girl at the time they said because of the tides. If you see here, high tide around the bay was 12.43 a.m., but in the cove it had to be earlier.'

Anya didn't follow.

'The winds, girl. The winds. The expert they got in didn't factor them. This was a sheltered cove. Missed the mark by a couple of hours.' He paused and seemed to wait for a sign of under-standing. 'Winds affect the tides, especially in a cove. That expert just averaged the times across the whole of the bay.'

'So what you're saying is that high tide was as much as two hours earlier than the police thought.'

'That's right. Willard told his mother he dragged the dead girl out of the water. Only thing is, I don't know how to prove he was telling the truth.'

'There might be a simple way,' Anya said. 'Do you know anything about crayfish larvae?'

'Not much. They live in the sea.'

'The pathologist found larvae inside Eileen Randall's chest cavity. The only way they could have got there is if they floated in through the stab wounds.'

Bill slapped his leg. 'So I'm right. The body was in the water. Willard told the truth.'

'In so much as we now know that the body was floating in the water at some stage. But it doesn't tell us when exactly.'

Anya thought that it seemed too simple to have been overlooked. If Bill Lalor was right about the tides that night, then Eileen Randall may have been killed before Geoff Willard found her.

She sat on the chair vacated by Snowie. Taking that into account and the lack of blood on his clothes, it was possible that Willard might not have stabbed Eileen Randall after all. If that was true, he'd just served twenty years in prison for a crime he hadn't committed.

Back at the cabin, Anya took copious notes about her discussions with Charlie and Bill. The crayfish larvae could only have got into the body via the water. If Willard had watched the TV show as he had claimed, Eileen may have been killed earlier and been floating in the water when he found her.

That would explain the smears on his shirt, if he carried her up to the beach. But why would he be dragging her? And there was the issue of a positive ID from Michele Harris, Eileen's friend. She circled that fact over and over.

This was the side of forensic medicine Anya loved and loathed. Answering questions was incredibly satisfying, but creating even more questions was a source of constant frustration.

She made a sandwich and pulled out a crime novel. Sitting on the small wooden balcony, she put her feet up on the second chair and began to read. She was yet to find one that wasn't full of inaccuracies, but she still enjoyed the stories.

The sound of children laughing on the beach reminded her of childhood holidays at Low Head – before and after Miriam had disappeared. That was such a sterile word for what had happened. She thought of her three-year-old sister building sandcastles and obsessively putting shells in a straight line on every one. That's what Miriam loved to do – build things and make them perfect. And then she was gone.

A young girl squealed with the thrill of getting wet, as her mother stood, huddled, wet up to her ankles. The little girl jumped and splashed, unaffected by the cold temperature. Anya wondered how kids could complain about a tepid bath but revel in a chilly ocean.

Putting the novel aside, she closed her eyes and drifted into a relaxing state with the sun warming her face and legs. Something about the ocean made everything seem insignificant, except Eileen Randall. The thought kept entering her mind. If she had been floating in the water, that would explain the clean feet.

Why would Willard confess to a crime he hadn't committed? It wouldn't be the first time the police had intimidated a suspect. And the emotions of the local community and police that night would have been feverishly high.

What was the name of the show Charlie Boyd mentioned? The seventh something. Damn. Anya hated not remembering a name. She grabbed her laptop from inside and connected to the Internet via the phone line. Within minutes she'd located a television guide on a nostalgia site. On the evening of the murder twenty years ago, at 11.30 p.m., a comedy sketch show called *The Eleventh Hour* was shown. It had been cancelled not long after, and faded into obscurity with so many other failed series, according to the website.

Willard had been right. If he had such an amazing memory for shows, he might have remembered some of it. Or was that expecting too much? She wondered if she could recall any of the sketches from revues during her university days. She could remember the funniest ones, but something from a weekly TV show? Only one came to mind. A brilliant impersonation of Brains from the *Thunderbirds* on her favourite show of the time, the *D-Generation*. Maybe Geoff Willard could come up with the same sort of thing.

She thought of phoning Veronica, but decided to wait to speak to her tomorrow. It was probably tennis time, anyway, she thought.

'Excuse me, are you Doctor Crichton?'

Anya turned and saw a woman about her age standing in harem pants, a tie-dyed shirt and a straw hat. She carried the card Charlie Boyd had taken. Anya wondered whether this was the rape victim he had mentioned.

'Yes. Please, come up.'

The woman slowly climbed the stairs and took off her hat.

'My name's Dell. Sergeant Boyd told me you were here asking questions. He assured me you're who you say you are.'

Charlie had obviously gone to the station to run a check on her. Fair enough, Anya thought. She explained her role as a forensic physician and the need to find out whether this was the same attacker who was assaulting women in the northwest of Sydney.

'Would you like something to eat or drink?' Anya suddenly felt awkward. She didn't feel in control outside her normal surroundings. This wasn't a consult but a conversation, she told herself.

'Tea. Weak, black, thanks.'

Anya boiled the kettle and used the same teabag for both cups.

'It's so nice on the balcony,' she said to the visitor. 'Do you mind?'

Dell looked inside then put her hat back on. 'I prefer to be outside, where there are people.'

Mid-afternoon meant the beach was at its most crowded. The pair sat in silence for a few minutes, as they watched the waves approach and recede.

Dell held the cup between both hands and studied the contents. 'Have you seen many rape victims?'

'Too many.'

'How do they react to having been through it?'

Anya took a sip. 'It varies. Everybody's different. Some are calm straight after, others are distraught and fragile. It can depend, too, on whether or not they knew their attacker. They all seem to go through a grieving process.' Steam floated above the meniscus of tea. 'Healing takes a long time.'

'It took me years. I still have flashbacks to that night.'

'Did you get counselling?'

The woman curled her top lip. 'Not around here. Back then, most people thought of counsellors and social workers as feminist radicals who'd created an industry for themselves. You just shut up and put up.'

'That must have been really difficult. You must have been so young.'

Dell looked towards the water. 'It probably would've been harder if I'd told people. They

227

also thought rape meant you'd led a boy on and then changed your mind when it was too late. You've got to remember that this is basically a mining community. They should have called the place Nickel Bay.'

Anya had seen the signs for the nickel mine on the drive in. 'So most of the men were miners?'

'It's always been a small group of locals and a large transient population. The shift work meant the men could surf on their days off.'

The breeze picked up and almost blew Dell's hat off. Anya studied the woman who spoke so calmly about the past. She had long fingers and odd splashes of paint on her shirt and near her wedding ring.

'There were a few rapes back then, but the police always put it down to the itinerant mine workers, never the locals. When I went to report my assault, Charlie Boyd assured me that Geoff Willard would be sorted out, unofficially, of course.'

The time seemed as appropriate as possible to discuss what happened that night. 'Do you mind if I ask you about your attack? What happened?'

Dell took a deep breath, as though she'd been postponing this moment.

'It was a few weeks before Eileen was killed. I was walking home after spending the evening listening to music at a girlfriend's place. It was probably about half past nine. I remember I had to be home by ten on a school night. Suddenly, I got

228

knocked to the ground and he was on top of me. He pulled my top over my head, so I didn't really see him, but he kept saying things. Like he knew I wanted it. How he'd watched me. From what I've read, most of them say things like that.' She held the cup in both hands. 'He had trouble keeping his erection and pushed harder, telling me it was my fault.'

'Did he hit you at all?'

'No, but he pushed pretty hard. I told him it was hurting and begged him to stop, but he wouldn't.' She put her head down. 'I wasn't a virgin, but it still hurt.'

Anya shook her head. Even women perpetuated the myth that non-virgins experienced less pain and trauma during a rape. One of the worst cases she had seen was a prostitute who'd been assaulted by a client.

'What happened next?'

'He got off me, told me he'd kill me if I said anything to anyone. He ordered me not to move, then he was gone.' She took another deep breath.

'I was so scared. I told Mum, but she didn't want Dad to know. Said he was under enough stress at work. I stayed in bed for a couple of days and Mum just told people I had the flu. After that, I got used to not telling people. The only other person who knows is Sergeant Boyd. I told him before Eileen's funeral.'

Anya instinctively reached over and placed her hand on the woman's forearm. After twenty years, this victim was finally able to tell someone without wondering whether she'd be blamed for what had happened.

Something bothered Anya about Dell's story. 'You didn't see the man's face, but Charlie Boyd said you identified Geoff Willard as your attacker.'

'When I saw Geoff on the news for killing Eileen, I just knew it was him.' She put the cup down on the table. 'I guess I was lucky.'

'Did you see his hands, whether there were any marks on them?'

'Sorry, but I couldn't see.'

'Did he say something to you about being hurt and loved?'

'No. That's it.'

'If there's anything else that you remember, anything at all about that night, please call me. It's very important.'

Dell stood and shook Anya's hand. 'Thank you for listening. I know it's been a long time, but it feels good to finally be believed.'

Anya realised that rather than stirring up pain of the past, their conversation had been cathartic for this woman. For more than half of her life, Dell had kept a painful secret. Maybe now she could gain some degree of closure.

Then again, if Geoff Willard had not committed the murder, or even the rape, the security of the community and victims like Dell was about to be shattered.

30

Back home late Sunday afternoon, Anya had three messages from Hayden Richards. Her mobile phone had been out of range over the weekend and with her continually forgetting to charge it, it was now flat.

The first asked her to call him regarding the causes of patchy white skin. He'd looked up vitiligo on the Internet and wanted to discuss that with her. The next message was checking to see if she was in yet. The third surprised her. She sat down to replay it.

A search warrant executed at Geoff Willard's home had found blood on a dark blue T-shirt that had been sent for urgent DNA analysis.

If DNA technology had been around when Eileen Randall died, Willard might have been exonerated. If someone else's DNA had been found on the body, it could have placed a greater onus on the prosecution to prove he had killed the girl.

Willard was either incredibly unlucky that his defence had not picked holes in the prosecution's case, or he had committed the crime and the prosecution was lucky to get a conviction.

She couldn't decide which, rubbing the tension from her temples. She'd spent the weekend finding mistakes in the police's handling of the Randall case that should have been enough to at least have raised reasonable doubt in the minds of a jury.

Anya phoned Hayden's mobile. They agreed to meet for dinner at a local pizzeria.

Arriving at the restaurant, the detective looked even more slender in jeans and a fitted shirt. Weight loss had also taken years off his appearance.

One breath of the wood-fired dinners had Anya salivating. The smell of garlic and cooked dough gave the décor an even more homely feel. Wooden tables and benches in a courtyard seemed the ideal place for a quiet conversation. Thankfully, Sunday evenings were the quietest night of the week.

'Where did you disappear to?' he asked as they sat and were handed menus.

'I went away for the weekend.' Anya studied the menu. 'The vegetarian pizza is to die for.' She grinned. 'Low in fat and packed with fabulous flavours – basil, eggplant, artichoke.'

The waitress lit the candle on the table and switched on an umbrella-shaped gas heater. Another brought fresh bread with a divided dish containing olive oil and balsamic vinegar.

'I happened to go over the brief in the Randall case myself, given we arrested Willard for the

Dorman murder based on similar pattern evidence.'

Anya dipped some bread into the balsamic vinegar. Her tongue savoured the delight. 'I hoped you would. What did you find?'

'Obviously, I'm not a forensic expert, but it seemed to me that the investigation was a bit thin on the ground. Most of it depended on Willard's confession.'

'Which he later recanted.' Anya chewed her second piece. 'Otherwise, there would not have been a trial.'

'Correct. There are definite similarities with Elizabeth Dorman's murder – the nature of the wounds, I thought, though, he would have had more blood on him if he'd stabbed Eileen Randall up close that many times.'

Anya nodded. 'I agree. You would expect a lot more blood.'

'So you have seen the report.' Hayden smiled and tried the bread.

'Just the PM. Oh, and I might have spoken to the officer who was in charge of the investigation locally.'

'Damn, you're good!' the detective said.

The waitress returned to take their orders. Hayden chose a seafood pizza with bocconcini, and they agreed to share the vegetarian pizza, some bruschetta and a bottle of lambrusco.

'Something must have bothered you, to go all that way.'

'Let's just say that in the past we were more specific about time of death. Places like the Body Farm in the US helped us realise that it's nothing like an exact science.'

'Okay, so time of death is dubious. What else?'

Anya felt free to speak to Hayden Richards. Facts didn't compromise confidentiality with Veronica Slater and what they were discussing could as easily have been deduced by any other competent pathologist.

'The body has to have been immersed in saltwater. The chest contained crayfish larvae. They're only ever found in the ocean.'

'Could she have breathed them in, if she went swimming first?'

The drinks arrived along with the bruschetta. Anya wiped her hands on the napkin. The detective poured half a glass for himself and a whole glass for his dinner companion.

'Thanks. No saltwater in the lungs. She didn't swallow the larvae. They had to have entered the chest via the stab wounds. The debatable point is that if you take into account the winds that night, the tide could have swept her out a couple of hours earlier.'

'How can high tide be debatable? It's recorded, isn't it?'

'For the main bay, but Koonaka Beach is a cove and winds that night could easily have affected the timing.' She explained what Bill Lalor had told her.

Hayden sat silently, staring at the bruschetta. 'But if she died that long before she was found, why were her clothes still wet? The blood on Willard's shirt was fresh. Wouldn't it have clotted and dried after two hours?'

'Not necessarily. The night was humid. Clothes don't dry when there's that much moisture in the air. The same goes for blood. Willard could have got the blood on himself if he carried her out of the water, like he initially said.'

'When she'd already been dead a couple of hours.' Hayden sipped his drink. 'But far-fetched, don't you think?'

'Not if he really was watching that TV show he described.'

Hayden sat back, studying Anya. 'You always find a way to surprise me. You have that insatiable woman's curiosity that could really bugger up the cases we just want to finish with.' He chuckled again, then became serious. 'Sorrenti thinks it's all cut-and-dried. With Willard in jail, there's only the brief to prepare. No other leads are being followed up regarding the northwest rapes.'

'What about the two who attacked Gloria Havelock? I know you think the mother and daughter rapes were unrelated, but what if—'

'Ah, you haven't heard. The blue sheet you found in Gloria's evidence bag and sent to the lab did have some DNA on it. Belonged to a guy called Eric Scholl. Arrested for assaulting a security guard at a nightclub. He was out on bail when he attacked the Havelock woman.'

That would be little relief to Gloria, but at least one of her attackers had been found.

'Have you interviewed him?'

The pizzas arrived and Hayden waited until the waitress had left.

'No chance. He was killed in a prison fight over drugs six months ago. Seems he developed a nasty cocaine habit inside.'

Anya's appetite waned.

'Do you know who his accomplice was?'

'He was arrested with a real loser going by the name of Gideon Lee and half-a-dozen aliases. Has an IQ of about eighty and couldn't mastermind a peanut-butter sandwich, let alone a burglary. Seems he followed Scholl like a puppy, but he's not admitting to raping anyone.'

Anya picked up a slice of pizza and oil dripped onto her wrist. Hayden had begun cutting up his meal with a knife and fork. She quickly wiped herself clean and continued eating, more delicately.

'Is there any chance Lee could have committed Melanie's rape?'

Dean Martin singing 'That's Amore' filtered through the outside speakers.

'No, he's still in jail. And he's Chinese, not exactly white-skinned.'

The white hands described by both victims still baffled her.

'I got your message about vitiligo. It causes depigmentation, or whitening of the skin. Michael Jackson is supposed to have it, I think.'

Hayden put down his knife and fork and finished chewing. 'You know, that's bothered me for a while now. Even though Melanie didn't see the white stripe Louise described, there's got to be something to it. Willard doesn't have a blemish on his arms or hands. Maybe our guy has this vitiligo condition.'

Anya left the crust and picked up another piece, this time not caring how uncivilised she appeared. 'Couldn't it have been paint on his hand?'

'I thought that as well. I know Willard is odds-on to have raped again, but something tells me that he's not the right guy this time. I can't shake this gut feeling that maybe he didn't do it.'

'Did you find the knife that killed Liz Dorman?'

'No. Maybe Willard's playing us for suckers and is a lot smarter than we think.'

The detective's phone chimed and he excused himself to answer it, swivelling sideways in his seat.

'Thanks for letting me know,' he said, and snapped the phone shut.

His face looked ashen.

'Is everything okay?'

'So much for our theories. That was the lab about the blood on Willard's shirt. Looks like it came from Liz Dorman after all.'

237

31

The following morning, Anya met Veronica Slater outside Long Bay prison. Every time she had visited, winds howled through the trees, giving the place an eerie feel, despite it being so close to the ocean.

It was unusual for Anya to see defendants, but Veronica stressed that it was important for the case. Being paid for her time was the only incentive Anya needed. After seeing the assault victims and the PM reports from the Dorman and Randall murders, she was curious to see what Willard was like and how he presented – whether he appeared intimidating, or came across as quite simple.

Outside the administration building, a number of camera crews stood waiting, as though they were expecting something to happen. Veronica's arrival had them racing to shove a boom microphone as close to her head as possible.

'Can you tell us whether Willard is on suicide watch?'

'Has he confessed to killing and raping more women?'

'Do you think he's going to die in prison this time?'

'Should he ever have been released?'

No one waited for an answer before firing off the next question.

Veronica acted surprised at the ambush. 'In this country, a person is deemed innocent until proven guilty. In fact, renowned forensic expert Doctor Anya Crichton is here with me to help prove Geoff Willard's innocence.'

Damn Veronica! She'd made out that Anya was on her 'side', not just providing an opinion based on fact. Anya ignored the cameras who chased her into the building, hoping not to give them good 'vision'. She fumed that Veronica could have compromised her credibility with the sexual assault investigation, police and judges.

Inside, Veronica stomped across the carpet floor to the enquiry counter.

'Who let the reporters know we were visiting Willard today? Vultures are out there. We've just had to run the gauntlet.'

The officer behind the counter shrugged and asked them to sign in.

'I'm sorry to have mentioned you back there,' Veronica said casually over her shoulder, 'but I was taken by surprise.'

Anya was yet to meet a barrister who couldn't react on her feet.

'Let's get something straight. You do not speak

239

for me, let alone tell the media I'm on your side. There's no excuse for the stunt you just pulled.'

'Like I said, they took me by surprise.'

Like hell, Anya thought.

Once past the multiple gates and security checks, and the lawyer's incessant complaints about having to give up her mobile phone for the duration of the visit, they were let into a fenced courtyard. Stark apart from white plastic tables and chairs, it was where families met on visiting day.

'He likes to be in the sun,' Veronica said, as though she cared.

Anya doubted the woman saw him as anything more than a fast-track to bigger, higher-profile, and therefore more lucrative, cases.

A few moments later, a guard escorted out a man in a green tracksuit who was considerably shorter than the witnesses had described. Anya thought of Quentin Lagardia saying that victims almost always overestimated their attacker's stature.

Veronica remained seated as Willard failed to make eye-contact with either of them.

'We haven't got long and it's important that we go over some things. This is a doctor who I've asked to check how you're being treated. I gather the police were unnecessarily rough with you when you gave yourself up.'

Willard sat at the table and looked down at his lap. So far he didn't appear very intimidating at all.

'Can you show the doctor your bruises?'

Geoff deferred to the nearest guard, who nodded.

'Excuse me,' Veronica said. 'Lawyer, client. Privileged.'

The guard took a few steps backwards.

Willard held out his arms. Anya noticed bruising on the back of his wrists, presumably from handcuffs. His fingernails had been chewed beneath the tips of his fingers. She wrote a brief note on the pad she'd brought in.

'The doctor wants to ask you some questions about the night Eileen Randall died.'

Willard looked up. 'Why? I'm not in jail for that any more.'

Anya couldn't work out whether the seasoned prisoner's naivety came from innocence, or was part of a polished act.

'I looked at the report, and I think Eileen's body floated in the water that night. Just like you said when you first went to the station.'

'That was a long time ago,' he said.

'Do you remember what show you watched that night, before you went out?'

He smiled, just perceptibly. 'It was funny. I laughed a lot.'

'Can you tell us its name?' Veronica spoke to him as though he were a baby.

'*The Eleventh Hour*.' He watched an ant on the corner of the table. 'It was a bit rude. Mum didn't like it.'

'Good boy,' Veronica said.

Willard may have been in a forty-year-old body, Anya thought, but the twenty years in prison hadn't allowed him to mature. He was emotionally frozen as an immature adolescent and should have been treated as one, not babied.

Anya tried to encourage him to open up. 'I checked, and the show that was on that night was never run again on TV. Can you remember anything about the episode you saw before you found Eileen?'

Geoff seemed far more interested in the ant. He put his hand out for the insect to crawl on. Anya noticed the dirt beneath his stumpy fingernails as the ant ran maniacally over one finger, then another. It was difficult to judge whether he was being kind or cruel.

'A man went up to a woman at the bus stop and looked up her dress. She slapped him in the face and stormed off. Then an old lady came up and hit the man with her umbrella when he wouldn't look up her dress.'

He continued to play with the ant.

Veronica clicked her pen on and off, on and off. She reached over and squashed the ant with her finger. 'You're facing life in prison if you get convicted of murder. We're busting our backsides here trying to get you out of this place and maybe even get you exonerated for the Randall murder. Do you know what that means? If we can do that, you'll be entitled to compensation. Lots of it. You could do anything, go anywhere you want, not rot in here for the rest of your life.'

He didn't react to what his lawyer said, just studied the insect remains.

Anya lowered her head to make eye-contact. 'Ms Slater is trying to help. I'm trying to find out about the tides the night you watched that show. Do you remember anything about them, like whether the tide was going in or coming out when you saw Eileen on Koonaka Beach?'

Geoff scratched the palm of his hand with the opposite thumb. 'I told the police I killed her. I tried to tell them what happened but no one believed me. Not even Mum.' He turned to Veronica. 'Now I want to see my picture.'

Veronica shrugged her shoulders. 'I don't know if I have it.'

Geoff's jaw tensed. He slapped the table and Veronica started, then pulled a photo from the back of her yellow notepad. It was a wallet-size snapshot of a girl with long, dark hair.

Geoff snatched it, and held it close to his chest.

Anya was no longer sure who was in control. She looked around for the guard, who was speaking to another visitor.

'I told you I'd look after it for you, and bring it when you wanted,' Veronica said. 'But you do not threaten me. Ever.'

Geoff hid the picture against his chest and sulked.

'Is that your girlfriend?' Anya asked.

'Not yet, but she likes me. She said so.'

'May I see?'

Quill looked at Veronica, who nodded, and then passed his prized possession slowly across the table.

Anya gasped when she saw the photo. The hair was longer, but it was probably taken a while ago. Even so, the candid smile unmistakably belonged to Melanie Havelock. And her address had been scrawled on the back.

32

'For God's sake, you're withholding evidence in a major crime investigation.'

'Keep your voice down,' Veronica Slater snapped as she went through the final security gate. 'It came with a love letter from the girl.'

Anya felt her temples pulse faster. 'Like hell it did! The police should know he's got the picture.'

'Well, neither of us is in a position to say anything. What happened in there just then was privileged. You go shooting your mouth off to your police buddies and no lawyer is ever going to hire you to consult again.'

Anya wanted to slam Veronica against the wall of the admin building. 'How dare you? He didn't show me the photo in a medical consultation.'

Veronica didn't waver or let on if she felt intimidated by Anya's anger. Instead, she seemed to feed on it.

'In a way, he did. You were there to assess him and he showed you his fantasy girl. Even told you how she liked him. That's sounding pretty delusional to me, which is, if you recall, a medical term.'

'This isn't about semantics. He has a photo of a rape victim, and he's under suspicion for committing that crime. It ties him to the victim.'

'Grow up, we're not in Kansas, Dorothy.'

The lawyer scratched the path with her heels as she opened the door to the admin building. Sarcasm only made her more repugnant, Anya thought – if that was possible.

'The moment he gets bail, the police find out.'

The door closed and Veronica turned. 'He's already been denied bail. But he swears he got that photo from the girl and I believe him. We all know psychos have made false rape accusations before. Maybe she's a complete nutter. Ever thought of that? Otherwise, it's easy to argue that anyone could have sent him the photo. Maybe he's being set up? Wouldn't be the first time the police have tried to stitch up one of my clients.'

Anya leant on the door. 'Don't play the victim, Veronica, it doesn't suit you. How many of your female colleagues have you bitten the heads off in your career?'

The lawyer smiled and shook her head. 'Resorting to personal attacks now your cognitive arguments have failed you? You've just proved how jealous you are. It's my *intimate* relationship with Dan. That's what all this is about.'

Anya felt the rash on her neck rise. 'You're the one who's delusional now.'

Some of the visitors began to appear along the

246

path. The two of them stopped talking long enough to collect their possessions stored in the lockers inside and sign out.

Anya was annoyed that she'd resorted to personal comments, but she could never think up good comebacks on the spot. One would probably come to her at four o'clock the next morning.

The press were still hanging around and Veronica was in full melodramatic mode. 'I'm worried for the mental health of my client, who is having trouble understanding why the police have arrested him again.'

Anya felt nauseated at the public performance and wanted nothing more to do with it. She headed towards her car, with a lot less respect for Dan Brody. Fingers shaking from anger, she fumbled with the keys in her lock.

'Shit!' She dropped the keys and bent down to see a pair of red stiletto heels approach. She stood up, bracing herself for another fight.

'We haven't finished. I still want that report on the Randall murder. All the inconsistencies you came up with.'

'Fine. You'll have it. But I can tell you now, if you want me to appear in court, what I say may not be so favourable to Willard.'

Veronica swung her briefcase like a schoolgirl and smiled – again. 'I thought as much. That's why I wanted you on this case.'

Anya didn't understand. Veronica just smiled wider.

'Let me explain it to you. I knew you'd come up with something to criticise Alf Carney's PM. We all know he's been a joke for years. With you working for the defence, the prosecution won't want to touch you. They'll know what evidence you've come up with to cast doubt on Willard's conviction, which would ruin their similar-pattern-evidence prosecution.'

'You're forgetting that I've done the examinations on all the assault victims.'

Veronica stepped closer. 'We all know that the medical examination in a rape case has very little to do with the outcome. In fact, it's almost insignificant. Besides, there are always experts like Lyndsay Gatlow who are happy to give an opinion on the evidence if required.'

Jesus! Veronica had nobbled her. She wanted her blocked from testifying for the prosecution and had set her up. Anya had done everything Veronica had planned, and more.

Veronica took advantage of Anya's stunned silence.

'If I'm not mistaken, you've already told one of your police mates about the discrepancies in the Randall murder, so they already know you're casting doubt on Willard's conviction. Looks like you're not testifying for either side now.'

Anya clenched her teeth, grinding them. 'Get away from me before I do something I may not regret.' She unlocked her car, got in and started the engine. The vision of Veronica's smug expression haunted her as she sped out of the car park.

33

Morgan Tully, the state coroner, rocked back and forwards in her leather chair. Peter Latham sat, elbows on the chair arms, index fingers meeting at his beard. Anya filled a glass of water for a distraction. She thought she could hear her carotid arteries pounding. If it hadn't been for Morgan Tully, Anya would have been somewhere else. Anywhere but in that conference room.

Directly opposite Morgan, Dr Seth Myer, head of the College of Pathologists, folded his arms and kept checking the clock on the wall. The empty chair at the head of the table had been reserved for Alf Carney. No one, it seemed, had wanted this day to come. A representative from the Medical Complaints Tribunal, a lawyer, was allocated the task of taking notes and serving as a witness to what was about to transpire.

'From everything I've seen,' Seth Myer said, 'he's using papers that are twenty years old to corroborate his findings. He's either sorely out of touch or he's committing perjury every time he testifies. He just selects studies that back his claims and refuses to admit that other possibilities exist.'

'In some of the cases I've reviewed,' Anya added, 'instead of referring to texts, he quotes his own previous autopsies as validation.'

The room went silent.

'Peter, do you have anything else to contribute?' Morgan Tully asked.

Peter Latham pushed his chair back, as if about to leave. 'There's not much left to say.'

'So we all appear to be in agreement,' Morgan said. 'If he won't retire, things could get rather unpleasant for him. As it is, we face countless reopening of cases and reviews of convictions.' She readjusted her scarf so the knot sat asymmetrically to the right.

Peter Latham hadn't moved. Anya felt guilty at being the one chosen to review Alf's decisions and wondered who else in the room saw her as the Judas Iscariot of pathologists.

Morgan glanced at Anya as if reading her mind. 'Doctor Carney needs to realise that this hasn't been a witch hunt, but a systematic review of countless cases he was responsible for. I've had pathologists in other states reviewing a dozen more cases selected at random, and their findings are pretty consistent.'

A tap on the door broke the tension. Alf Carney appeared, with a leather portfolio under one arm. Despite a dark charcoal suit and College tie, he looked unsure of himself.

Morgan stood up and checked her watch.

'We weren't expecting you for another half-hour,' she said.

'I want this on my terms, not yours.'

The coroner indicated where she would like him to sit. He was already perspiring and barely acknowledged the others in the room other than with a quick scan.

Anya had wanted to leave by the time he arrived, but was now caught in the room. She studied his face. It appeared bloated and he looked like he hadn't slept for days. For the first time she could remember, he wore polished black leather shoes instead of suede lace-ups. He'd taken today very seriously. He sat slowly, unbuttoning his jacket.

'Before you speak,' he croaked, then cleared his throat, 'I'd like to say a few words.'

'By all means,' Morgan said.

He pulled out a number of pages from his portfolio and donned a pair of half-lens glasses from his pocket.

'I understand that in the last few months there have been numerous enquiries about my work over the last thirty-five years. It disappoints me that I had to hear about this from the medical grapevine, not from my most trusted and respected colleagues.'

Peter Latham didn't move.

'With more litigious criminals, a glut of lawyers and a media ready to lynch anyone for the slightest perception of wrongdoing, I accept that someone who has been involved in some of the nation's highest-profile cases would come under scrutiny. It's not the first time.' He took a deep breath. 'However, this appears to be motivated by something more personal, something deeper than defence lawyers appealing for their clients. It is saddening to learn that colleagues who have worked alongside me have, at the same time, been undermining my authority and accusing me of the worst failing in the medical profession – negligence.'

Morgan Tully interrupted. 'We're not at the Salem trials. You're not invited here to defend accusations, Doctor Carney. Please understand that we all have your best interests at heart today.'

For the first time, Peter Latham spoke. 'We're all subject to peer review and quality assurance. None of us is immune, nor should we be. We may not be advocates for living patients, but we none-theless need to ensure that we adhere to uniform standards.'

Alf Carney removed his glasses. 'Let's talk about professional standards, shall we? When I was a family doctor in country Victoria, there wasn't anyone within a five-hundred-kilometre radius who would do police forensic work. Not a single member of *our* noble profession would help. When a young girl was raped and murdered in the middle of nowhere, the police had nothing without a post-mortem. Stupid me did it out of a sense of duty. Next thing I know, my practice is suffering because I'm suddenly the police surgeon, district pathologist and anything else the community needed. I took on a role nobody else wanted.'

He directed his comments towards all four in the room. 'Pathology wasn't fashionable, not like today. It was like some macabre secret society that voters didn't need or want to know about.' He rubbed the bridge of his nose. 'People didn't even want you round to dinner any more.'

Morgan Tully remained businesslike. 'We're not here to discuss how you entered the field. We're concerned with current scientific practice.'

Carney's face flushed, highlighting the number of sun-spots on his ruddy complexion. The veins in his neck distended.

'As the country doctor, I helped retrieve bodies. Kids I'd known half their lives pulled from wrecks or mangled by farm machinery.'

He pointed to his breast-bone with both hands and spoke through almost clenched teeth. The emotion and pain he couldn't hide made Anya want to rush out of the room. The man's career was over, and he knew it.

'*I* was the one who had to try to resuscitate the fractured bodies, then break the news to the family. Then *I* had to do the stinking autopsy as well. There was no technician to help out with the dirty work, no one to share on-call with. No one to discuss cases with. No such thing as debriefing and no one to ask how I felt after the funerals.' He wiped his forehead with a handkerchief. 'So don't lecture me about standards. I worked my tail off to study as much as I could to deliver the best bloody service I was capable of. Where were the College members when I needed support or time off? Sitting on their shiny arses in the cities.'

Seth Myer shifted. 'We all did it tough back then. But times have changed and we've had to move with them. Everything we do has to be scientifically validated. We're more answerable than ever before.'

'So that's it,' Carney said. 'I'm too old so I'm being hung out to dry. Clean out all the old fools and make way for the new.'

'That's not it.' Peter Latham broke his silence. 'No one disputes that you've been an outstanding provider of desperately needed services. But ongoing education is essential, and there is some concern that you may not be applying current best practice.'

'I thought better of you than this.' Carney stood. 'Don't bother saying what you'd planned. I'll save you the trouble.' He pulled an envelope from his portfolio and slid it across the desk.

'It's a copy of my resignation. And if anyone tries to sully my reputation, I'll have you for defamation or libel faster than you can snap your fingers.'

He walked towards the door, head held high and

255

shoulders back. He was going out with dignity, if nothing else.

Morgan Tully stood first once he'd gone. 'Anyone for lunch? I've got an inquest resuming at two.' She behaved as though nothing had happened.

Peter Latham hurried out the door without speaking.

Anya collected her papers and felt a knot in her chest. It was so easy to criticise someone else's work with the benefit of hindsight. She wondered if one day it could be her being accused of medical negligence. For the first time, she felt great pity for Alf Carney.

Being right wasn't any consolation.

34

Tired and frustrated by the events of the past two days, Anya didn't feel like a confrontation at police headquarters, but Hayden Richards had told her it was important that they meet. Thankfully, Meira Sorrenti had already left for the day and the other detectives had better things to do. No one took any notice of her as Hayden escorted her through security.

Once inside the office, he offered her a chair near his paper-covered desk. 'I really need to talk to you about the Dorman murder. Willard's mother says the shirt that had the DNA on it hadn't been worn yet. She'd washed and ironed it, but he'd never put it on.'

'And you believe a mother?'

'No, listen. I rang the lab this afternoon. The shirts were taken after crime scene used luminol at the home. They found traces of Liz Dorman's blood on not one but two of his shirts.' He handed her a faxed report and trotted off to make coffees.

Maybe Geoffrey had taken a change of clothes and got some from his skin on the second shirt.

Anya twice read the comments on the page. These traces were small smears, nothing like you would expect for such a blood-spattered scene.

From the amount of blood at the Dorman house, the shirt should have been saturated, or at least covered in splatters. The small amount of blood on Willard's shirt at the site of the Randall murder bothered her more than the tide discrepancies. The similarities between the cases became more odd.

Maybe Willard had had an accomplice if he did kill Liz Dorman. When the detective returned, she raised the possibility of a second attacker. 'When Gloria Havelock was raped, there were two men there.'

'Yeah, the dead one and Captain Moron.'

A cup with the remnants of someone else's lipstick faced her along with two plain biscuits. Anya turned the cup around and drank with her left hand. She could taste unrinsed dishwashing liquid on the rim.

'When they robbed her, they took wallet-sized photos of her daughters. Did they ever turn up?' Anya asked carefully.

'Not that I know of. The officers did a search of Captain Moron's cell yesterday and didn't find anything apart from tennis magazines.' Anticipating his guest's next question, he explained. 'Girls, mini skirts. It's the closest thing to porn Lee could get. Sorrenti went over there to interview him and got nowhere. The little bastard wouldn't talk.

Kept saying he'd answer one question for every time she showed him her tits.'

As much as Sorrenti grated on Anya, she shouldn't have had to put up with that.

'Does the guy still have his gonads?'

Hayden laughed. 'Only just. Sorrenti was incredibly ticked off. She didn't get anything out of him.'

'Willard was in jail when Gloria was raped, but don't you think it's too much of a coincidence that her daughter was attacked in their house once he got out?'

Hayden crunched on a biscuit, trapping crumbs in his moustache. 'You know the stats: just about every woman I know has had to deal with a pervert some time. The girl's kind, pretty and would automatically turn heads.'

Anya knew that the detective hadn't meant to implicate Melanie in her assault, but he was right. All it took was one sexual deviant to notice her.

Anya needed to find out how Willard had got that photo, without letting on that Willard had it. As galling as it was, Veronica had her rattled. Telling the police about Melanie's photo could breach confidentiality, in which case Veronica would make sure everyone heard about it. Perhaps there was a chance Hayden would work it out himself. It was pretty clear in Anya's mind that Melanie would never have sent it with a love letter. But in a world of dysfunctional people, bizarre things happened.

'Was Willard ever in prison with Gideon Lee?'

'Don't think so. Lee's been in Goulburn jail, Willard served at Long Bay.'

'Could Geoff have had contact at any stage with Lee's dead partner?'

Hayden looked confused. 'Unlikely. Willard was incarcerated for a long time. Am I missing something?'

'No. I'd like a link between Melanie and Gloria's attackers, that's all. It still doesn't sit right that they were both random victims.'

Hayden shrugged. 'How do you explain the shirt results?'

Anya decided not to pursue the issue of Melanie's photo – for now. The DNA evidence needed to be discussed.

'The small amounts of blood on the clothing don't make sense. Maybe Willard, or someone else, threw out the really blood-stained shirt and accidentally got blood on his other clothes.'

Hayden bumped the desk with an elbow and nearly spilt his drink. 'I was thinking more about the chances of contamination in the lab. To the naked eye, the clothes were clean when we picked them up.'

'So they'd both been washed?'

'Yep,' he said, breaking his diet and munching on two more biscuits. 'Luminol showed up the stains again at the lab, which is why they were tested properly.'

The detective flicked through the papers on his

desk, pulled out some photos and handed them across. 'We had his cousin under surveillance when Willard was on the run. This character's a bit smooth for my liking, and he's got an answer for everything. He lives at the house and could have been an accessory after the fact.' He cleaned his moustache with the back of his hand. 'Fancy a little trip out there for a chat?'

Anya wondered if that were appropriate. 'I thought priests were the only ones who popped round for visits just in time for dinner.'

'It's when the punters are most likely to be home.'

Hayden had obviously planned that she would go along. 'Aren't you risking trouble if you keep investigating without Sorrenti's permission?'

He put down his half-full cup and collected the papers into a pile before locking them in his desk drawer. 'The investigation only begins with the arrest. That's when the fun starts, trying to put together the brief. That's all I'm doing, nothing more, nothing less. A woman might have better luck with the cousin.'

'You mean I'm a distraction to get him to let his guard down?'

'Doc, you are a looker, and it might just work.'

Anya opened her mouth wide, not sure if he were serious or joking. Going by the grin on his face, he was joking. She hoped.

She felt like a hanger-on, but what Veronica Slater had orchestrated made her more determined to find out what had really happened to Eileen Randall and Liz Dorman. She wondered if her criticism of the Randall autopsy results would lead to a guilty man getting away with Liz Dorman's murder.

Maybe she was no different from Alf Carney after all. She tried to block the thought from her mind.

35

Nick Hudson opened the door without releasing the chain.

'We're about to eat,' he said. 'It's not a good time.'

They heard a frail voice call from inside. 'If it's reporters, tell them to leave us alone.'

'No, Auntie, it's the police. They've got some more questions.'

A few seconds passed and a petite, grey-haired woman in a floral apron opened the door.

Hayden held up his badge. 'I'm sorry for the timing, but this shouldn't take long.'

'I don't know how we can help. We don't know anything,' said Mrs Willard, leaving the door open as she scuffed her way to the living room.

Two fold-out trays were set up in front of the lounges. The TV was switched to a popular teen-age soap-opera.

'Do you mind if we eat before it gets cold?' She detoured to the kitchen, returning with two meals. Well-done chops, boiled potatoes and greens comprising peas and beans. Mrs Willard kept the most burnt piece of meat for herself.

'You might as well sit down,' Nick offered, before leaving the room. He returned a moment later with a bottle of barbecue sauce.

Hayden and Anya sat at the end of the longer lounge and waited for the pair to have a few bites of their meals. A black bass guitar stood propped on a stand, next to its speaker. No sheet music was in sight.

'Do you play in a band?' Anya asked.

Nick puffed his chest. 'Some mates own a pub and we get a gig now and then.'

Men always thought being in a band impressed women. Anya thought of Liz Dorman's boyfriend playing at a pub while someone took her life.

The smell of burnt meat reminded her of the days before her mother knew what 'medium-rare' meant. The sole purpose of cooking was to kill the bacteria in the meat and the only way to do that was by burning it to a piece of carbon that was almost inedible. Anya used to mock her mother for their evening meals. Ironically, with all the diet trends over the years, the old meat and three vegetables was now being accepted as one of the healthiest. Her mother had actually known best.

'You lot already ransacked the place and got most of what Geoff had. There's not much left to pinch,' Nick proclaimed with a full mouth. Judging by his reaction, something he'd stuffed into his mouth was still hot.

She sympathised when Nick drowned what was

left of his dinner in sauce. He was eating quickly because they were there.

'We wanted to ask you about the night Eileen Randall died,' Hayden began. 'I gather Geoffrey confessed.'

'Yeah, so?' Nick seemed more interested in the teenage drama on the screen. 'You bastards verballed him.'

'I thought his lawyer told him to change his story.' Mrs Willard looked confused. 'It was a long time ago.'

'Why do you say he was verballed?' the detective asked.

'Did anyone see him confess apart from that local copper who interviewed him? Back then, Geoff would've admitted to starting World War II if he was scared enough. What would you do if someone threatened to stick your mother in jail?'

Hayden pulled out his small black notebook and wrote something down.

'It seems as though he initially told the police that he found Eileen in the ocean. Doctor Crichton here went over the reports. They found crayfish larvae in the body, which can only get there in the water.'

Silence made it unclear whether the pair had heard or understood.

Anya broke it first. 'I spoke to someone about the tides that night who is convinced the body would have been floating when Geoff was still at home with you, Mrs Willard.'

'Why are you bringing this up now? It's all in the past.'

'Hang on, Auntie.' Nick stopped chewing. 'Let her talk.'

'There's a chance,' Anya said, 'that Geoff might not have murdered Eileen Randall.'

Mrs Willard put down her knife and fork and seemed to sink lower in the chair.

'That's not possible,' she managed.

Anya found it difficult to comprehend how a mother hadn't considered the possibility that her son was not guilty. If he was innocent, the pain that must have inflicted on Geoff Willard was immeasurable.

'You don't understand,' Nick explained. 'No one wanted to say anything after the way she died, but Eileen Randall was no bloody saint. She was the town bike and a prize bitch with it.'

'Stop it, Nick. The girl is dead, for heaven's sake.'

Nick lowered his head at the reprimand.

'What my nephew means is, she had a reputation.'

'She earned it. Half the guys in town and even more from the mines had been through her. She'd even boast about who she'd slept with.'

Mrs Willard collected her tray and excused herself.

'Did you ever have a relationship with Eileen?' Hayden spoke quietly.

Nick nodded. 'Everyone did. I was going out

266

with a girl and Eileen couldn't wait to tell her. It was how she got her kicks. She was a trumped-up little slag.'

Anya tried to imagine the Randall girl. Fourteen was still legally and emotionally a child. Every male who'd had intercourse with her had committed statutory rape. And now Nick sat, taking the moral high-ground.

'Did she sleep with Geoffrey?' she asked, trying not to sound judgemental.

'Shit no. She used to call him a retard and make fun of him. She'd tease him and come on to him, then tell him he was disgusting to make her friends laugh. You couldn't blame Geoff if he did it. She asked for it.'

Hayden interrupted. 'If she was so horrible, why did you sleep with her?'

'Because she offered. Hey,' Nick shrugged, 'I'm only human.'

The theme song for the show came on in the background and Nick filled his mouth again. He reached for the remote control and changed over to another soap.

Hayden referred to his notebook. 'Does the name Melanie Havelock mean anything to you?'

'Long, dark hair? She's the one who has it bad for Geoff.'

Hayden shot Anya a glance. Anya held her breath. Nick had just given Hayden the connection he needed between Melanie and Geoff without Anya having to disclose the photo.

'You know her?' Hayden said.

Nick swallowed. 'Not personally, but I found the letter she sent Geoff. Pretty steamy stuff.' His eyes didn't leave the television screen.

'She wrote to your cousin? When?'

'Dunno exactly, but she sent a photo, too. Oh yeah, she put it in his pocket when he got out. She kinda scared him with all the sex stuff. She's pretty wild, by the sounds of it.'

Anya could not believe Melanie would ever write to Geoff. 'Can we see it?'

'Do you think I'm stupid? You just want to use it to get to Geoff.'

'Actually, no,' Anya tried. 'It's possible that your cousin might have been set up and the letter would really help us out.'

Hayden suppressed a smile as Nick left the room. He returned with a stuffed dog under his arm, about two feet tall.

Anya sat back out of instinct.

'It's okay,' he said. 'This is Brown-Eye, me old mate. Dead as a doornail.'

'I didn't know taxidermy was back in fashion,' Hayden uttered. 'How long's he been like that?'

'Had him seven years before he got run over, um, about fifteen years ago. Never go far without him.' He put Brown-Eye on the carpet and unfolded a letter hidden underneath its collar.

'Police didn't think to check him out. Seemed a good place to stick it,' he said, handing it to Hayden with a wink for Anya.

As the detective unfolded the letter, he read the first few lines aloud.

'*Dear Geoff, I could hardly wait for you to get out so we can be together . . .*' He scanned the rest. 'After that, she talks about wanting him. Then it gets really lewd.'

Anya only half-listened. She remembered unidentified dog hair found on Eileen Randall's body. The timing fit. Nick owned the dog at the time of the murder. 'Must have been a loyal dog,' she said.

'Sure was.' He patted its belly. 'Wouldn't go with anyone but me. Couldn't even fart without him being there.'

'One more question,' Hayden said. 'Did you see Eileen the night she died?'

Nick clutched the dog. 'No way! After she shot off her mouth to my girlfriend, I never wanted to see her again.'

Anya could see how defensive he had become. 'Is there any chance I could borrow Brown-Eye for a couple of days?'

Hayden raised both eyebrows.

'Only if it has something to do with helping our Geoff?' Nick looked nervous.

Anya smiled. 'It could be a big help. I'll bring him back as soon as I can. He's such a good specimen, I'd like to show him to a friend at the Australian Museum. He's doing DNA research on preserved dogs. If we're lucky, it may just help Geoff out.'

'I don't see how.'

Mrs Willard entered the room and gestured to her nephew to hand over the dog. Puffy eyes indicated she had been crying.

Nick watched his aunt and softened. 'Sure, if it'll help.'

Surprised by the power Geoff's mother wielded, Anya carried the dusty animal to the car, followed by Hayden, who remained silent until she had strapped it into the back seat.

'What the hell just happened in there?' he asked from the driver's side.

Anya gloated, for once knowing more than the detective.

'Come on. What has a stuffed animal got to do with the murder?'

'There was dog hair on Eileen Randall's body. If Nick Hudson killed the girl and the dog went everywhere with him—'

Hayden nodded slowly and grinned. 'You're going to get the dog tested for a match. Damn, you're good.' He started the engine. 'Without the technology and the case looking strong, no one would have bothered with dog hair back then.' Holding the handbrake, he checked his side mirror. 'So, here's my next problem. Has Melanie Havelock been dicking with us? Did she actually come on to Willard?'

Anya exhaled heavily. 'Difficult to believe, but that's what we're going to have to find out.'

36

Anya found a car park just off College Street in the city. Sunday mornings were the best time to visit the museum, although families were already lined up before opening time.

Ben could barely contain his excitement. 'Remember when we came to the Egypt exhibition, and saw the dead mummies?'

How could a mother forget seeing her son wrap his own tiny kewpie doll in a bandage in the activity centre, then colour in a cardboard sarcophagus? It sat on her desk as a constant reminder. His litany of amusing questions that day had caught the attention of a visiting Egyptologist, who later sent him a wonderful book on the pharaohs.

'Sure do. I got an email from that English archaeologist recently, asking how you're doing.'

'Cool,' he said. 'Can I pat the dog again?'

Anya had brought Brown-Eye with them and hidden him under a rug. She hadn't wanted to scare the children, but the rug seemed to pique the curiosity of everyone in the queue. Ben didn't seem to mind that the dog wasn't actually alive.

'Where are we going first?' he asked, unable to stand still for more than a couple of seconds. 'Can we go to the skeleton room?'

Anya checked her watch. The taxidermist wasn't due for half an hour and had agreed to meet them in the Search and Discovery Centre, an interactive room full of preserved specimens, microscopes and computers.

'We've got plenty of time. Skeleton room it is.'

The man behind the ticket counter chuckled at the parcel in her hands. 'No dogs allowed,' he said, pretending to be stern. Anya happily explained the purpose of the visit, and he let them through:

'Hope he's toilet-trained, or you'll be cleaning up the mess,' he added, and chortled.

Ben slipped his hand into Anya's spare one as they followed the signs to the skeleton room.

'Wow! Check this out,' he said, and hurried to the centre display. A human sat in a rocking chair flanked by a dog, cat and rat, all in skeletal form.

'What's that?' he asked, pointing at the animal bones.

'That one is the dog, chasing the cat, chasing . . .'

'That's a giant mouse! It's the biggest one I've ever seen.'

Anya laughed and wondered how many mice her son had actually seen. 'It's a rat. They're bigger than mice.'

Ben's hand grabbed his mother's again. 'Is that what you look like inside?'

272

'Sure is,' she said. 'Come and see this one.'

She steered him over to a human skeleton riding a bike behind glass. On the visitors' side was another bike.

'If you hop on, you can see what parts move when we pedal.' She put the dog down and lifted Ben up but his legs didn't reach the pedals. Instead, he sat on the seat and pretended.

'Your turn,' he said. Anya lifted him off and climbed on. She pedalled as fast as she could and Ben hooted at the skeleton's movements. 'Can I stop now?' she begged after a minute. 'I'm puffed.'

They wandered along, looking up at the giraffe. 'Wow!'

'Did you know that the heart has to pump incredibly hard to get blood all the way up to its head? If it bends down and gets up too quickly, it can faint.'

'I've seen them in books getting down to drink. Their legs go like this.' He stood, legs as far apart as he could in a side split, then toppled over, much to his amusement.

Anya laughed. 'Look, over here.' On the other side of the room behind glass was a full dolphin. The bones in the fin for some reason surprised her. She'd never thought about sea mammals in that form before.

'Is it an elephant?' she asked.

'NO!' he guffawed.

'A goldfish?'

'NO!' Giggling, he said, 'Mum, it's way too big for one of those.'

'What is it then?'

'It has a dolphin nose and dolphin fins . . .'

'I know! It's a whale!' she announced in a goofy voice.

Ben keeled over with laughter and patted her back. 'NO! It's a dolphin!'

Anya loved the way they played. Being silly with Ben was one of the best things about parenthood. Despite being so caught up in death and trauma in her working life, simple pleasures like this were what mattered most. She wished more people realised that, and bent down to give him a kiss. He returned it with a hug.

Carrying Brown-Eye didn't detract from their fun. Apart from the odd stare, they could have been sharing the day with the family pet. It didn't seem out of place in a building full of preserved birds and specimens.

After two laps of the room, Ben declared the 'Bone Ranger on its horse' his favourite. At half past ten they found their way to the Search and Discovery Centre.

'Wow! I love this place,' Ben declared. 'Mum, can I please go play?'

'Sure can.' The man behind the information desk stood up, displaying an official white coat. 'That's what it's all here for.'

Ben headed for the smaller specimens and the man turned to Anya. 'I'm guessing you're

Doctor Crichton. Tim Weston. We spoke on the phone.'

'Thanks so much for coming in today,' she said.

'My pleasure. Let's have a look at what you've got.' He took the dog and rug to a side exhibit with benches of stuffed lizards, reptiles and marsupials. Brown-Eye looked overgrown in comparison.

Anya glanced at the near-empty room and saw Ben kneeling on a stool to reach the eyepiece of a microscope. Tranquil music played over the speakers.

'Mum, they've got spiders and flies!' he called, staring down the lens. She had to smile. A room full of animals and a boy is most impressed by things he could see at home.

'It's been frozen, this one,' Tim announced, referring to Brown-Eye.

'I didn't think that worked.'

'Not a lot of people understand taxidermy. Those who do it don't often talk about it, especially the ones who do big-game animals for hunters.'

Coming from a scientific background, she'd only associated taxidermy with places like museums, not trophy rooms in homes around the world.

'What sort of dog is it? Looks like a crossbreed.' Tim sniffed the coat.

'Does it matter?'

'Yep. Pure breeds are almost impossible to link

to a DNA sample. There's so much inbreeding, the profiles look pretty much the same. Now if it's a mongrel like this one looks to be, we've got a chance.'

'What are you smelling for?'

'There are a couple of ways to preserve the animals. One is by stretching the pelt over a wire frame made with wood and wool or coconut fibre. To prevent insect attacks, you rub either borax or naphthalene on the inside.' He got even closer to the pelt and inhaled.

'Looks like museum beetles have already eaten away some of the skin. By the stench, someone's sprayed it with insect killer.'

Anya was always enthralled when people spoke passionately about their areas of expertise. She'd once spent two hours listening to a fly-fisherman tell her about the various ways to make flies and was absorbed the whole time. Taxidermy wasn't a topic she was likely to come across again soon.

'What's the other way?'

'Looks like this fellow's been freeze-dried.'

The image of a dog in the family freezer came to mind, albeit briefly. The whole thing seemed grotesque, but then she'd never been so close to a pet as to want it around as a perennial piece of furniture.

'It's not what you're probably thinking,' Tim said. 'The animal's posed and then frozen in a unit. It extracts the water, which goes from ice to vapour, hence the term "freeze-dried". The process takes weeks to months. They do it for lizards, pets, but it's a bit trickier with fish.'

Ben had moved on to a round table with animal bones and was assembling some kind of skeleton. He looked up with a cheeky grin, waved to his mother and continued building. A little girl about the same age sat on the other side of the table. The pair had already struck up a conversation, as kids are prone to do.

Anya admired the room's brilliant design. Parents could be in one section and still keep an eye on their children without being on top of them. The long warehouse-style facility had been tastefully designed with a row of overhead spotlights shining from a drop rail, giving the place a studious but relaxed feel. One side of the room was filled with bookshelves, with the space divided by multiple stations and comfy-looking lounges.

It was the sort of place Anya could spend hours in, and, thanks to Ben, often did.

'Did you get the original sample sent to the laboratories?' she asked, keen to go and play with her son.

'To be honest, I was surprised it had been kept, but it arrived from the archive yesterday. Seems all those years ago some lawyer brought it in with an explanation of where it had been found. No one at the lab knew what to do with it and they never heard from the lawyer again. It was dated and has been filed in our archives ever since. Good thing we're all hoarders in this business.'

A group of children came over and jostled to see what the man in the white coat was doing. Pretty quickly, they became distracted by a game someone else was playing with a turtle shell. They squealed with enthusiasm.

'How will you get a sample?' she asked.

Tim studied every aspect of the specimen. 'There's still dried meat inside the feet, mouth, lips. Marrow in the bones as well. We could take cartilage from the ears but the easiest way is to cut a small piece out of one of the toes. You'll never notice. Part of the left back foot is already missing. Probably dropped off in the freezer.'

Maybe it wasn't just pathologists who were pragmatic about deceased parts, she thought.

'How long before you get a result?'

'Should be in a few days.'

He disappeared and returned with a scalpel and some fine scissors. Part of a back toe was collected along with a scraping of skin from under the belly.

Anya thanked him and wandered off to find Ben, who had moved on to a computer.

'Don't forget your friend here,' Tim called.

She rolled her eyes and rewrapped the dog in the rug. Brown-Eye was going to be with them for the day, it seemed.

As Ben played a puzzle game about rainforests, she thought about Nick Hudson. Could he have been so casual about Eileen Randall if he had killed her? He obviously despised the girl and had no remorse for her death. She looked at Brown-Eye, who was propped on the desk.

Pretty soon they'd know whether the dog that never left Nick's side had been at the crime scene that night.

The following morning, Ben was up at his usual six o'clock and Anya struggled to adjust to the early start. Seeing him every second weekend made her want to make up for lost time, but trying to cram two weeks into two days was at times almost too intense for both of them. She constantly tried to find the right balance and treat Ben like he was with her all the time.

The gentle knock on the front door made her flatten her hair with her hands and grab a wind-cheater from the lounge room to cover her pyjamas.

Standing on the doorstep was a weary-looking Peter Latham.

'It's early, but I was on a walk and saw your lights on.'

Never a fan of exercise, Peter maintained his ideal weight by skipping meals, usually unintentionally.

'We're up,' she said, hugging him. 'Come on in.'

For a moment, Peter looked uncomfortable until he saw Ben run from the kitchen and launch himself into his godfather's arms.

'How's my favourite little man?' he said, dropping to one knee. He was one of the few people who got down to Ben's level to hug.

'The way you looked around when you came in – don't tell me you thought I was entertaining a man?' Anya teased, unsure whether she should be flattered or insulted. 'I'm doing microwaved scrambled eggs if you'd like to join us.'

'I'd love to, but only if I'm not interrupting. I know how precious your time is together.'

'Please stay, Peter,' Ben said. 'I can show you how to do a noisy trick.' He released the hug and ran his hand under his shirt, cupping it under his armpit. With a few levers of the other arm, he demonstrated.

'Wow, I was seven before I could do that,' Peter said, laughing.

'With all he can do, he's proudest of armpit noises,' Anya said, shuffling in her slippers to the kitchen to the strains of Ben's latest performance trick. In a way, she was proud of his boyish crazes. The thing she feared was having a child who felt socially inept. That was what had crippled her so much in her teenage years. Behaving like a four-year-old was what he was supposed to do, without inhibition.

Whisking eggs, she thought for a moment of Geoff Willard and wondered if his mother had harboured the same fears when her son was a child. She found it difficult to understand the woman's reaction to the possibility that Geoff might have been innocent, as though the thought had never occurred to her before.

She added a little milk to the glass bowl and put it in the microwave. Two minutes on medium and she'd check it again. Meanwhile, she made the toast. The smell of bread cooking on a Sunday morning made her want to gorge herself. Today was no exception.

In the lounge room, Peter and Ben were competing for the better body trick. Ben could roll his tongue, but the more senior of the two could wiggle his ears, a talent that Ben immediately tried to mimic.

The microwave beeped and Anya stirred the sloppy mixture.

'Couple more minutes and we'll be ready,' she called to the now silent pair. Wiggling ears took intense concentration. She'd have to remember that if she ever wanted Ben to be quiet for a few minutes.

'Smells yummy.' Ben appeared and sat at the table.

Anya placed knives and forks and dished up the toast and eggs.

Peter had arrived just in time for a large pot of coffee. After the exhausting week, Anya would probably drink it all day. She poured two cups.

Handing Peter two plates, she took the cups and they sat together. 'Are you all right?' she asked quietly before flicking to her son. 'Careful, Ben, it's hot.'

282

'I know,' he answered, blowing on the first mouthful.

Peter sighed. 'I saw Alf Carney last night. He's taken it pretty hard.'

That was hardly surprising, given he had just been deemed incompetent and could even face criminal charges if the police felt he had fabricated evidence.

They ate in silence until Ben had finished. 'Thanks, Mum. Can I watch cartoons, please?'

'Of course you can,' she said, and kissed his forehead as he squeezed past.

'What's Alf planning to do?'

'He's talking about suing for defamation, but I think he'll change his mind once he's cooled off. He's threatened it before when someone questioned his decisions, but has never followed through.'

Anya wondered if that was how he'd got away with incompetence for so long. Threatening anyone who questioned him with legal action was one way of stopping people challenging him or going public with their concerns. Without open discussion and peer review, incompetence could go unchecked indefinitely.

'How could he have continued working for so long? He must have known that his decisions were way off-base.'

Peter chased a piece of egg around the plate with his fork. 'He suffered depression for a very long time. He's getting help now, but that probably affected some of his decision-making.'

'I'm sorry, but he should have known better. To refuse treatment is irresponsible.'

'It's not that simple. Insurance companies can deny you income protection and reputations can be ruined if anyone hears about it. A pharmacist recently rang a doctor, to let him know that a GP with depression was working in his practice. The thing was, the sufferer was better on antidepressants than off.'

'Okay, that was inappropriate, but Alf is a different story. His decisions affected so many lives. People could have been falsely imprisoned or acquitted when they were guilty.'

The theme to *Looney Tunes* sounded from the lounge room.

Anya took the plates to the sink. 'What isn't clear is why he started out being pro-police, conveniently narrowing down time of death to the only time suspects didn't have alibis. All the cases I reviewed were the complete opposite. He went out of his way to exclude anything other than death by natural causes.'

Peter collected the salt-and-pepper shakers and cups. 'He talked about that last night. Seems he was very trusting of the police and then became pretty disillusioned.'

Anya scraped the leftovers into the dustbin and one-third filled the sink. Tight water restrictions due to a statewide drought meant using the dishwasher as little as possible.

Peter picked up a tea-towel and stood next to the draining tray.

'Years ago, he gave an opinion on a series of infant deaths from the one family, attributed to Sudden Infant Death Syndrome. This was about the time some pathologists, including Alf, started believing that there was no such thing and that every case was murder in disguise.

'A pretty aggressive prosecutor got a conviction for a young mother who'd lost two children, based on Alf's evidence.' He held up the first plate and let it drip into the sink before wiping. 'She'd been in jail about fifteen years when Alf did an autopsy on the woman's baby niece. Turns out there was a metabolic abnormality that ran through the family. Alf went back and rechecked the specimens on the other babies. They all had the same disorder. An innocent woman had been convicted of murdering her children.'

Anya listened in silence, but knew that with the benefit of hindsight and better technology for testing, there were probably many similar cases from the past.

'Around the same time, Alf's wife delivered a stillborn and he thought it was a sign from God, punishing him for that woman's wasted years in jail. That's when he started exploring alternative medicines and became obsessed with Vitamin C deficiency.'

Anya pulled out the plug. 'What happened to the woman?'

'She was released and exonerated, but the husband had left her and she was unable to have any more kids. He's kept track of her all these years.'

'That is tragic. Reality is that we probably would have all come to the same conclusions at that time. But Alf didn't help anyone by over-compensating and crippling the police investigations into genuine homicide cases. In some cases more than one child in the family lost its life to abuse. Don't you think that's criminal?'

Peter nodded. 'I just don't think anything is that simple any more.'

Anya dried her hands and touched his arm. 'Normally I'm the one trying to right all the wrongs and you're the calming realist.'

'Maybe the student has outgrown the teacher.'

'Never!' She smiled. 'I was going to ask your advice about the Willard case.'

Peter folded the tea-towel and hung it over the oven door-handle. 'I remember that one from all the publicity.'

Anya put the plates away, banging the cupboard door in haste. 'The file's in my office, if you'd like to take a look.'

They passed Ben, who was lying on his stomach drawing what looked like a truck in his scrapbook, while watching Sylvester try to catch Tweety Bird.

As they entered her office, Brown-Eye stood guard, and stared through his glass eyes.

'What the—'

'It's going back to its owner tomorrow. Don't ask,' she said, handing Peter the autopsy reports for Eileen Randall and Liz Dorman. He studied them for a while before speaking.

'There are distinct similarities, but the time of death is most certainly wider than the window defined here. The girl could have died well before, especially if she were floating in the water, which she must have been.' He scanned down further. 'A quick immersion wouldn't have resulted in that many crayfish larvae finding their way into the chest cavity. And the post-mortem wounds are interesting. You don't often see exploratory wounds like that after a frenzied killing.'

'What if,' Anya said, 'someone other than Willard killed that girl on the beach and sexually assaulted her, and he merely pulled the body out of the water?'

'That could explain the smear of blood on his shirt.'

'Don't we have an obligation to at least check, to right a potential wrong?'

Peter frowned. 'I think I taught you far too well.' He ran his eyes over the reports again, scratching his beard. 'All right, what would you like me to do?'

38

On Monday afternoon, Hayden Richards arrived at the SA unit. Anya had just finished examining an eight-year-old girl allegedly abused by her mother's de facto. The local doctor had referred the girl after noticing some inappropriate sexual behaviour, but the mother refused to separate from her boyfriend. Family services would have the girl in a foster home by this afternoon.

Anya had taken twice as long as usual to examine the young girl, accompanied by a gynaecologist from the hospital. The pair concurred and the magnitude of their decision was not lost on either of them. If the girl stayed in her current situation, she would be subject to more abuse, but the child didn't want to be taken from her mother.

The sounds of the girl crying when told she would be placed in a temporary home still rang in Anya's ears. She double- and triple-checked the evidence. The photographs weren't clear and didn't help.

'You look like you've lost your last penny,' Hayden said as he tapped on her open door.

'Guess we're all suddenly questioning ourselves, hoping we've made the right decisions.' Her head throbbed and she tried to ease it by rubbing the pressure points at the base of her skull. It made the pain worse.

'Is that such a bad thing?' He leant against the door with a videotape in one hand. 'Want to talk about it? I'm a pretty good listener.'

She rested her head in her hands after gesturing for him to come in. 'I just took a child away from her mother. What if it isn't the right thing?'

'None of us is infallible. Come to think of it, maybe you should be having this conversation with Sorrenti.'

'Speaking of whom, how did you get off the leash?' The moment she said the words, she wished she hadn't.

Luckily, Hayden just raised his eyebrows and sat down. 'It is a bit like that, especially after Willard's arrest. Unless his former conviction for the Randall killing is overturned, he's going to stay on remand for the Dorman murder. The similarities are far too close for any judge to let him go. Sorrenti's got him pegged for your knife-rapes as well. She doesn't want to consider any other suspects.'

He looked like Anya felt. Tired, disillusioned and fed-up. Like someone who had lost his spark, whatever that was. Anya studied him. Each time they met, it seemed as though more weight had melted off his frame. For a moment she wondered whether he was in perfect health, or whether there was a more sinister reason behind the massive weight loss. Whether the cancer scare was merely that.

Then she thought of Meira Sorrenti. It couldn't have been easy working with someone who knew a lot less about investigating sexual assaults.

'Guess we're all under pressure.' She lifted her head. 'So what brings you to this salubrious part of town? Have you come to tell me Melanie wrote that letter?'

'Nope, handwriting doesn't match. We've also turned up a number of rape cases that could fit the pattern, but victims are proving hard to find.' Hayden threw the tape into the air and caught it. 'To cheer you up, I brought Geoff Willard's initial confession.'

There had to be something unusual about it, or he wouldn't have bothered. Anya moved to another room and returned with a portable TV/video. She plugged it in on the desk and inserted the tape.

A young-looking Willard appeared in black and white. The quality of the picture was poor, but she could make out that he was sitting at a desk in an office. The uniformed officer, a younger, thinner Charlie Boyd, sat with his back to the camera.

She turned up the sound.

'Here comes the good bit,' Hayden pre-empted.

'All right.' Willard wiped his nose with the back of a blood-stained hand. 'I'm hungry and I wanna go home.' He had the look of a rabbit startled by a shooter.

'You tell us what we want to know, and we'll let you go,' the policeman said. 'And your mama will stay out of prison, too.'

'All right, I killed Eileen Randall. I saw her and stabbed her to death on the beach.'

'And what else did you do?' A beardless Charlie Boyd tapped the table with his pen.

'I stuck my penis into her insides.'

'You mean you raped her vaginally?'

'Yeah, I guess.'

Charlie Boyd noted the time and date Willard had confessed.

Before he could shut off the tape, Willard asked, 'Can I go home now? I said what you wanted.'

Anya stopped the tape. That wasn't a confession. It was a frightened adolescent saying what he was told. He was scared and probably didn't understand what had happened.

'That last bit didn't get heard at the trial,' Hayden said. 'The local cop thought he was doing the right thing. Screwed up big-time with that effort.'

The confession should never have been shown at trial. It failed the most basic standards of policing.

'After I saw that, I decided to do some checking. Nick Hudson's no cleanskin. He served some time in Queensland for assault in the early

1990s. He's got a charge-sheet for minor offences, but no other convictions.'

'Nice family.' The timing suggested Nick hadn't been in prison with Gloria Havelock's rapists, so would not have had access to Melanie's photo. Three questions remained: why Geoff had small amounts of blood on two shirts, who'd written him the letter and how he'd got Melanie's picture.

'Have you checked out where Nick was the night of the Dorman murder?'

The phone rang and Anya answered it, gesturing her visitor to give her a minute. He wandered into the corridor while she spoke to a victim's local doctor. When the conversation ended, Hayden returned to the doorway.

'Hudson works at a local pub. No tax records, just cash in hand. He says that on the night in question, the owners went out and asked him to cover the bar. The owners confirmed it and every dropout from Fisherman's Bay frequents the place, so the guy's got a firm alibi.' He leant his head on the door again. 'They all know someone who recruits at the local chicken factory. It's like some kind of magnet for them all.'

Anya wondered if Hayden had a back problem and was more comfortable standing.

'For all we know,' he said, 'there could be more fatal cases, ones we're missing because Willard was in jail at the time. I'm thinking our killer's struck before.'

'Funny you should say that.' Anya swivelled back in her chair to the empty fax. 'I was wondering the same thing.'

'Damn!' he said, sat and pulled the chair between his legs. 'You know something.'

So much for the bad-back theory, she thought.

His foot met Brown-Eye, who was temporarily deposited under the desk. 'Jeez, you've gotta take that back. It's disgusting.' He screwed up his nose. 'And it smells worse than ever in here.'

'Thanks for that.' She wondered what other smell he was referring to, one when Brown-Eye wasn't there. 'It's going back tonight. I just want to grab some paracetamol and check the other fax. I'll be right back.'

In a few moments, Anya returned with a blister-pack of tablets and a glass of water. Under her arm, she clutched some papers. 'This just came through – your timing's impressive.' She squeezed past the detective to get to her seat and deposited the papers on her end of the desk. 'A friend did a search of the National Coroners Information System. I can't access it from here.'

The NCIS had been established in 1998 to collate autopsy findings around the country. Its purpose was to identify clusters of disease, trends and similar cases to reduce preventable death and injury. Its role had become important in occupational health and safety, pinpointing the types of work-related deaths, occupations most at risk, and equipment linked with deaths.

Pathologists also found it useful for looking up similar pattern injuries. She'd ring and thank Peter Ludlam later.

Hayden wanted to get in first. 'Well, I came up with a case from three years ago. A woman up north was stabbed to death in Port Macquarie. Local police thought it was a break-and-enter gone wrong, and never even had a suspect. No fingerprints or DNA at the scene. Hard to say if anything was taken. The investigation was pretty sloppy.'

Anya looked through the faxed sheets. 'Leonie Turnbull?'

'Bingo!' Hayden suddenly looked brighter. 'What have you got?'

'I'll tell you in a minute.' Anya gulped the tablets and read the report. She recognised the name of a locum pathologist who'd done the autopsy. Thankfully, Alf Carney hadn't been involved. The deceased, Leonie Turnbull, was in her mid-twenties, five foot two and weighed fifty-five kilograms. Cause of death was massive blood loss due to thirty-eight stab wounds. Some were superficial. One penetrated the thoracic aorta, which was probably the fatal wound.

'Looks like she was stabbed multiple times; wounds look confined to the chest and neck, some deep, others superficial. Some look like they'd been done after death.'

'Anything to suggest she'd been sexually assaulted?'

'Not according to this, but that doesn't exclude it.'

Hayden flicked through his notebook. 'Apparently she was a medical student from Sydney sent there for a country rotation. She'd just returned from a few days off. No one even knew when exactly she got back, but she was having problems with her supervisor. Seems she didn't really like the place and wanted to get back home.'

'Any patients bother her?' Anya knew that a young medical student could easily attract unwanted attention in a small place. Doctors were at a much greater risk of being stalked than anyone else, given the relationship they had to forge with patients. Even the most innocent exchange could be misinterpreted and deemed intimate by someone with dysfunctional thinking.

'Not that we know. According to the supervisor, she looked young, but her work was fine. He thought she was bright, shy and a bit strange, but he wouldn't explain what he meant. He thought she was irresponsible when she just took off for a few days. Sounds like he's pretty guilty about what happened to her. Thinks he should have spoken to her more.'

Hindsight was 20/20, Anya thought. Everyone would do things differently if they had the benefit of what medical people termed the retrospectoscope.

She wondered about the young woman's sudden disappearance. Hayden's mobile phone rang and he excused himself to get better reception.

Anya flicked through the list on her notice-board and dialled Port Macquarie hospital. The medical-records department proved surprisingly helpful when she explained the need for information. No one named Leonie Turnbull had been admitted. The sexual-assault service had been run by the local clinic for many years. Anya doubted a medical student would want to be examined by people she worked with if she'd been assaulted.

She dialled a friend at the Newcastle SA unit, the closest major centre. After explaining how important it was to know whether Leonie had presented three years ago, her colleague agreed to check and promised to call back. Anya thanked her and flicked through the remaining pages from Peter Latham.

A case from six years ago involved a more elderly woman who had been stabbed in her home multiple times. This woman had ligature marks on her wrists and ankles from being restrained on the bed. Judging by the trauma to the vagina, uterus and bowel, the poor woman had been raped with a sharp instrument prior to death. The details were horrific. After the rape, the perpetrator slit her throat, shearing the carotid arteries on both sides. The stab wounds weren't confined to the chest and involved the face and limbs as well. As far as murders went, this was one of the most sadistic. The killer had even urinated on his victim.

When Hayden returned, Anya passed him the pages. He read in silence, shaking his head at various stages. 'Hard to imagine what sort of animal can do this,' he said.

'I doubt it's the same killer. The pattern of injuries is very different.'

Hayden studied the page. 'I agree. What did Quentin Lagardia say about our guy? The gentleman rapist?'

'Exactly. In relative terms, he's not that sadistic. Whoever did this wasn't role-playing with the old lady. Everything he did was angry, brutal and degrading. Look at the urination. That's something either an anger-retaliatory or anger-excitation rapist would do.'

'Our guy doesn't kill them *when* he rapes them. And the ones who were stabbed to death weren't raped at the same time, as far as we know, except for maybe Eileen Randall, and that could have been consensual going by her reputation.' He took a deep breath and rubbed his forehead. 'This old lady was a goner as soon as she opened the door.'

Either way, Anya knew she would be happier if Hayden followed up on whether or not anyone had been convicted of the old lady's murder.

As if in response to her thoughts, he said, 'I'll still check it out just to be sure we're not jumping to the wrong conclusion.'

Anya's mobile phone rang in her handbag. She fumbled to grab it on the fifth ring.

'Thanks for getting back . . . She was? . . . She

did? On the twelfth of June? . . . Brilliant. I'll need to talk to her about the details later on. Thanks.'

A counsellor knocked on the door.

'Sorry to interrupt, but we've just got word. A woman is coming in who's been tied up and held captive for two days. Casualty is checking her out. If she's well enough she'll come here, otherwise they'll ask you to examine her over there,' she said. 'I brought you these,' she added, presenting a plate loaded with buttered scones.

'Fine, thanks.' Anya's headache suddenly felt worse. This would take hours to complete.

Hayden smiled and took the plate, thanking the counsellor.

'I think we could both do with some of these,' he said, tucking in to the first scone. 'If we think the same person killed Liz Dorman and Leonie Turnbull, Willard can't be guilty. He was in prison at the time. Unless we find a concrete link between Turnbull and Liz Dorman, Geoff Willard's looking at life and I'm likely to be pulled off the case.'

Anya had almost forgotten. 'That call was from Newcastle. It seems Leonie Turnbull had good reason to take off suddenly. She'd been raped outside the clinic four nights before she was murdered.'

39

Exhausted and with every muscle aching, Anya strapped Brown-Eye's carcass in the back, climbed into her Corolla and instinctively pressed down on her lock, securing all the doors. All she wanted was a bath, a long soak and ten hours' sleep.

The mobile rang. She closed her eyes and thought about ignoring it, but checked the caller ID, just in case it was important. Elaine. She hadn't checked in with her secretary all day.

Breathing out, she picked it up. 'Hi, Elaine.'

Ever efficient, Elaine rattled off the routine and then emphasised the priority messages. Dan Brody had asked for another meeting. He could damn well wait, Anya thought. She wasn't at his beck and call, and no doubt Veronica Slater had spun him some story about their argument at the prison.

Only half-listening, she let her mind wander. Nick Hudson was anxious to get his stuffed dog back. The drive out to the house would take about thirty minutes, maybe more in traffic, but Brown-Eye had already made her car reek, not to mention her office at the SA unit.

'That's about it,' finished Elaine.

Relieved that everything could wait, Anya said goodnight and headed over to the Willards' place.

'Brown-Eye, big fella.' Nick greeted his dead dog like he would a best friend.

'Sorry about the timing, but I couldn't get out here any earlier.'

'My aunt's in the kitchen, and we're just watching the box.'

The scene was relaxed and homely. Anya imagined it echoed in millions of homes across the country.

By the fumes, meat was on the menu again, and *The Price is Right* was the focus of Nick's attention. On the lounge sat a thick-set woman sorting washing. The abdominal girth could have been fat or pregnancy, but from that position it was difficult to tell. Anya had no intention of taking the risk of asking, When are you due?

'This is Desiree Platt, another old friend from the Bay. She stays sometimes for company,' Nick said. 'When her husband's away working.'

Desiree cupped one hand beneath her bulge, put the other behind her as an anchor, and arched her back to get herself up off the lounge. She was definitely pregnant.

'Hi,' Anya greeted her.

'You must be the doctor Nick's been telling me all about.'

Nick scuffed the floor with his feet like a schoolboy. 'Don't you have to be somewhere?'

'Yeah, the toilet. This kid's been using my bladder as a trampoline all afternoon.'

Mrs Willard came out from the kitchen and wiped her hands on her apron. 'Dinner won't be long. Would you care to join us this time, dear? We've got an extra tray.'

Anya sensed she was being set up with Nick, who could just be a rapist and/or murderer. 'No thanks, I can't stay. I have a meeting to go to.'

Mrs Willard grabbed Anya's left hand. 'No ring. You career women are missing out on the most important things.'

'Come on down,' cried the game-show host.

'How's the investigation going?' Mrs Willard asked, releasing her guest's hand.

Anya thought twice about divulging information concerning the case, but the pleading look in the woman's eyes made her want to give the mother something, some kind of hope, without giving away too much.

'We found another murder, one that Geoff can't have committed, that is very similar to those of Eileen Randall and Elizabeth Dorman. It happened when he was in jail.'

Mrs Willard's eyes moistened. 'Thank you for telling me. I'll try to see Geoff tomorrow and tell him the good news.'

Anya paused. 'The shirt the police took, that you said Geoff had never worn. Was it new?'

'Goodness, no. He couldn't afford new things,

301

and there are perfectly good clothes at the local op shop.'

'So it came from there?'

Mrs Willard nodded. 'We have to make do. When he came out of prison, he had nothing but a donated pair of trousers and a shirt. They didn't even fit properly.'

Desiree returned from the bathroom, wiping her hands on the oversized Black Sabbath T-shirt she wore over black leggings. 'What's the good news?'

'The police have got some evidence that Geoff didn't kill Eileen Randall or that other woman.'

'What?' she said, clutching her belly. 'But he did it. He even broke into our place. God knows what he would have done if Nick and Luke hadn't come in. We all know what he's like.' Her voice became shrill and she began to hyperventilate. 'Oh my God, it's a contraction.'

Anya couldn't believe the histrionics. 'It's probably the baby moving.'

'I know you had a scare.' Mrs Willard led Desiree to the lounge. 'But he didn't hurt you. He wanted somewhere to hide out for a while. Maybe he has changed after all these years.' She straightened out her apron. 'I'll just check the dinner. After that, I'll help with your folding and we'll get you home.' She turned to Anya.

'Doctor, would you mind staying with Desiree for a few minutes, to make sure she's all right?'

In the few days since they had met, Geoff's

mother looked like she had aged years. Nick seemed annoyed and left the room. His aunt followed him to the kitchen, and Desiree calmed down.

Anya wanted to run out the door more than ever, as a crowd of people shouted and made hand movements on the screen.

'Got a boyfriend?' The woman opened her mouth and revealed what looked like a piece of food clinging to a tooth.

Anya felt her face flush and became flustered. 'I really just came to drop off Nick's dog.'

The sound on the TV became louder, with members of the audience shouting and gesturing numbers at the pair on stage.

'Wouldn't blame you if you were shit-scared of getting involved. Men can be real bastards.' She rubbed her abdomen again and her shirt moved with what was probably a kick. 'Lucky I got a good one. We got married once we knew the baby was on its way, before I lost my figure.'

Judging by the size of Desiree's arms and the broad hips, the figure she referred to was full. The tooth didn't have food on it, either. It was some kind of crystal embedded in the enamel.

'Congratulations,' Anya managed, backing to-wards the entrance.

'Nick's a great bloke,' Desiree continued. 'You could do a lot worse. And he's a great kisser.'

'I'm sure he is,' Anya blurted, wondering why the words came out of her mouth. 'I really have to go.'

Desiree propped herself to get up and Anya gestured to stop her.

'I'll let you out.' The woman smiled and lumbered to the door, which had been deadlocked. As Anya stepped out onto the porch, Desiree said quietly, 'From one woman to another, I hope you find someone.' Looking weary, she arched her back and rubbed her belly. 'I know this little one's gonna cause me pain. God knows, it already has with the morning sickness, reflux and backache. And don't start me on about the haemorrhoids.'

Anya had no intention.

'And from what everyone says, the birth is going to be agony. But I've gotta go through it to have this baby.' She rubbed the back of her neck, as though massaging out another sore spot.

'You know, my friends back home used to have a really wise saying. "If you can't be hurt, you can't be loved."'

Before Anya could respond, the door clunked shut.

40

Once outside, Anya stood at her car. Desiree's words repeated in her mind.

If you can't be hurt, you can't be loved.

Did Desiree somehow know that the rapist used that particular phrase? Was she sending Anya a message? Had she, herself, been raped? Was she saying that the baby was a product of the assault?

The words were disturbing. It wasn't something expectant mothers would normally come out with. She drove off, wondering whether Desiree was warning her about Geoff or Nick. The thought made her check her rear-view mirror to make sure no one was following. A few minutes passed and, after running an amber light, the hairs on the back of her neck relaxed. She wondered why she'd felt so threatened. Why did Desiree say 'friends back home'? What friends, and where exactly were they from? Fisherman's Bay?

She thought back to the minimal conversation they'd had. Desiree had said something about men being bastards but that she'd found a good one.

Anya turned on the radio and a news update

rapidly faded into the background. Desiree's comment could have been innocent. The woman was not far off giving birth. The labour would be on her mind already. To increase the focus, a pregnant woman was a magnet for everyone with a birthing horror story. Even strangers felt the need to regale mothers-to-be with the most horrendous tales of excruciating agony culminating in third-degree tears, stillborns or permanent incapacity.

At least that was Anya's experience and that of her friends. Not once had any of the well-meaning scaremongers bothered to say that pain relief was available and that there were no prizes for being a martyr in the delivery room. Or that most women who gave birth chose to do it again.

If either Geoff Willard or his cousin was the serial rapist, and Desiree had spent time with them, it was possible she'd picked up the phrase, having no idea of its sinister meaning. Maybe it even came from Lillian Willard. It was a strange 'tough love' sort of expression. No, it couldn't have been just a coincidence, she decided. There was no such thing.

Anya hit the indicator and pulled into a breakdown lane on the M2. Immediately she put her hazard lights on to save anyone running into her. Multiple cars passed. No one slowed or stopped. Thank God, she thought, that chivalry was dead. The last thing she wanted was some man or men stopping. She'd seen rape victims fall for that one many times. Locked in, she dialled Hayden Richards.

'Jesus Christ! She really said that to you?'

Great. The detective didn't come out with comments about over-reacting or panicking for no good reason.

'Where the hell are you now?'

'On the M2. I'm fine. Just heading back home. Look, it was said in innocence, I'm sure. They were trying to hook me up with Nick Hudson.'

'Christ! How did you get out of that one without ticking him off?'

'I behaved like a professional and sneaked out the door.'

She could hear Hayden's voice go up half an octave. 'Nothing like the rejection of a woman. I wouldn't have picked you as the skulking-away type, not until the end of the game-show, anyway.' His voice returned to normal, much to Anya's relief.

'How about you go straight home and get some sleep and we'll talk again in the morning.'

Something in his tone suggested he was more concerned than he wanted her to know. She was about to hang up when he spoke.

'Can you do one thing for me? Promise you'll lock all your doors and windows.'

Anya felt as though someone had just walked over her grave.

41

The following morning, Anya felt hung-over from tiredness. She'd had nightmares again, just like she used to have when she had oral exams at medical school. In the recurring dream, she'd sit in the exam and watch, helplessly, as two examiners dissected her body with scalpels.

She leant against the kitchen bench, sipping herbal tea, and made an effort to think things through rationally. Dismally, she admitted to herself that there was a lot to worry about.

Veronica Slater had affected her more than she wanted to admit. The biggest concern was that the solicitor had virtually ruined her chances of consultancy work for both the police and defence attorneys. That didn't give her many other options in private practice. Her income would plummet.

Sorrenti would not want Anya to give evidence in any rape trial involving Geoff Willard. The fact that Veronica had asked her to consult on the case – very publicly thanks to the staged press-conference outside the prison – wasn't surprising, but still distressed her. Veronica never intended to use

Anya's findings. She had no obligation to use any opinion that might hurt her case. She might have to go through twenty specialists to find one who gave her client a favourable slant, but she would. The media would be anticipating Anya's evidence at a trial. Her omission could hurt the reputation she'd worked so hard to forge.

Things seemed to be getting out of control. Even the most basic housework seemed overwhelming. Suddenly she could see mess and dirt all over the house. So much for the plan to get a cleaner. She might not have enough money to pay the mortgage by the end of the year.

She picked up the kitchen rubbish to take it out the back door and deposited yesterday's dirty clothes in the laundry on the way. What faced her was the piled-up washing, impossible to ignore. Deciding to put on a load of whites before Elaine arrived, she put out the bin and quickly sorted what she was most likely to need sooner rather than later. Adding some powder to the full load, she switched it on to the fast-wash cycle.

Whenever she put in a load of washing, it reminded her of a case she had seen a few years ago. A baby had suffered a severe head injury from being placed in a bouncinette on top of the family washing machine. The baby had slept, but when the cycle hit the spin-dry phase, the baby bounced right off, onto the concrete floor. The mother didn't seem to understand how it could have happened. Unfortunately, stupidity wasn't a good enough reason for community services to remove the child from the mother's care.

Anya checked her answering machine. There were three messages. Martin had given her address and number to a mother from preschool, so Ben could play some time. The mother would call during the week. Anya didn't recognise the friend's name, but that was hardly surprising. She had only been to preschool a few times to collect her son.

Dan Brody's message asked if they could have a chat about the Willard case. Anya felt her pulse race again at his arrogant tone. She didn't want to speak to him, not today. She deleted it before he'd finished.

Lastly, her father had phoned. He'd be in town next week and asked if they could have dinner.

She sat down, and wrote down the phrase that Desiree had used so casually. The way she'd behaved was a little possessive towards Nick, yet she made a point of saying how happy she was with her 'good man'.

What was Desiree's last name? She strained to remember. Watt? Putt? Patt? Sounded like a hair-do – Platt! That was it. She circled it on the page for when she next spoke to Hayden.

She also wrote down what they knew about the Dorman murder. Two of Geoffrey's shirts taken from the house had traces of blood that were consistent with Liz Dorman's. The DNA evidence against Willard was pretty damning, let alone the similarities to the Randall stab wounds – the number, distribution and types. He also had no alibi for the night Liz Dorman died.

Anya concluded that the same killer was most likely responsible for both deaths.

Did Liz's rape have anything at all to do with her murder? But the photo that had been stolen from the fridge during the rape was found in the garbage bin after her murder. She was unaware of any serial offender who took souvenirs of their victims and then returned them to the scene.

The rape *had* to be related. So was Geoffrey Willard the serial rapist? Or did he work with a partner? Maybe Nick?

Elaine arrived with a cheery 'good morning' and removed a scarf and coat.

'You started early,' she said. 'Anything I can do?'

'Just going over a case. Just when I think I've worked it out, something comes up to confuse me all over again.'

Elaine rubbed her hands together. 'Do you mind if I put the heater on?'

'No,' Anya said, lost in thought again.

Mrs Willard had told her one of Geoff's shirts had come from the opportunity shop and he hadn't even worn it. But it was possible the mother had lied to protect him.

Was there a possibility the shirts he bought already had Liz's DNA on them? She clicked on to the Internet and googled Willard. He'd been released four weeks ago, and Liz died just over a week ago. It was unlikely he'd worn the same donated shirt and trousers for three weeks, especially if they didn't fit. Still, Hayden could check the dates with the shop receipts. Maybe he had borrowed Nick's clothes in the interim.

'Oh, Anya!' Elaine called from the kitchen, her voice impatient.

What now? She stood up, not realising how cold her fingers were until she passed through the lounge room and felt the warmth of the sun in the kitchen. Elaine was behind the kitchen in the laundry, bending over the washing machine.

Anya had begrudgingly accepted that Elaine liked to mother even when at work. Sometimes that meant helping out with household tasks. Today Anya had no objection.

'The machine was bouncing across the floor. You put an unbalanced load in,' the secretary said, standing up with two mottled pink shirts, both of which had originally been white. 'I can't believe you did this again.'

Anya had thrown the clothes in without checking inside the machine. Ben's missing red sock had been in there, forgotten from the last wash. Her favourite pair of capri pants were ruined as well. Things were not getting better.

'When I duck out with the post, I'll get you some of that dye remover,' Elaine said. 'If we wash it straight away, the colour might just come out.'

There was no point stressing over a pair of

trousers, Anya thought. She went back to her office. Just as she sat, the idea of dye running in the wash made sense.

'Elaine, you're a genius!' she called. 'You've just helped me with a case. Why didn't I think of it sooner? I've got to go out for a while. I'll be back soon.'

She grabbed her handbag from the kitchen bench and slipped into her shoes at the door, pausing to say, 'That dye remover is under the sink. I bought a spare in case it happened again.'

42

Anya stood in the forensic-science student lab at the University of Technology in the city. Renowned for its forensic-science degree, the university had developed an excellent post-graduate research programme.

The director of the degree course was a biochemist who was so passionate about the science that he was a major instigator in the World Congress of Forensic Medicine, organising conferences in Sydney followed by Montpellier in the South of France.

Jean Le Beau was a small man with the blackest hair and dark brown eyes. He had the sort of eyelashes that mascara companies would die to promote, had they been on a woman. It was the only feminine thing about the gifted scientist. Jean was intense, and his face seemed set in a perennial frown. Anya often questioned whether supreme intelligence was a constant burden.

'Hello, Unya,' he said, in an accent that could melt the coldest heart. She knew it was shallow, but at the forensic conferences she'd been to, married women would find excuses to talk to him, just to hear his voice. His presentations were always standing-room only. Not bad for someone with relatively little charisma before he spoke.

'Do you come to teach or to learn today?'

'I have a hypothetical question, and you, or one of your students, may be able to answer it.'

Jean's brow furrowed deeper as he pulled a stool from the lab bench and took a seat. 'I am ready,' he said, as though about to start a quiz.

Anya felt like a student again, sitting at a chemistry bench. The whiteboard, sinks and gas-taps could have been at any university or high school. They were strangely comforting.

'I've been involved in a homicide case where a woman was repeatedly stabbed in her house. The suspect was found to have a shirt in his home with DNA that matched the blood from the crime scene. His mother tells us that the suspect had bought the shirt second-hand and that it was washed, but that the suspect had never worn it.'

'How much blood was on the shirt?'

'That's the interesting thing. Small traces, it seems, which also appeared on another shirt confiscated from the house.'

'Ah, I see the problem. Your question is, how is this possible? Why would there be such little blood? Stabbings are messy, blood spurts every-where. Yes?'

The scientist used his hands to emphasise the movement of blood.

Anya smiled. 'Actually, I wondered if there'd

been some kind of error at the lab, contamination of samples, perhaps?'

'There are other possible explanations,' he said, pulling his hands to his chest, while maintaining the frown. 'The shirt from the murder may have been placed on top of the other shirts, in the laundry basket or perhaps in a cupboard. Come, we will see.'

Anya followed him along a tiled corridor with offices to each side. He kept his head down as they passed a couple of students laden with texts and backpacks.

Around the corner, he knocked on a door. The door had been wedged open, presumably for ventilation. The room was even more compact than Anya's office at the SA unit. With shelving along one side, it had probably been a storage cupboard in earlier times.

A female with long brown hair kept off her face with an Alice-band worked at a laptop computer. 'Just a minute, I need to back up.' She saved to a disc and removed it. Turning, her face broke into a warm smile. 'Professor, sorry, I didn't realise it was you.' She stood up, eager to please, it seemed.

'This is Doctor Crichton, a forensic physician who 'as an interesting case. Doctor, this is Shelly Mann, one of our honours students. She might be able to 'elp.'

In the doorway, Jean explained the scenario and Shelly's eyes widened.

'Your research might be applied in a police case

sooner than you thought,' he said, sounding for a moment like a proud father. 'You should take Doctor Crichton to the testing centre.'

Anya felt like she was about to attend the unveiling of a top-secret weapon. Instead, they arrived at a lab containing half-a-dozen washing machines.

Shelly's posture straightened as she entered a more comfortable environment. Her professor excused himself for a moment and disappeared down the corridor.

'My thesis is about transfer of DNA material in the wash.' Shelly picked up a plain white T-shirt to explain. 'We know it happens with spermatozoa, but the properties of blood differ. It coagulates and flakes when it dries. To start with, I bought six identical shirts and washed each one first. I pricked my finger and let some drops of blood spill onto the first shirt. I then washed the shirt with another control.'

The student spoke quickly, being so familiar with her experiments.

'After drying, some of the DNA material from the first shirt had transferred onto the second. It seemed to collect in the seams. I repeated the process and found that with further washings, smaller amounts were transferred to the other shirts. Even so, it was still discernible.'

'Blood's pretty difficult to get out without cold water. Did you do it in hot or cold washes?'

'Both. Heat sets the stain, so I needed to use cold

washes as well. Even though the stains weren't visible to the naked eye, they showed up with luminol. I'm planning to repeat the whole process with semen.'

Anya didn't ask about the source of the semen. It was probably the student's long-suffering boy-friend, or one of the other students. Such was the shoestring budget for research.

She tried to absorb the information. If this were true, suspects could merely claim they had washed their clothes in a communal laun-dry as a form of defence. The implications were enormous. 'Has your work been pub-lished yet?'

'No,' she said, 'I'm still working on the con-clusion to stage one with the blood-testing.'

Jean Le Beau reappeared with some papers. 'Do you mind if Doctor Crichton has a look at the draft? I've made some comments.'

Shelly shook her head. 'If this could be applied to a case already, I'd be thrilled.'

Anya thanked them both and returned to street-level. All she could think about was the DNA on the shirts owned by Geoff Willard. The pile of washing that Desiree was sorting was more than you'd expect for two people. If she used the machine at Lillian Willard's home, it made sense that she did some of their washing, too.

Outside, she hastily dialled Hayden Richards. His phone diverted to voicemail.

'Hayden, please call me. It's urgent. Geoffrey Willard really could be innocent. You should be looking at his cousin, Nick, and Desiree's husband, Luke Platt, before more evidence washes away.'

43

'What the fuck do you think you're doing?' Meira Sorrenti almost spat the words.

Anya unlocked her front door, frowning and glancing over her shoulder at a mother and toddler walking along holding hands. 'We should discuss this inside. I don't just work here, this is my home.' She'd watched the little girl trying to avoid stepping on the lines of the footpath before being distracted by Sorrenti's outburst.

The detective came as close as possible to Anya, speaking through gritted teeth. Everything about her approach was meant to be intimidating. So far, it was effective.

'You stay the hell out of my investigation, or I'll charge you with obstructing justice.'

Sorrenti obviously didn't know how ridiculous she was being. Anya clenched her fists by her side and decided it was better to let the woman vent before tackling her with logic. The mother and child quickly crossed the road and hurried away. Sorrenti remained oblivious, it seemed.

'Richards ordered a tail on Nick Hudson. What the fuck's that about? My men are wasting time when we've already got the guy who raped and killed Liz Dorman.'

She began to pace along the path, hands in her suit pants. 'Do you have any idea how much of the budget has just been blown on this fucking joke? What are you up to? Trying to get me sacked so Richards can get back into the job?'

'I'm trying to save you from making a serious mistake.' Anya instantly regretted her choice of words.

'Funny, from where I stand you're trying pretty bloody hard to make a fool out of me.'

She came closer again. Anya chose to remain on the doorstep, giving herself the slightest height advantage.

'This is about finding the truth. And if you go to court with the evidence you have against Geoff Willard, you'll be making sure he gets acquitted. Is that what you want?'

'Don't turn this on me. I want to nail the prick. I saw what he did to that woman. And we've got DNA evidence to place him at the scene. End of story.'

Anya waved hello to 'Mrs Bugalugs', as Ben and Martin called the next-door neighbour, who had conveniently come outside to check her letterbox even though the postman delivered much later in the day. Despite claiming to be deaf and blind, the nosy woman managed to appear at the first sign of visitors or noise.

The elderly neighbour's presence seemed to affect the detective.

'The DNA evidence you have is ambiguous. The distribution doesn't fit with an attack and it's on more than one shirt.'

'So?'

'So, even a first-year law student would blow your case out of the water. Science can make a case, but it can more often than not destroy one.'

'Is that what you and that Slater bitch are doing? You're so desperate to make names for yourselves you'll prove Willard didn't do it at any cost. Oh, and going on TV news was a pretty gutless way to let us all know where you stood.'

Being linked with Veronica Slater made bile rise in Anya's chest. The idea of colluding with the woman to further her career was nothing less than disgusting. Anya felt like hitting something – hard. Slater's head came to mind first. Sorrenti came a close second. She tried to control her anger and opened and closed her fists.

'Detective, I think we should—'

'Stop there! There is no "we".' Sorrenti's face looked ready to explode. 'You have nothing to do with this case. I don't want you involved. You're poison. You may have already shafted Alf Carney, but you sure as hell won't screw me over.'

She swung around down the path, stopping to call 'Have a good day' to Mrs Bugalugs, who responded with a grin and a wave.

Then she stopped at the end of the path and

announced, 'Oh yeah, and Nick Hudson is threatening us with a harassment suit. His lawyer mentioned your name, too.'

Anya leant against the door, feeling like she'd just gone a few rounds in a boxing ring. Inside, the phone rang and she wearily pushed open the wooden door. There was no sign of Elaine; she must have been at the post-office.

Anya's hands were shaking when she picked up the receiver. The museum wanted her to know that the DNA on Nick Hudson's dog had been analysed. It didn't match the animal hair found on the body of Eileen Randall.

There was nothing to connect Nick Hudson with the murder.

Anya slumped onto the calico-covered waiting-room lounge. Maybe Meira Sorrenti had been right. She *was* searching for holes in the Randall murder because Alf Carney had done the autopsy. Despite the doubts she had about the time of death, it was still entirely possible that Geoff Willard had raped and killed the girl and then done the same to Liz Dorman.

The last thing she needed was a lawsuit. She tried to convince herself that Geoffrey was the serial offender, but something inside niggled. The supposed love-letter and photo from Melanie Havelock and the woman killed while he was in prison didn't fit at all. And why did Louise Richardson describe her attacker's hand as having a sort of stripe on it? She decided to go back to the start and review the evidence she'd taken in the sexual assault cases, in case she'd missed something – anything.

44

When Anya arrived at the SA unit, Mary Singer was sitting at her computer, frowning. Her tousled hair was more uncontrolled than normal.

'I was just about to call you. Have you seen today's papers?'

Current news was the last thing on Anya's mind this morning. She shook her head.

'There's an article in the *Herald* about a victim's photographs being posted onto a rapists' website.'

'Oh shit! The poor woman,' Anya said. 'What country?'

Mary looked over her granny glasses.

'Anya, it has to have come from one of our units.'

Phones rang unanswered.

'We've had victims calling all morning, checking to see if it was their photos.'

This was exactly why Anya thought photos should never be taken. A black and white pencil drawing of genitals held little interest for paedophiles and sex offenders. A scandal like this would do irreparable damage to the unit and the trust they had all worked so hard to establish with victims and the community. She had no doubt that the number of people presenting would rapidly diminish.

'There isn't much we can do until the police have done their computer checks and tracking. I'll be in my office.'

Mary returned to the computer. There was nothing else to say until the source of the leak had been identified.

Anya hid in her bunker for over two hours. For once, the space felt more like a sanctuary than a cubby-hole. She appreciated that no one wanted to spend time in there unnecessarily. It gave her the chance to think and go over the evidence that had bothered her until now. There had to be something she was missing. Something obvious.

Desiree Platt's comments about being hurt and loved still bothered her. Had she come into contact with the rapist as a friend or victim? Nick mentioned that she stayed over when her partner worked or was away. Maybe she'd been attacked and was too afraid to be alone? Or she could have been carrying on with Nick Hudson while her husband was gone? How many friends who might have used the phrase were back at Fisherman's Bay?

The victim named Dell she'd met up there had said that most men worked at the nickel mine. That could mean a huge pool of men to draw on, and it would be difficult to trace many of them twenty years down the track.

She tried another angle and phoned the government's analytical laboratory. The number of rapes in which a condom was used was rapidly on the rise, possibly because of rapists' fear of sexually transmitted infection. More likely, it was so the offender didn't leave biological fluids at the scene.

For each assault case, forensic physicians at the unit had taken an extra swab in case a condom lubricant could be identified. Another of Jean Le Beau's students had done groundbreaking work on identification of specific condom lubricants. Each manufacturer had its own formula, which was like a chemical fingerprint. Isolating the brand might just help catch the rapist.

After being transferred, she spoke to the head biochemist, Ethan Gormley. With the names and dates of the cases, he checked his computer.

'You were right,' he said. 'Each slide you took had the same kind of silicone-based lubricant, which means—'

'He used the same brand each time.'

Anya listened. Serial rapists who used condoms commonly used the same brand. As far as most people were concerned, one brand equalled any other, but apparently not to some rapists.

'Exactly. It's an imported one called Fluidity, for originality.'

'Thanks, Ethan. Can you email the results?'

She wondered about the assault on Eileen Randall. Twenty years ago, had the same brand existed? What were the chances?

A piercing series of bleeps interrupted her thoughts.

Before picking up the pager, she automatically pulled the papers together in a pile. One leak from an SA unit was bad enough, and interruptions were how people got distracted and left rooms without putting things away.

She checked the number, which, oddly, was the hospital switch. Ordinarily, they put calls through to the unit secretary.

'There's an outside call,' the operator said. After a click, Hayden Richards' voice rasped.

'Can we meet? It's urgent.'

'Look, Sorrenti made it pretty clear—'

'I heard, but I've got some information you may want to hear.'

Anya sighed. 'Where are you now?'

'Outside your unit. You can practically wave to me.'

The cloak-and-dagger charades were beyond a joke. Anya didn't have the patience, not today, not ever. First Sorrenti, now Richards being childish.

'Talk to your colleague and leave me out of it!' She slammed down the phone. Within a moment she had left her office, locked her door and stomped off towards the detective.

As she walked down the path she could barely control her irritation. 'What puerile games are you people playing?'

'Good thing I phoned first to calm you down.' Hayden put both hands up. 'Hey, I wanted to protect you from any more of the crap Sorrenti pulls.'

Anya stopped and took a few deep breaths. 'I don't need protecting, thanks all the same. And you can sort whatever problem you have with her yourself. Leave me out of it.'

'There's already been a lot of shit going on in the department, and Sorrenti's under pressure to slam-dunk Willard and move on to any number of serial cases that are still on the books. After the photo scandal, it looks like she'll be sacrificed to the media before the end of the week. The Commissioner's already making moves.'

'But that was a Department of Health directive.'

'Yeah, but she's in charge of protecting evidence in SA cases. And her arrest rate isn't impressing anyone.'

Protecting digital photo images should have been a computing issue, but that was not Anya's fight. 'So why the secretive phone call?'

'Think about it. The Independent Commission Against Corruption is investigating how those pictures got released. It's tapping all our phones, so I rang the hospital switch. I could have been making an appointment to get my prostate checked. After Sorrenti's rampage, I wasn't sure whether it was safe for a cop to just walk in on you.'

Anya noticed the sunshine for the first time in days. It felt good to be outside, in a fresh breeze. 'Let's walk.'

They strolled along a path, down past the entrance to casualty. An ambulance rolled along the road, diverting to deliver its load. Hayden seemed more tense than normal. 'We've had the dogs on Nick Hudson.'

'Sorrenti told me you'd ordered surveillance. She didn't seem too happy about that either.'

'Yeah, well, I had to go over her head for approval. My butt's on the line for this one.'

Great, Anya thought. Now her decisions affected someone else's career. A blue-green parrot flew past them, barely missing a car slowing for a speed-bump. Students carried bags and textbooks on their way to lessons. An elderly man stood by a tree, smoking the last dregs of a hand-rolled cigarette. The sickly tobacco wafted uninvited in their direction.

Hayden seemed to pause to inhale.

'I forgot you'd given up.'

'It's like being an alcoholic. You still take one day at a time, but sometimes the cravings get pretty strong.'

For the first time, Hayden appeared vulnerable, more human than ever. It made her a little uncomfortable.

'Anything on Nick turn up?'

'He fits the rapist's profile. His aunt may look small, but she rules that household. She's a domineering woman in his life. Apart from under-the-table pub work, he's unemployed so has time to stalk and doesn't have to be up early in the mornings. Lots of free time on his hands.'

Anya remembered the fingernails. 'What about his hand?'

'His hand didn't have two skin tones. I looked for that when we were at the house. He spends time with that woman Desiree and her husband, Luke Platt. And get this, Platt has a job. He's a taxidermist. Stuffs fish for a living.'

Anya thought of Brown-Eye and the grotesque cat in attack-pose they'd seen on Liz Dorman's mantelpiece. 'What about dogs and cats?'

'I did some checking and the Dorman woman had hers done by a company Luke Platt used to work for.'

The breeze picked up, sending dust swirling in their pathway. Both turned their faces to avoid hurting their eyes. A car alarm sounded in the background, which everyone seemed to have no trouble ignoring.

'What about his skin?'

'Thought about that. He's done time in prison for fraud and petty theft. Charge sheet says he's got a tattoo of a dog's head on his right hand. Pretty much rules him out. Besides, he's used to working up and down the coast and surveillance has seen him with Hudson and says he's pretty tanned. His credit-card records show he was away on a job the night of Dorman's killing. He spent the night in a motel down the south coast. I'm beginning to think the eye-witness accounts are unreliable.'

'Not necessarily,' Anya said. In her experience,

rape victims were incredibly aware and observant given the smallest window of opportunity. There had to be a logical explanation for what the women saw.

They veered off the path, past an emaciated woman in a wheelchair. The woman sat, eyes closed, in the sun. For a moment, Anya considered checking for a pulse until she saw one of the slippered feet move. The breeze picked up and another gust brought more dust. They waited until it settled.

Hayden began, 'Nick Hudson is still my pick for being involved in the Dorman murder, if not the rapes as well. When Leonie Turnbull, that trainee doctor, was killed, he was visiting some mate up north, not far from where she died.'

'What's the taxidermy link?'

'Maybe his friend, Platt, has a big mouth? Maybe Nick helped out in the business sometimes, for cash. No tax record of him ever working. Shit, we've got to be missing something here.'

'Who wrote the love-letter to Geoffrey Willard with Melanie's photo? You still haven't explained that.'

Hayden shrugged his shoulders and shoved his hands in his baggy trouser-pockets. From a couple of steps behind, it looked as though his backside lay flush with his spine.

'I know. There's a lot I can't explain.'

'When you searched the Willard home, did you find any packs of condoms?'

'We don't usually put them on search warrants. It's the used ones we're after. Why do you ask?'

Anya chose an empty bench to stop at. They both sat and waited for a group of nurses to file past.

'This morning I phoned the lab, to chase the smears for each of our rape victims. The lab has matched the lubricant used in each case. If you can match the condom brand in the house, you'd have something stronger to go on.'

Hayden stared at his shoes. 'Hang on, does this guy take time to use a lubricant during the rapes?'

'Sorry, I didn't explain. Almost every condom sold in this country comes already lubricated. The manufacturers put it on to stop the latex getting stuck to itself. It also helps stop it perishing, but not indefinitely. That's why the packs have use-by dates on them. The labs matched the lubricant in a brand called "Fluidity".'

'Well, guess we'd better go condom-hunting.'

The pair stood and headed back towards the unit.

'Why the frown, doc? You still don't look happy.'

Anya couldn't understand why they had only seen three women who had been attacked in the same way. A serial rapist like this one usually performed many more assaults than this. However, it was possible that he had done, and many had gone unreported.

'I've checked with the other SA units in the

state. If the rapist, whoever he is, has attacked at least three women in the last few weeks, why haven't we seen a lot more cases, before and since? Has he just moved here? If so, where's he been, and why haven't we seen any more with the same pattern?'

Hayden nodded. 'That's bothering me, too. If Geoff Willard didn't rape and kill that girl twenty years ago, then someone's been out there for a long time cooling their heels, only to surface the same time Willard gets released.'

'Then the murder of that young doctor, Leonie Turnbull, when Willard was in prison, was the offender's big mistake.'

'Yeah, at this rate it looks like it's the only one he's made. If finding a brand of condom in his house is the only evidence we can manage, we're stuffed. Whoever raped and killed those girls is smart. And from where I stand, he's way smart enough to get away with it.'

45

Anya could hear heavy metal, something from the 1980s, pulsing into the street. She nervously knocked at the address from the Internet listing for *L and D Platt*. After a minute the music went quiet. Desiree opened the door. Despite being afternoon, her hair was wet and she smelt of coconut. This time she had a different oversized shirt on. With maternity clothes so expensive, wearing a man's clothes made a lot of financial sense.

She seemed understandably surprised to see Anya.

'I hope you don't mind. I wanted to see how you were, after the pain you had the other night.'

Desiree squinted. 'Oh yeah, those contraction things. I get them all the time now.'

'They're pretty normal later in pregnancy.'

They stood in an awkward silence.

'So you're all right?'

'Uh, yeah.'

'You have a big yard,' Anya volunteered, unable to find anything more positive to say about the unkempt lawn and metre-high weeds.

'With Luke working so much on weekends, it's hard to keep it under control. One day we'll have something better, for the kids.'

Anya made up an excuse to stay longer, with the hope of finding out more about the rapist's catchphrase. 'I didn't know taxidermists travelled.'

'Oh, yeah, he has a mobile freezer on a trailer for when he has to get bigger pieces, like the game fish. That way they are better preserved if he gets them fresher.'

'It must be difficult, with your husband travelling.'

'I don't like it. I used to go with him but he's been doing it so long now he stays with mates and bunks on a couch. We can't even afford a washing machine, so motels are out of the question.' She patted her belly. 'But that's gonna stop when the baby's born. I'm going to make sure he gives up his job and stays at home all the time.'

Anya coughed a few times, and tried to clear her throat. 'Would you mind if I had a drink of water before I head back into town?'

'Sure.' Desiree opened the door. Inside, magazines lay piled on chairs, along with catalogues advertising every must-have baby product. 'Have a seat and I'll get you that drink.'

The woman returned with a cartoon-painted glass, the sort that started off as a peanut-butter jar. The rim was immaculately clean.

'Thanks for this.'

Her hostess lowered herself into a single-seater lounge and seemed to study her visitor. Anya responded by feeling more self-conscious than usual.

'Something you said the other day made me curious.'

Desiree flicked a strand of hair over a shoulder. 'Was it about Nick? He's a good guy, you know. You could do a lot worse than him.' She picked up knitting from a bag next to the lounge. It looked like lime green was in for baby jumpers right now. Either that, or she wasn't sure of the sex of the baby and played safe with a neutral colour.

Anya decided to pursue this line of conversation. 'Have you known him a long time?'

Desiree smiled. 'Nick and I used to go out when I was in high school. Back then, he couldn't keep his pecker in his pants, if you know what I mean. But,' she added, 'he's changed now. That was when he was young and stupid.'

'You do go back a long way.'

Desiree stopped clicking the needles and reached for a photo on a side table. 'This is me, Nick and some other friends. Luke's the one sitting on the grass in the front. There's Badger, Carrot, and some others, too. I don't like those two that much, but they're good mates still. After all these years.'

Anya moved across the room and took the photo, returning to her seat. The faded colour showed girls in shoulder-pads and teased hair and boys with mullets. Each face smiling with the promise of the future.

'When did you leave the Bay?'

'Oh, after Luke left. I bummed around fruit-picking for a few years, shacked up with a real loser and didn't have the money to leave. A few years ago I caught up with Nick and there was Luke. We didn't know each other that well in the Bay, but I knew right there at that nightclub that he was the one.'

Anya returned the photo to its place and took a sip of water. 'Do you like Sydney?'

'Sometimes people can be a bit stuck-up, but it's a good place for kids.' She did a couple more stitches. 'We're better off in a big city. At least our friends are all here. You know, there aren't many of the old crowd left in the Bay.'

'I came back from England and it's taken about a year to settle in.'

'We've been here three months next week.'

Anya needed to broach the idea of sexual assault, but was having trouble steering the conversation. Desiree looked tired. Black semi-circles underscored her smallish brown eyes – the kind of fatigue pregnancy always brought on.

Desiree sat forwards a little, breasts folding over her abdomen. 'I read in the paper you look after women who've been raped.'

'That's part of my job,' she answered, relieved that Desiree had brought up the subject.

'It must be horrible. They get attacked when

338

there are plenty of women out there just itching to have sex with anyone.'

'It is.' Anya was surprised by the comment and tried to read the expression on the face of the mother-to-be. 'Sometimes memories of an assault can be triggered by pregnancy.'

Desiree nodded and unwound some more wool. 'They asked me about that at the antenatal clinic. They said pregnancy could bring back all kinds of stuff about abuse and all that.'

'That's true. It's part of the routine questions they ask all the women who go there.'

The conversation stalled.

Anya needed to recover it. 'I was thinking about what you said the other night about having to feel pain to be loved. That was quite profound.'

Desiree laughed and waved one hand at Anya. 'Yeah, the boys at home used to say it before they had sex with a girl. Turns out, most of the time it was true. At least, until I met Luke. He says the opposite. But then you're a doctor, you'd know about all that.'

It saddened Anya that young women could be coerced into accepting painful sex because 'that's the way it is'.

'Is Luke looking forward to being a father?'

'He's getting used to the idea.' Desiree sat forwards, inching herself along the cushion. 'Let's just say sometimes nature needs a little help.'

Anya didn't follow.

'You doctors aren't that smart, are you?' she

mocked. 'I put pin-pricks in his condoms.' She jabbed the air with a knitting needle, as though piercing an imaginary balloon. 'Tiny holes that he'd never notice. That's our little secret,' she said, and slid back in her seat.

Anya could not believe that Desiree would proudly boast about deliberately getting pregnant. Maybe they did come from different cultures.

Something about the photo drew her back to it. 'What were they like, the boys back home?'

Desiree laughed. 'They thought their shit didn't smell because they played football. The Pit-Bull Maulers hadn't been beaten in years so it made them all a bit full of themselves. Except Luke. He was always quiet.' Knit one, purl one. 'The girls loved them. Treated them like popstars. Guess I did, too. You could always pick them with their tattoos.'

'What tattoos?'

'They got pictures of pit-bulls on the back of a hand. It was part of being on the team. Everyone except Nick did it. He whinged about how ugly the dogs were.'

'Did Luke have a tattoo?'

'Oh yeah, he was one of the boys, but was a lot nicer to girls than the others.'

Anya could just imagine a group of adolescent males in a country town, thinking they owned the place because of their sporting prowess. Like a gang, they hung together with a tattoo for membership. Sadly, young girls probably helped perpetuate their misogynistic attitudes by idolising them.

If you can't be hurt, you can't be loved.

No wonder Geoffrey Willard had never fitted in.

Any one of them could have killed Eileen Randall.

46

'What the hell were you thinking, going in like that alone?'

For the second time this week, Anya was being berated by a police officer. Hayden Richards paced around the office, hands in his pockets.

Anya couldn't really explain why she had gone to the house, except to find out about Desiree's saying and whether she was one of the rapist's victims. The excuse seemed feeble now, considering what she had discovered.

She sat on a chair, trying to come to terms with what she had done. She was only in the room because Hayden and Sorrenti needed to know exactly what Desiree had said. 'At least now you know that Luke Platt, "Badger" and "Carrot" lived in Fisherman's Bay as well when Eileen Randall was killed. Luke's a taxidermist and had contact with, or at least knowledge of, Liz Dorman. Maybe she recognised him, which is why he went back to kill her.'

Hayden stood at a whiteboard. Across the top was a timeline with the names and dates of the rape victims. In bold were the names of the three murder victims. He wrote Luke Platt in the left-hand column.

'We know he was down the south coast at the time Dorman died.'

Meira Sorrenti stood next to a partition, jaw clenched. 'The motel clerk remembers him. Said he was more polite than their usual clientele.'

'But Desiree said he bunked on couches while away. Then again, if he were paid cash, why not stay at a motel and get some proper sleep?' Anya wondered why the female detective was being more agreeable than expected.

Hayden crossed out Platt's name. 'Alibi's rock-solid and he was interstate when Leonie Turnbull died.'

The rest of the detectives in the room remained silent. Anya suddenly felt embarrassed at trying to justify herself. She had crossed a line by going to the house alone and everyone in the room knew it.

'We borrowed the group photo from Desiree Platt last night,' Sorrenti began. 'Mrs Platt was co-operative once we explained that her husband wasn't a suspect. So we are aware that a group of them from Fisherman's Bay live in the local area. They all played football together and called themselves the Pit-Bull Maulers. It seems each had a tattoo of a pit-bull's head on the back of one hand, except Nick Hudson.'

'Willard didn't have one,' Hayden said, as if part of a twin act. 'He was never part of the group.

343

His cousin played, but says he chose not to have one because of Geoff missing out.'

Hayden and Sorrenti were working as a team. Anya wondered what had prompted Meira's change in attitude.

The senior officer took the lead.

'One of these guys is a real possibility. Barry Lerner. Goes by the name of Badger. He's got a record of violence against women and was accused of sexual assault, but the woman withdrew her statement.'

'Any chance of interviewing the woman or seeing her medical records?' Anya ventured.

Hayden anchored one arm over the whiteboard. 'She just vanished. He could have killed her, too, and disposed of the body.'

Anya remembered the cubby house at one of the victim's homes. 'Did anything turn up at the Davises' house? If he were stalking Jodie from the cubby, he must have left some piece of himself.'

'Couldn't get jackshit to tie Lerner to that rape.'

There was no DNA left at the scene.

Sorrenti put both hands on her hips. 'Now, I want to know this bastard's movements for the last twenty years. Everywhere he's been, worked and visited. Check registrations in every state, leases, rental-bond boards, phone accounts, whatever you have to. And I want a tail on him. I want to know when he eats, sleeps, craps and even takes a leak. Everything.' She paced across the front of the room. 'The others from the Bay, the rest of the gang. I want to know everything there is to know about them as well. They should be checked for tattoos and scars. Don't go by police files, check them out for yourselves. I want to know *everything*, no matter how insignificant it might seem. This Lerner is our major suspect, but I'm not excluding any of the others just yet.'

Another detective looked puzzled. 'Why are we looking for ones with tattoos?'

Sorrenti's patience seemed to have run out. 'Because they all had the same fucking tattoos, like a gang. Maybe some got them removed and they left scars. Scars don't get suntans, so look whiter than the rest of the hand. These guys stick together like shit to a blanket. They could even be in this together.'

The junior detective persisted. 'If they still hang out together, why would they have them removed?'

'Maybe they just grew up,' Hayden said, 'and realised that the job-fairy didn't deliver to anyone with flesh-eating dogs all over their skin.'

Anya offered another explanation. 'Part of prison rehab involves the option of removing tattoos. The system pays for dermatologists to remove them, usually with laser. The most visible would be removed first for the same reason Hayden suggested. To increase the chances of finding work once out of jail.'

Anya needed to raise an issue, aware that it

would probably aggravate Sorrenti. 'Is it possible to get the case against Geoffrey Willard dropped? He's still on remand. It might flush out the real killer.'

'You've got to be kidding.' Sorrenti sniffed. In another era, she could have spat tobacco in Anya's direction. 'Not until we've thoroughly reviewed the Randall case. Does anyone know if the evidence still exists?'

Hayden screwed up his moustache. 'Since the case had been closed and Willard imprisoned, no one will have thought to keep the clothes and physical evidence. For all we know, they were destroyed years ago.'

Sorrenti sat on the table, one leg swinging. 'I've seen the alleged Willard confession from the night Randall died. Having seen it, I have to agree with Hayden's assessment. Willard didn't know shit from clay that night. The police set him up for a confession. We could get the case reopened if we had some physical evidence, but so far we've got nothing to tie Lerner to Eileen Randall.'

'Or Elizabeth Dorman, for that matter,' Hayden added.

'Maybe you can get what you need,' Anya said. 'It's just occurred to me. I think I might know where that missing physical evidence could be.'

47

Morgan Tully listened to Anya's plea, but sat at her desk, stony-faced.

'I appreciate what you're saying, but the area doesn't have the funds to go chasing cases that were closed decades ago. We're struggling to keep up with the samples taken from current crime.'

She pushed back her chair, stood up and closed the office door. 'It can take eight months to process a sexual-assault kit as it is. I'm afraid this isn't a priority.'

Anya put the brown paper bags on the desk. Judging by Morgan's response – a sneezing spasm – she was allergic to dust. When Charlie Boyd souvenired them after the trial, the world forgot about them – until now. It had not been the first time that a policeman had squirrelled evidence from a trial away, particularly in the biggest case of his career. Thankfully, he had been forthcoming, believing that Willard's guilt could be proved with modern science. The retired policeman had not considered the possibility of science exonerating an innocent man.

'These have been kept in a police-officer's shed

for twenty years, while Geoffrey Willard served time for a crime he probably didn't commit. There's at least enough doubt to hold another inquest.'

Morgan took a tissue from the counter and turned away to wipe her nose. 'You need to talk to the DPP.'

Anya had already tried that. The official line from the office of the director of public prosecutions was that a jury had convicted Geoffrey Willard on the basis of evidence, motive and opportunity. Since DNA hadn't been operational back then, he had not been wrongly convicted based on DNA evidence.

She had hit a brick wall. They wouldn't test Eileen Randall's clothing unless someone else was found guilty of the Dorman and Turnbull murders. By that time, the killer would be serving two life sentences. It would be a waste of time testing the Randall evidence because no one would spend money trying a killer for another murder if it made no real difference to the sentence he would serve. Crime and justice were about money and practicality.

Twenty years might have been wrongfully stolen from Geoff Willard's life, but nobody cared because it was in the past. He would have a better chance of being exonerated if he were still in jail for that crime.

'The DPP don't want anything to do with it,' she admitted.

Morgan sat down again. 'I can see why. I'd need a better reason to hold another inquest into Randall's death.' She clasped her hands, as though about to pass judgement. 'Do the family want it?'

Anya stood head down with both palms flat on the desk. 'There's no family that we know of.'

'I see.'

'There are two other murders with similar pattern injuries, one of which was committed while Geoffrey was in jail. If Barry Lerner's DNA turns up on this underwear,' she put her hand on the dirty bag, 'it'll go a hell of a way to proving Lerner's guilt in the recent murder too.'

'And therefore Willard's innocence.'

The coroner pushed the bags to the edge of the desk and wiped her hands on another tissue. 'And therein lies the problem.'

'Pardon?' Anya lifted her head, confused.

'After serving twenty years in prison for a crime he didn't commit, then being rearrested for another crime – again, that he didn't commit? Imagine the compensation.'

Finally, Anya understood. Conveniently, exonerating Willard was a low priority, which also saved the government millions of dollars and extreme embarrassment. How could she have been so naïve?

'I can't hold an inquest until you have something more substantial on the Dorman killing.'

'How about another body? Maybe, if we're lucky, the killer will stab someone else.'

Morgan took a deep breath. 'Don't do this to yourself. The system isn't perfect and never will be. With people like you on the job, there will be fewer people going through what Geoffrey Willard has endured.'

That wasn't much consolation. If testing was about money, she had a better idea. 'How about I wipe the bill for my reports on the Carney cases?'

The coroner sneezed again and delicately dabbed the tip of her nose.

'That should just about cover the cost of examining the clothes, I'd say,' Anya persisted.

Both women smiled and understood.

Anya reached over and shook the older woman's hand. 'I owe you for this one.'

'Take those dusty bags off my desk and we'll be even.'

Back at the SA unit, Anya felt victorious. Finally, something was going in a positive direction. Then she saw Mary Singer's solemn face.

'Did you get my message?'

Anya checked her mobile phone. She'd forgotten to charge it overnight. 'Sorry, it's flat.' With annoyance she realised that in her haste to see Morgan Tully, she'd left her pager at home as well.

'There's a woman in the waiting room. She's been here two hours and hasn't said a word. It's like she's catatonic.'

Anya followed the counsellor to a room filled

with lounge chairs. It served as a waiting room and was used for counselling sessions as needed.

A young blonde woman sat staring out the window. Dressed in trackpants and a windcheater, she had her bare feet on the chair, knees pulled up to her chin. The disturbing thing was how she rocked. Not much, but repeatedly.

Outside the door, Mary whispered, 'She's been like this since she got here.'

'Do we have a name?'

'Her licence says Emily Mirivac. She's eighteen.'

Anya entered the room first, and knelt down on the floor in front of the young woman.

'Emily, my name is Anya. I'm a doctor, and I'd like to help you.'

Emily stopped rocking and turned her face towards Anya. A bruise on the left side took in part of her eye, but most of the impact had been taken by the cheekbone.

'That looks sore.' Anya shifted her weight onto the other knee and reached over to a bar-fridge. In the freezer section she pulled out a gel ice-pack and wrapped some paper towel around it from the tea-tray on top.

'This might help,' she offered, and Emily made eye-contact. As she took the ice-pack, their hands touched, and it was enough to break Emily's emotionally frozen state. The young woman blinked back tears.

'Will you pray with me?' were the first words she spoke.

351

Anya flicked a look at Mary, who had sat down in a chair across the room.

All three women bowed their heads and Emily asked for forgiveness for what she had done, and the strength to go on. Anya wondered what she had done to the person who attacked her.

She concluded with 'Amen', and the two others in the room echoed the sentiment.

'Emily, can you tell us what happened?' Anya moved to a position next to the teenager and tried to straighten her stiff knees.

Clutching the ice-pack with one hand and Anya's with the other, she began to explain. 'Mum and Dad had gone away for a couple of nights, on a church camp. My little brother was staying with a friend. I got home from scripture at about nine thirty. I remember locking the doors before bed. Next thing I knew, I couldn't breathe. There was someone on top of me, holding me down.'

She squeezed Anya's fingers tighter.

'He hurt me. I was so scared, I didn't move. I told him I was saving myself for marriage.' She blinked a few times and a lone tear escaped down her purple-red cheek.

'He raped me,' she managed, 'and told me it was for my own good. He said that if I can't be hurt, I can't be loved.'

48

With Emily's permission, Anya phoned Meira
Sorrenti after the examination. It took less than
half an hour for her to arrive with Hayden Richards.

They chose to interview Emily in the same
room in which the young woman had sat to steel
herself for what lay ahead, and sat down to wait.

While Emily finished showering and speaking
to Mary, Anya took the opportunity to brief the
detectives.

'This one's got all the hallmarks of the others.
Same kind of vaginal tear, same saying, and the
knife mark on the clavicle. She's pretty small and
slight, so the mark isn't continuous. But it looks
like the same weapon was used.'

'Did you get a photo?' Meira spoke and then bit
her lip.

'Not this time, no.' With the chance of any
images being leaked, Anya refused to photograph
any more injuries. 'I've measured it and recorded
it on a diagram.'

Hayden was surprisingly quiet and let Sorrenti
take the lead.

'Fucking Lerner,' Sorrenti said, rocking on her toes.

Hayden added, 'Surveillance didn't pick him up until this morning. It was almost as if he knew. Platt and his wife swear they didn't say anything to him, but he's got to be smart enough to know why you were sniffing around their place.'

Meira pulled a face. 'My guess is Platt spilt her guts.'

Hayden smiled. 'By the way, we found the condoms in Lerner's garage. And it looks like we got the weapon that killed Liz Dorman. It's fairly new and had been cleaned, but there were still traces of blood on it, mostly up near the handle.'

'What kind of knife?' Anya asked.

'Boning, really pointy blade. He's our boy, for sure.'

Meira stuck her hands in her pockets, like a child caught stealing from the lolly jar. 'Looks like you were right about Willard,' she said. 'Lerner has been round at Lillian Willard's home. He could have hidden the bloodied knife in the laundry basket, or even wiped it clean with Geoff's shirt.'

Anya knew that was the closest thing to an apology that the detective was capable of giving. There was no point holding a grudge.

'You surprised me the way you still looked into the anomalies.'

Meira flicked her fringe and shifted uncomfortably. 'I may be gullible and pig-headed, but I'm definitely not stupid.'

'Agreed.' Both women smiled.

Emily entered the corridor and appeared more child than adult. Her frame seemed more delicate silhouetted in the light. Anya excused herself to let the detectives take their statement.

Thinking about how Emily's world had forever changed, she desperately hoped that Lerner would be stopped before he hurt or killed again. She found herself saying a silent prayer, just in case God was listening.

The detectives reappeared. Hayden took a call on his mobile in the corridor and signalled for Anya to wait. She walked further away, not wanting to eavesdrop.

'Shit,' he said, rubbing his mouth. 'That was the lab. There are two types of blood on the knife. One is Liz Dorman's, but the other doesn't belong to Lerner.'

Anya considered, 'So, either he's not the killer . . .'

'Or there's been another victim, only we haven't found her yet. My money's on the rape victim who withdrew her statement and hasn't been seen since.'

Sorrenti began to dial. 'We'd better liaise with homicide and pick this bastard up.'

49

Anya parked her car and dragged her green bag full of milk, vegetables and bread through the front door, automatically locking it once inside. Her body relaxed when she realised Elaine had left for the evening. Right now, she didn't feel like talking to anyone. No one asking about her day or offering sympathy for what she had seen. With soft light streaming through the lounge-room window, there was still time to just enjoy the peace and quiet before darkness fell. Ben would arrive after dinner for another weekend, and there'd be noise, cuddles and laughter in her house. She couldn't wait.

After unpacking the shopping, she kicked off her shoes and sifted through her mail on the lounge. Bills, more bills and a letter from her brother, Damien, in England. The rest could wait, along with email and phone messages. For once, she wasn't on call and was happy to let someone else deal with whatever presented to the SA unit.

With stockinged feet tucked up beneath her, she read the letter and couldn't help it when her smile burst into a laugh. Damien had a wonderful way with words and could make the most boring anecdote about being lost in London sound like a thrilling adventure. She missed him, and wondered about what his letters didn't say. There was nothing about a girlfriend, or his social life. He talked about his work as a forensic scientist, but the absence of anything personal made her think he was lonely. She'd give him a few hours for work to start in England and then call, once she had put Ben to bed.

She checked her watch and switched on the TV with the remote control. A game-show caught her attention for only a moment. It was much better without sound. Light fading, she decided to have a quick shower and freshen up.

As she undressed, a vague image of Barry Lerner came to her. She went over the facts in her mind. The knife with Elizabeth Dorman's blood was pretty damning. She could only imagine how the women felt when he surprised them. Did fear stop them from fighting? Melanie Havelock must have been paralysed with fear to stay in the bedroom while he helped himself to dinner. Knowing the police had him under arrest meant women would sleep better tonight. She just hoped that this time they did have the right man. Why he raped and returned to kill only two women gave her a frisson of uneasiness, though.

With the gas water-heater set to forty-two degrees Celsius, she turned on the hot tap. Steaming water surged over her flexed shoulders and neck.

She thought about the effect Lerner had had on so many people's lives. Ever since the assault, Melanie had showered in a swimsuit, too afraid to be naked. Jodie Davis had sold her house and disappeared with the family, possibly to the US. Louise Richardson might never again work in her chosen profession.

Steam fogged up the shower screen. With the tap on full, water cascaded over Anya's skin. The heat stung, but the sensation felt like a pulsing massage. The fine line between pleasure and pain, she thought. Far different from having to be hurt to feel love.

Every muscle felt fatigued, like she'd run a marathon. Thank God she'd reached the finish line. She closed her eyes and savoured the time to herself.

The list of Lerner's victims just kept getting longer. Crime had a ripple effect, which spread through the whole community. There was never just one victim. Lerner had irrevocably changed the lives of the victims' families and friends. It was like an irreversible chemical reaction. No one could ever go back to how they were before he had struck. The lives of the investigating police had changed as well. Anyone dealing with the effects of Lerner's attacks would remember the case for years to come.

There was nothing more she could do except focus on Ben. With rain predicted, they could spend all day inside playing games like Battleship and Mousetrap. And she could deliberately lose the Concentration card game – not by too much, but so it looked close. Even small children loved to beat a worthy opponent. The thought made her grin with pride.

Out of the shower, she quickly slipped into the blue pencil skirt she had bought on their last shopping expedition. It wasn't overly practical, but her son liked the colour and feel of the wool. On top of her bra she pulled a loose jumper, another of his favourites, and her ugg boots. At last she felt warm.

Facing the mirror, she threw her head forwards to towel-dry her hair and froze when she saw the shoes behind her. A man blocked the doorway.

Pulse racing, she flicked her head back and clutched the towel in her hands. The heat and sudden movement made the room fade in and out for a moment.

'Turn around slowly! Don't think about trying anything,' he said, playing with something metal in his hand.

She turned to face him, trying to stem the rising panic. He raised his eyes, which she saw beneath the black cap. She had seen that face somewhere before.

'I've been watching,' he smirked, letting his eyes roam down to her legs and back to her chest. 'You've got a great-looking body.'

He'd been there while she showered. God. The adrenalin surge made her want to be sick. But she had to think. Quickly. The small en suite only had one door and no real escape options. A hairdryer was the only possible weapon.

As if anticipating her next move, he revealed what looked like a crucifix on a chain in his hand and pressed a button so she could see. A long blade released, just like the one she'd described to Hayden; the one that left the marks on his victims. Jesus, he wore the knife around his neck.

Heart pounding, she made a split-second decision. She wrapped the towel around her left arm.

He laughed. 'What do you plan to do with that? Dry me to death?'

She clenched her left hand around the end of the towel. If this didn't work, he'd try to stab her. The towel might cushion the blow. She nervously waited for the right moment.

He stood staring, and took a step forwards.

Right then, Anya grabbed the hairspray from the bench, lunged with all her strength, spraying at his face. With the other arm she hit out at the knife. All she needed was the chance to get away.

The force made him stumble back. He grabbed at his eyes. She ran towards the open bedroom door. The stairs were only feet away.

Suddenly, her head whipped backwards as pain shot through her scalp.

He twisted her hair to get a better grip. 'You stupid bitch!'

Anya clawed at his hand, desperate for him to

let go. Unaffected, he dragged her along the floorboards, back into the room. Towards the bed.

Jesus! He was going to rape her! She knew she was helpless on her back, and flipped over onto her knees. He breathed hard but couldn't swing a hand to hit with her so close. She couldn't see the knife and struggled to her feet.

With one movement, he picked her up and flipped her onto the bed. Before she could resist, he was sitting on her chest, knees pressed hard on her upper arms. She had to fight to breathe and gasped small amounts of air.

His face distorted with rage and he slammed a fist down hard on her chest, forcing what little air was inside her lungs to escape.

Then she saw the knife again and braced herself.

50

The pain from the blade on her collarbone forced her head off the bed. Every muscle strained against his weight. For a moment he sat back, knees still pinning her arms above her head. Then he unbuttoned his belt and unzipped his trousers. The smell of ketones in his sickly sweet breath made her gag.

Anya swallowed hard and struggled to think how to stop him. 'My ex-husband will be here any minute with our son. He's got a key,' she lied. 'You could get away if you go now. I won't say anything.'

The words sounded hollow, even to her.

The man cocked his head to the side. 'Don't look at me,' he hissed, and landed a punch to her cheek. 'Don't make any noise.'

The thumping of her heart was almost deafening, and she was sure he was enjoying the sound of air straining to move through her lungs. Is this what excited him – the fear and terror?

Suddenly he froze. 'There's someone downstairs,' he said, zipping his pants with his left hand. The knife stayed put at her throat.

Anya was too afraid to scream.

'Let's go,' he said, and yanked her up by the hair. Standing, he pulled her head underneath his left arm in a tight headlock, like a footballer holding a ball. Her feet slipped on the floor as she tried to get a grip. The ugg boots had come off on the bed. She didn't have any control of her legs. The bedroom floor flashed beneath her. The rug slid towards the window in the struggle. A pair of flat shoes were under the bed. She couldn't reach anything. She tried to get her fingers between his arm and her throat. She needed to breathe. Trying to make a sound, a cough was all that came out. If he had someone else downstairs, she would have no chance of getting away. Maybe one raped and the other killed?

The cold metal pressed harder against her face. It took all her strength to suck in air filled with the stench of body odour.

Slowly, her feet slid down the stairs. Blackness was all she could see. How many stairs were there? She tried to remember. That way she'd know when they were at the bottom. First chance, she'd run for the door.

Light flashed when they turned the corner. The silent TV was still on.

She tried to think. She had to get away, try to get some kind of control. If the police had arrested Lerner, who was attacking her, and why? Maybe Lerner murdered the women but did not rape them.

363

'Who's there?' her captor demanded.

He was not expecting anyone! Anya prayed for someone to be here, anyone to save her.

They stood in silence for what felt like minutes, Anya hunched over with the knife in her face. Then he relaxed his grip, just enough to ease her breathing.

'Guess we're alone after all,' he said. 'Now, where were we?'

Anya needed to buy time. Any time at all. She thought of the smell of his breath. Ketones meant he hadn't eaten.

She managed through the arm-hold, 'You must be hungry. Don't you want to eat something first?'

He seemed to pause for a moment then released her, still hanging on to her damp hair.

At least she had the use of her hands, she thought.

'What's for dinner?' he asked, as casually as if he were home for the evening with his girlfriend.

Anya remembered the profile. Wants to role-play the loving partner. Fantasy rapist. Gentleman. She had to play along.

'There's a bottle of wine you could open, and some lasagne. It's cold, but I could heat it up.'

'Do it.' He tightened the grip on her hair. 'But don't try anything. I've still got the knife. And don't look at me.'

Hands trembling, she lifted out leftover lasagne and removed the cling-wrap, feeling the pull on her scalp each time she moved. 'Could you put on the light, please, so I can turn on the oven?' She tried to sound casual.

'No lights,' he said. 'And use the microwave. Got any beer?'

'No,' she said. 'I thought wine was more romantic.'

She felt him loosen the grip on her hair. The knife remained around her chest – for now. For the first time, she thought she might talk him into leaving her alone. She had to gain his trust, get him to open up. She hoped like hell that the profiler had been right. If not, she was about to get herself killed.

She unscrewed the wine bottle. 'Pour it,' he said, waving the knife at a glass in the drip-tray. They stepped towards the sink, with his hand still attached to her hair. She could feel his hot breath on the back of her neck.

'You smell nice.' He inhaled again. 'Real nice.'

The flesh on her neck and shoulders contracted. She shuddered uncontrollably. He responded by licking her neck. Then he gulped the wine and shoved the glass at her for a refill. The microwave hummed, the light illuminating the clear kitchen benches.

Anya had the knives high up in the pantry, so no little fingers could get to them. Neither could she. Even if she could reach a knife, she was afraid he'd be too strong and turn it on her.

The microwave beeped and steam rose off the lasagne. 'Get a fork,' he said, still with the cap low over his eyes. 'I'll eat it here. You can feed me.'

By the way he devoured the leftovers, he hadn't eaten for quite a while. With his hands still on the knife and her hair, Anya was trapped and had no chance of escape right now. She had to wait. Light flickering from the TV couldn't be seen from the street. Somehow she had to let Martin know she was home. Somehow she had to get the lights on.

As he chewed, she felt him watch her face as the metal blade depressed her cheek.

She had to play along with the fantasy. It was her only chance of getting away.

'I've been waiting for you to come,' she said.

He swallowed hard and stared into her eyes. 'How did you know I would?'

'I saw the other girls. I wanted to know what it was like to be with you.' She moved his hand from her hair to her cheek.

He bent forwards and brushed his face against hers. The muscles in her face quivered with revulsion, but the gesture worked. Her hair was free of his hold.

'I know you didn't mean to hurt any of the women,' she whispered. 'You were just showing love.'

He raised his head and one of his eyes squinted. She still didn't know who he was.

She had to be more convincing. Her stomach wanted to purge, to vomit all over him. She swallowed.

366

'I'd like to get to know you better, you, as a person.'

Don't cry, she told herself. Stay calm. 'I know how intelligent you are, and what you feel about love.' Her voice quavered, so she pushed some hair across his forehead. 'That's why I want this to be right.' Her rapid pulse throbbed in her neck.

'It's going to be perfect,' he said. 'What else is there to eat?'

'If you like, there's chocolate in the cupboard.'

'Get it,' he snapped, and grabbed her hair again. She complied as slowly as she could.

With a piece of mint-chocolate in his mouth and another in his knife hand, he said, 'It's time to get what I came for.'

He was between her and the back door. She couldn't run, his grip was too strong. If she could bite the hand holding the knife, he might drop it.

Before she could try, he pushed her into the lounge room and threw her face-up onto the lounge. As her back hit the cushion, he landed on top again, knees pinning her arms by her side. This time he let her breathe. With her legs curled up beneath her and the woollen skirt pulled tight, he couldn't get his hand between her legs. For a second he looked like he'd cut it open, but pulled back.

His breathing became faster and more shallow. He lifted her jumper, exposing her bra. Taking his time, he bent down, pushed away the material and licked her breasts. She turned her head to the side and swallowed again, trying not to cry.

367

His mouth quickly made its way to hers. She didn't struggle, despite gagging when his tongue mauled her mouth. She tried to ease her hand free to switch on the lamp.

Martin should be here by now. She needed to let him know she was home.

'I have to tell you something,' she said. 'I've got an infection right now and I don't want you to catch it.'

He stopped trying to force her legs apart. 'No problem.' A condom came out of his trouser pocket. The zip went down again.

She arched her back, trying to sit up. 'But you could still catch it. I'm a doctor, remember? A condom won't protect you completely. It's fungal and makes your skin itchy. It's incredibly painful when the skin starts to peel.'

He squinted both eyes and grimaced. The thought of an infection near his penis must have bothered him.

'I'll be better in a few days' time. Why don't you come back and we can do this properly? We could make it a magical night. I promise.'

He muttered something she couldn't make out.

'The police have been watching you. They could be here any minute. You've got to go before they find you.'

The man sat up, still pressing on her with all his weight. His eyes flicked around the room.

Jesus. He might go, she thought. With a little more pushing, Anya really believed she could get away. She took a deep breath. 'I'll get you some food to take with you, and see you back here next Saturday, when it's dark, so no one sees you.'

He smirked again. 'You're a stupid fucking liar.'

A chair scraped the floor in the kitchen and Anya felt relief flood through her. Martin!

The man held the knife against her throat again and froze.

'This is going to stop now,' said a woman's voice. 'Right here, right now!'

For the first time, Anya saw fear in the man's eyes.

51

Martin pulled up in front of Anya's neighbour's house. The old woman would no doubt complain, but she whinged about everything.

'You ready?' he asked.

'Dad, why is Mum's house all dark?'

Martin checked his watch. 'She's probably held up somewhere. Just like usual.'

Ben didn't respond and continued to play his hand-held computer game.

'I'll check anyway.' He got out of the car and knocked on the front door, studying the small jade plant in a pot near the path while he waited. It was a plant they were given when they got married. For luck, supposedly. It had always been healthier when Anya looked after it.

No answer.

He climbed back in the car and undid the window. 'Guess we wait a few minutes. Her car's there.' He pointed to a blue Toyota Corolla, two cars ahead.

'Maybe she's gone to get bread.' Ben zapped another couple of aliens.

'Either that or she took a taxi this morning.

We'll give her a few more minutes,' he said, flicking on the radio.

The man stared over Anya's shoulder at the intruder.

No one moved as they heard the knock on the door. The man shoved his hand over Anya's mouth, muffling her attempts to call out and restricting her vision. There was no second knock.

Anya's eyes welled. Why hadn't the woman reacted, she wondered.

'Get off her.' The strange woman's voice sounded familiar. 'Now!'

Without taking his eyes off the woman, he complied and slowly rose to his feet.

Anya sat up and moved backwards to get away from him.

'Stay there!' He leant towards her with the knife. 'I'm not finished with you.'

In the shadows, Anya could make out the woman's shape and the glint of metal reflecting from the TV. It didn't make any sense.

'How did you get in?' He sounded nervous.

Anya braced herself to run.

'Luke, I know you. You always leave the back door open.'

Anya realised that Desiree Platt was in the house with a knife in her hand.

None of this made sense. Why had Desiree come to help her? Did she know her husband was a rapist?

371

Luke inched his way along the side of the coffee table. 'Des, what are you doing?'

'I can't believe you'd do this to me,' she blurted. 'I trusted you.'

'Calm down, Des. It's not what you think.' He held one arm out like a peace offering. 'How'd you know I was here? Did anyone follow you?'

'No one knows I'm here.'

Anya's heart hammered. How could a heavily pregnant woman overpower Luke? Her breathing quickened and her fingers began to tingle.

Desiree sounded angry. 'I saw the way you listened to Nick talk about her. That's how I knew you'd come.'

Luke leant forwards. 'I'm sorry. I'll get help this time, go to counselling, whatever it takes. It won't happen again.'

'You promised! No more women,' Desiree cried.

He kept advancing slowly. 'Don't do anything silly. If you just put down the knife.'

'Not yet . . .' Her voice trailed off.

She was no physical match for Luke. Once on the ground, she wouldn't stand a chance. If Anya moved, he could get to her in a lunge. But Desiree was standing even closer.

Anya had to distract him, so Desiree could get help.

She leapt over the arm of the lounge, shouting, 'He's got a knife. Desiree, run, get help!'

As her elbows hit the wooden boards, Platt had

her hair in his grip again. Pain shot through her arms and knees.

'You stupid fucking bitch!' he said, and thumped the back of her head with something like a rock.

It felt like her head exploded. Dazed, she scrambled to pull free, disorientated by the blinding sensation.

He dragged her back onto the lounge and she felt the metal dig into her cheek again. 'Don't move a fucking muscle.'

Head throbbing, she hoped Desiree had got away. She could cope with almost anything if she knew help was coming quickly.

Clutching her head, she looked across. Her chest tightened. Desiree stood where she had been, frozen.

'The father of my child is a good man,' she said calmly. 'You won't take him away from me.'

Anya didn't understand. She couldn't process what was going on.

'You're right, Des.' With one hand, Luke slid the coffee table to his left, clearing the path to Desiree. With his right hand, he kept the knife pointed in Anya's direction.

'What about Elizabeth Dorman?' Anya put pressure on her throbbing scalp.

'Don't you get it?' Luke's voice strained as he shook the knife. 'It was Willard. He did it, just like he killed Eileen Randall.'

Anya hesitated. When he was in control, she had no chance of escape.

If he lost control, he might do anything. She had to risk it. 'Geoff Willard didn't stab Eileen. She was already dead when he found her. I know because I've got the evidence to prove it.' If he came for her, she'd dive and roll. Maybe he'd reach her legs, but not her body.

Luke panted loudly. 'You're lying. Willard killed Eileen. Des even saw him do it.'

'Shut up, Luke! She's messing with your head. Just like the others did.' The knife glistened again. 'She wants to seduce you. She's exactly like the others.'

What others? Anya didn't understand. What was Desiree doing? The whole moment seemed surreal with *The Simpsons* playing silently on the screen.

Platt began to pace and bumped his knee on the coffee table.

About ten metres and she could make it to the front door. Her muscles tensed in readiness.

'Honey, you need to go now,' Desiree said calmly. 'I'll stay and sort this out. We can meet at that kiosk where we had lunch last month.'

He froze. 'What do you mean, sort it out?'

'I forgive you, Luke. The baby does too. I know it's not your fault that women seduce you. They were all just affairs that didn't mean anything.'

374

Anya slowly edged one leg over the arm of the lounge. Desiree was more unstable than she had thought.

'I told you not to fucking move!' Luke yelled, and the knife jolted closer again.

'I saw you,' Desiree said. 'I know where you went when you were supposed to be working. Sometimes I even followed you. I could see the Dorman bitch inside her house, prancing around with the lights on. You always went around the back so no one could see you.' She sniffled and her voice broke. 'I'd wait outside, knowing what was going on in there night after night. Do you have any idea what that felt like, every time you went there to see her?'

Suddenly, it became clear. Desiree thought Luke had been having affairs with his victims. She had watched him stalk them and maybe even sat outside while he committed rape. The woman was delusional.

Anya tried to move her leg, which had gone numb underneath her.

Luke stayed still. 'Affairs? You stupid bitch. What have you done?'

'I protected what was mine, and our child's. What I did was for us. Our family.'

'Oh fuck, oh fuck, Des. You killed that teacher.' He rocked on the spot, almost in time with the TV flicker. 'I've got to think.' He squatted down on his knees. 'We've got to get out of here. But what do we do with her?'

Desiree bent down to put a hand on his shoulder.

'We can move somewhere new, start again. Change our names and give the kid a chance. Maybe some town in New Zealand.'

They were both going to kill her. Anya swung her other leg over and ran for her life.

'No, Des, don't! Leave her alone.'

She spun and saw Desiree coming towards her, knife next to her shoulder. Like a cat, Luke landed between the women. Desiree thrust and stumbled forwards into his arms. Anya ran for the door, not looking back.

A muffled moan came from behind her, then a horrible sucking noise. Someone had been stabbed. She had to get out. Fast.

She flicked on the light so Martin would know she was home. Nothing. *Shit!* Someone must have cut the power to the lights. The door wouldn't open. She'd deadlocked it earlier and the keys . . . Where were the keys? *Shit.*

Running into the office, she pushed hard on the locked window. It too was deadlocked. She swung around, trying to think. Pain still pulsed in her head. A chair. What if she threw it through the window? Someone would notice.

She ran round the desk but could not get the chair out from behind. She tried to lift it, but her arms couldn't take the weight. Oh God, she had to be quick. Then she thought of the back door. It was open.

She sidestepped out of the office, ready to sprint for her life. Then she saw the figure blocking the hallway.

Desiree stood, with the knife poised to attack.

The sucking noise had to be coming from Luke.

'You bitch, see what you've done? You've killed him!' the woman almost squealed. 'You're going to die, just like the others.'

Anya held both hands up in front of her, showing she had no weapon. Her arms and legs were her only defence, despite Desiree's pregnancy. She could hear Luke struggling to breathe.

Terror filled her. Desiree had come here to kill her. Luke was all she cared about.

'I'm a doctor, remember. I can help him.' She kept her hands at face-level. 'If you kill me, he might bleed to death.'

Desiree lowered the knife. 'If he dies, I'll slit your throat.'

Anya kept her arms forwards, feeling her way in what little light there was. When she reached the lounge room, the sucking noise became louder and more frequent. She felt her hair yanked again as her captor pulled her over to Luke. He was lying on the floor near the coffee table. Anya knelt down and felt the wetness seep through her skirt. He was haemorrhaging and there was probably little she could do.

The gurgling, sucking noise came from the stab wound into his lung. It sounded like a tension pneumothorax, sucking air in and compressing his heart.

God, please don't let him die yet, she thought. Feeling for a carotid pulse, her hopes faded. It was barely palpable, thready, rapid and weak. She leant back for the rug from the lounge and felt her scalp tearing.

'Can you get me the rug?' she pleaded. 'I need something to compress the bleeding.'

Desiree threw it at her. 'Do it.'

Luke was barely conscious as life drained from him. Anya put pressure on his chest, which did little for his condition.

'What's happening? What's that sound?'

'It's just air escaping from the wound,' Anya lied. 'If I keep pressure on it, his breathing will slow and he's likely to pass out. It's his body's way of saving oxygen.' She just hoped Desiree knew nothing about first aid. 'This is serious. You've got to call an ambulance. There's a mobile in my bag over there.' She pointed towards the kitchen.

'Don't try anything stupid,' Desiree said, stepping backwards to the handbag. Anya knew she was being watched. Her hands kept still, but with her knees she tried to mop up as much of the shiny liquid as possible. Even Desiree had to know he'd lost too much blood to survive.

'It's not working!' She came over and held the knife between Anya's shoulder blades.

Anya flinched as she remembered. She'd let the

phone go flat and hadn't recharged it. 'What about the landline?' she urged.

'It's dead,' Desiree said desperately. 'You're gonna have to save him.' She stuck the knife deeper, piercing Anya's skin. 'Remember, if he dies, you do too.'

52

Martin turned down the radio and checked his watch again. Shit! Why did his ex-wife have to be so annoying? She knew he was bringing Ben. You'd think that, of all days, she could leave her precious work a bit earlier to meet them. He and Nita had plans to celebrate his new job. It wasn't every day he was named manager of a product line.

Anya's mobile wasn't answering; neither was the phone. He had to admit, this wasn't like her. He looked up and down the street. No sign of her. Where the hell was she? Inside the adjacent terrace a figure watched through the curtains.

He opened the electric window on his son's side and stepped out of the car. 'I'll be right here, you can see me. I'm just going to say hi to the lady next door.'

'You mean Mrs Bugalugs?' Ben said, continuing with his game.

Martin just hoped the old woman didn't take offence if Ben let it slip one day.

He buttoned his jacket and, shoulders hunched, opened the gate. No doubt the old busy-body deliberately left it rickety so she could hear every squeak it made.

With the porch light on, he knocked on the door, looking back to check his son. Ben waved and watched, suddenly curious.

The door opened a few inches, as if she didn't know who was there.

'Hi, I'm Anya from next door's ex-husband. I was wondering if you'd seen her this afternoon or tonight.'

The woman opened the door further and clutched her cardigan with knobbled arthritic fingers.

'I don't like to spread gossip,' she said, peering towards his car. 'Have you got the little fellow in there?'

'He's here to spend the weekend with his mother, only she's not here. But her car is out front.'

'You'd think she could have waited until her son wasn't visiting.'

'Pardon?' Martin said. 'Waited for what?'

She leant forwards and gave an exaggerated blink. Martin saw her yellowed teeth up close for the first time.

'To entertain. To entertain that man who went in there.'

The idea made Martin feel uncomfortable. He'd never imagined his ex-wife with another man, although he'd been with other women. Anya had always seemed married to her job. Except

381

when that smarmy lawyer, Brody, had been sniffing around a while back.

His irritation turned to concern. This didn't make sense. Anya wouldn't do that to Ben, or him. One of the things he most respected about her was how she put her son's emotional needs above her own. He began to feel queasy, like something wasn't right.

'Are you *sure* she's home?'

'As I said, I don't like to spread gossip,' she replied, and closed the door.

He knocked again, and waited for her to return. She couldn't have been more than a few feet from the door, but she made him wait for at least a minute. His right leg twitched, like it did when he was nervous about something.

'I'm sorry to disturb, but would you mind just keeping an eye on my son while I go next door?'

She seemed to consider the request. 'I suppose he can sit out here on the porch. I don't like kids in the house.'

Martin hurried back to the car and grabbed Ben. 'Put your jumper on, it's cold out here.'

'But Dad—' His arms disappeared, reappearing inside the jumper.

'It's just for a minute. I'm going to see if the house is unlocked.'

'But Dad, she's creepy.'

'Shhhh. Don't say that. And I'll only be a minute. Okay?'

Martin began to perspire as he led Ben up the path.

'I'm watching,' the woman said through the partially opened door.

Martin wasn't sure whether that was threatening or reassuring, but he didn't have any other options right now. At least if Ben was out the front, he could hear if his son called.

Martin hopped the fence into Anya's yard, landing on a bed of violets. He listened and didn't hear anything. Around the back, he noticed an open window and his stomach lurched.

Anya never left anything open. She was obsessive about locking everything, which was one of the things he disliked about her. Something was wrong, really wrong.

Instinct told him to bang on the back door, but if Anya were in trouble he could make it worse. What if something had already happened to her? How would he cope? She was such a good mother, Ben would never get over it.

What if she was having sex? Wiping sweaty hands on his trousers, he put the thought from his mind. He decided to break in the back door. Maybe he could kick it in. Shouldering it only worked in the movies. He looked around for something to use as a battering ram. Then it occurred. What if there was more than one man inside? How would he fight? He'd never been in a fight in his life. What if they had weapons?

Ben could lose both parents if he didn't think this through properly. Heart speeding, he decided to get help before he went in. He ran back and jumped the fence again.

Mrs Bugalugs was sitting on the porch next to Ben.

'That man who went in,' he said. 'Did Anya let him in the front door?'

'No, he sneaked around the back. He's probably married,' she added.

'Call the police,' he said. 'Someone's broken in. I'm going back to help.'

They heard a smash and Martin knew he didn't have a choice.

'I knew that woman would bring trouble,' the old lady said as he hurried back over the fence.

53

Luke Platt's pulse became erratic. The rate slowed with each breath. A few more gurgles and it was over. He exhaled and the noises stopped. Anya put down the hand and a scar reflected the light. The white patch. She almost vomited. He'd had the tattoo removed.

Desiree had hurled the phonebase at the television. The screen smashed, sending sparks flying. Anya turned her eyes away. Hopefully someone had heard the noise, she thought. Maybe the woman next door.

'Come on, Luke, that's it, you're going to sleep but you'll still be able to hear us.' She kept pressing on the rug and pretending to feel the non-existent pulse. 'You're doing really well.'

She glanced up at Desiree, unable to see the woman's face. Lights flashed across her retinas every time she blinked, thanks to the screen damage. She hoped like hell that Desiree couldn't clearly see Luke's face. Even without good vision, the knife back between her shoulder blades meant moving was too risky.

'Desiree, you should talk to him. Tell him how you feel. It'll help.'

The pregnant woman started to cry, but the knife moved millimetres deeper. Anya arched her back to try to avoid the blade's tip penetrating further and felt a warm ooze down her spine.

'I didn't mean to do it, baby. I just wanted to protect you.'

Anya felt for the absent pulse again. 'You're doing well, Luke. Hang in there. I think we've stopped the bleeding.' She used part of the rug to hide the blood pooling around the body, seeping along the floor. 'You're in shock, I need to keep you warm.' She did not know how much longer she could keep up the charade. Pretty soon it would be obvious that Luke was dead.

A noise near the kitchen caught her attention. Desiree didn't seem to notice.

Then she heard it again. Someone else was in the house. God, she hoped Desiree hadn't brought anyone with her.

Out of the corner of her eye, she thought she saw a shadow. It stayed still. She spoke to let whoever it was know where they were.

'I can't help Luke with you sticking the knife in my back. I can't get away. You know that.'

'Shut up. Just fix him.'

The shadow was close, then moved quickly.

Anya turned her head too late. Something solid whipped her head back. She fell to the right, clutching her face as the thud landed.

'Annie, get the knife.' Martin's voice was breathless. 'Hurry! I've got her down.'

Relief pulsing through her, Anya crawled, feeling her way on the floor. The knife had to be up the hallway. Grasping and groping, she couldn't find it in the dark. It could have been anywhere. The sound of a siren approached. She'd never heard anything sound so good, except Martin's voice a moment before.

The lights were out, but the appliances weren't. She crawled back behind the lounge and around to the lamp. She flicked the switch, trying to catch her breath.

Martin lay on top of Desiree, who was trying to buck free. It was like seeing a turtle on its back.

'Use your knees to pin her arms,' Anya advised.

Martin held her wrists down and crept up, avoiding her abdomen, and sat straddled over her, knees trapping her elbows. The woman hissed and spat like a trapped animal.

Within seconds, the police arrived and entered via the back door, followed shortly after by Hayden Richards and Meira Sorrenti.

'We need an ambulance, there's been a stabbing,' Hayden yelled into his mobile phone.

Anya slumped to the floor, aching and exhausted. 'Where's Ben?'

Meira bent down. 'He's with one of the constables.'

'Platt's dead,' she said. 'She stabbed him when he got between us.'

Desiree wailed, 'Liar! You killed him. You said he was gonna be all right.'

The ambulance men arrived and one ran to Anya, who'd only just realised she was covered in Luke's blood. 'I'm all right,' she said. 'The blood's not mine.'

Meira remained at her side. 'Nasty hit to your face. Did Platt do that?'

'No, that was my ex-husband.' She smiled and the movement split her lip open. 'What did you hit me with?'

'My foot. I dived on the woman. Only I misjudged a little and kicked you. Sorry.'

Two uniforms lifted and hand-cuffed Desiree before leading her away. Martin stood watching the commotion. He had seen death during his years as an intensive-care nurse, but he had never been involved in a crime. His whole body trembled. Hayden Richards moved over and took him outside.

All Anya could think of was that at least he was respectable enough for Ben to see once he got over the initial shock. Whereas she'd have to get cleaned up first.

Meira asked one of the Crime Scene Officers to swab and photograph Anya straight away, so they could bag her clothes and let her get clean.

'Could you hold out your hands, please?' asked the gloved constable. A white cotton swab dabbed at one of the bloody spots. Then another. 'Did you scratch your assailant?'

388

'No . . . I mean, yes, I think. When he had me around the neck.'

The constable swabbed beneath her nails and then cut them, placing the cuttings in a plastic jar.

'We need to do this to tie up the loose ends.' Meira sounded sympathetic.

'All done until we do the clothes. When you undress, could you place this paper sheet beneath you?'

'I know the routine,' Anya said.

'Come on.' Meira put her arm around Anya's shoulder. 'I'll help you upstairs.'

Meira waited until they were alone in the bathroom. 'Do you want to tell me what happened?'

All her adrenalin spent, Anya had trouble mustering the energy to go over the last few hours. 'He came to rape me but he didn't get the chance.' The words came out, but it was as though she were talking about someone else. 'Desiree arrived and stopped him.'

The detective seemed relieved. 'You used your wits. They saved your life,' she said. 'You're a strong woman. You'll get over this.' She rubbed Anya's shoulder. 'I'll wait here while you have a shower. Chain of evidence and all that.' Any sentimentality was erased from the moment.

When Anya closed the bathroom door, she heard, 'And there's a kind of cute kid next door busting to see you, so could you hurry it up?'

Staring at the shower, Anya decided to scrub herself down from the sink. The thought of Platt staring at her while she washed was too fresh. Stepping out of the blood-soaked clothes, she took a wet face washer and began to wipe off the red stains.

54

'Welcome back.' Hayden Richards stood in the office doorway with a cactus plant in his arms. Around the base was a bright yellow ribbon.

Anya stared at the plant. 'What's this in aid of?'

'I call it "The Crichton". It's hardy, practical and can survive almost anything. It's like a rose, only it has prickles instead of thorns.'

Anya pushed back her chair and stood up.

'It's a really nice gesture,' she said, taking the plant. 'Thank you.'

'So how was the holiday?'

'Good,' she said. 'The salt air was just the thing. Ben and I had a ball.'

He put his hands in his pockets. 'And your ex?'

She put the plant down on the desk. 'He's doing okay. It was good to spend some time together, I guess. He's nowhere near as angry as I thought he would be about my work. Ironically, it's mellowed him and rekindled respect. I think he was genuinely impressed that I talked my way out of getting raped and killed.' She moved the plant closer to the centre. 'Can I make you a coffee?'

'Why not?'

The pair retreated to the staffroom. Light filled the area and the surrounding trees gave it a sense of calm. Someone had kindly already made a pot.

Hayden sat on one of the padded vinyl chairs and stretched his legs. 'Thought you might like an update on what's gone on.'

Anya was ready to hear about it. She'd prepared herself to listen to every detail.

'Turned out Lerner was just a thug. There may be up to twenty-eight rape cases that Luke Platt committed, judging by the unsolved cases we've tracked down and the stash of souvenirs Platt had hoarded. Some of the details are patchy and they cross three states, but getting information from victims is not easy. Not surprising, given how much he's moved around. We should be grateful he did get around. It made it harder for Desiree to follow him at night. Otherwise there would have been others killed.'

'Why didn't she kill more?'

'They only hooked up about three years ago.'

Of course, Anya thought. Desiree had told her that. 'What about before Luke?'

Hayden looked out at the view. 'Before that, she lived somewhere remote with a farmer. They barely left the property. He says she wouldn't let him. A real control freak, always accusing him of being unfaithful.'

Anya needed to hear. 'How could she think Luke was having relationships with these women? Is she still delusional?'

'Technically not, according to the trick-cyclist. Then again, trust a psychiatrist to think Desiree is sane. He reckons it was reasonable to assume Luke was having affairs. All the secrecy, sneaking out, lies, he could have been any unfaithful husband. Besides, he stalked them, so he kept going back to the same house. If you were in denial, you would think he was having an affair. And the few times she followed him, she didn't see the gloves. He kept them in his pockets until he went around the back. She didn't see him climb in Liz Dorman's window, or so she says. Either way, she knew right from wrong when she stabbed her victims.'

'It's lucky more wives don't take the same course of action.' Anya poured a couple of cups. 'What about the blood on the knife?'

'Ah,' he said. 'That belonged to Desiree herself. She must have cut herself during one of the three murders.'

'Three? Elizabeth Dorman, and I'm presuming Leonie Turnbull. Who was the third?' She passed Hayden a black coffee.

'Ta. Eileen Randall. She confessed to everything.' He grinned and massaged his top lip. 'There you go, maybe she is crazy. Even told us about planting the murder weapon in Lerner's garage after you went to her place. She knew we were digging around and chose him because of his reputation for domestic abuse.'

'Desiree was very calculating. It makes me feel better that Willard didn't do it.' She sat next to the detective, feeling a sense of pride at helping to vindicate an innocent man.

'Yeah, well, apparently she was on with Nick Hudson when he did the deed with Randall. Seems she's had trouble with pathological jealousy for a bloody long time.'

Anya couldn't believe fourteen-year-old Desiree would kill Eileen Randall over a boy. Desiree may have been legally sane, but she was incredibly disturbed, even if she'd escaped being labelled delusional. She was psychopathic, having not an ounce of remorse for what she'd done. She had even let Geoff Willard take the blame and spend twenty years in prison.

'What about the connection with Melanie Havelock and Willard?'

'Desiree again. She tried to set him up, too. Luke Platt got the photo from a pen-pal – Gideon Lee, the guy who raped the mother and stole her wallet. Rapists these days have a network, through which they swap their trophies. Seems Desiree found the photo with the name and address on it, presumed it was someone Luke was having an affair with, and decided to pass it on to Willard. Luckily for the other women, she didn't find any other of Luke's souvenirs. He usually stashed them in a tin in his mobile freezer. Now there's a creepy place!'

Anya wanted to get back to Willard. 'How did she set him up?'

'She found the photo – before Luke attacked Melanie – and wrote that sick note, hoping Geoff would hurt the girl when he got out, or mess her up at least. One way of breaking up a relationship, I guess. At least she didn't decide to kill Melanie. Or if she did, she couldn't find her because we'd moved her. On the news footage you can see her outside the prison, shoving something into Willard's pocket when he was released. Clear as daylight. Luke must have wondered where the photo had gone, but he remembered the address, so it didn't stop him from making Melanie one of his victims. And maybe this time Desiree was worried about her baby getting hurt, which is why she set up Willard. She knew more about him than we did.'

So Willard hadn't been guilty of anything. Anya thought of the injustice of his treatment, from the time he was born, right up to now.

'The dog hair found at the scene, can you explain it?'

'Ah, you'll like this,' Hayden said, and blew on the drink. 'Matched an ugly stuffed mutt we found in Desiree's bedroom. Her beloved puppy from the good old days.'

Anya straightened. Her back still ached from the ordeal. Bruises healed, but the strain from bending over Platt and tensing for that long had taken its toll. Thankfully, the stab wound between her shoulder blades had been superficial.

'Where's Sorrenti now?'

Hayden stood and reached over for a cream biscuit from the table. 'Still on the job. Seems the computing dicks found the source of the picture leak. They traced it to the house of one of your colleagues.'

Anya sat forwards, unable to imagine who would post victims' genitalia photos on the Internet.

'Damn, you're good, but you're not that good! You wouldn't have heard. Seems your friend Lyndsay Gatlow decided to study the pics at home, so she emailed them to her own address. She didn't figure on her teenage son seeing them and passing them on to his friends, who passed them on, and on. You know how it goes.' He munched, and more crumbs lodged in his moustache. 'In my day, models in bikinis were enough to excite a schoolboy.'

The irony of photography's greatest proponent ruining the pilot programme wasn't lost on Anya. Sometimes life was just.

Poor Geoff Willard, she thought. At least now he could clear his name and begin to get on with his life.

'Is the Willard family seeking compensation? Maybe I can help.'

Hayden sat forward. 'That's the funny thing,'

he said. 'Willard's been arrested for stalking some girl who works at an opportunity shop.'

Anya put the cup on the table. 'We've got to help him. This guy's been through hell.'

'You might want to reconsider. The sample you got from the old cop up north, the one with the DNA, came back.'

'And . . .'

'The semen on Eileen Randall's panties and inside the vagina belonged to Geoff Willard.'

'But how could it?' Anya bit her bottom lip. She sat down again, comprehending what had occurred. There was only one possible explanation. He'd pulled Eileen out of the water, and sexually assaulted her dead body. That would explain the blood smears on his shirt. By pressing repeatedly on her body during intercourse, he would have caused small amounts of diluted blood to spurt from the chest cavity.

'Took me a minute to connect those dots, too. Guess the guy is a pervert after all. He just happened to get lucky that once.'

Anya's mind raced. That's why Desiree was so cocky about not getting caught for the Randall murder. 'Desiree knew what Willard had done. She probably saw the whole thing.' Anya thought of Dell, the woman she'd spoken to at Fisherman's Bay. Willard may well have been responsible for that assault after all.

'The family are smart enough to know that if they go for compensation, it's likely to come out.

Besides, a judge will probably think that if he was sick enough to do that to a young girl, what else is he capable of?'

Anya stood at the window, staring out at the leaves waving in the breeze. The sun warmed the room. She thought about the Dorman murder, and how Desiree could have set up Willard by putting blood on his shirt.

'What about the blood smears on Willard's shirts after the Dorman death? How did Desiree put them there?'

'She didn't. But she used the Willards' machine to do her own washing all the time, so it was just a lucky accident, lucky for her, that is. My guess is, the blood was either still wet when it touched his shirts, or it transferred in the wash, as you said.'

'Which explains the odd distribution.'

They were yet to discuss Luke Platt. 'Did Quentin Lagardia give you any insight into Luke?' she asked.

Hayden finished his cup and licked his lips. 'He was an only child, abusive mother. Was always the good one at school. Then somehow he hooks up with some sex offenders and starts to act out his fantasies. Control-freak Desiree must have made him worse.

'Quentin doesn't think Platt ever really believed that he hurt the women. He may not have even known about Leonie Turnbull's death, since he had moved on by the time that happened. That was Desiree's second murder, after Eileen.'

That made sense to Anya. He had stepped between her and Desiree, to block the knife. In a perverse way, he had tried to protect her. 'And when the DNA evidence on Liz Dorman came to light, he thought Willard did that one too? He must have presumed Willard had been following him.'

'Yep.' Hayden rose and hitched up his pants. 'Guess I'd better get back to it.'

'Hey, is everything okay? You're still losing weight.'

'Yeah. I'm the only one not complaining. My doctor says it's inflammatory bowel disease and wants me to stay on prednisone. Only thing is, my appetite's come back.'

Relieved it wasn't a more sinister diagnosis, Anya showed him out of the unit's front door, knowing they'd cross paths again with another case soon. Life was getting back to normal.

She closed the door behind her and admired the cactus. In her pile of unopened mail sat a postcard from her friend, Kate Farrer, who was returning to work next week, and a letter from Dan Brody. She wondered if he was severing their working relationship thanks to Veronica Slater and her spiteful altercation. No point delaying the inevitable, she thought, and ripped open the envelope.

Inside was a card covered with a photo of an English garden. She opened it.

I'm sorry to hear about your unfortunate dealings with Ms Slater over the Willard case. In no way do I endorse her behaviour. For your information, she has received both a verbal and written reprimand from the barristers in these chambers in lieu of a formal complaint to the Law Society. Of course, you are within your rights to submit your own complaint, should you choose to do so.

Ms Slater is currently serving a period on probation and is excluded from further dealings with you. For future cases, you will be dealing directly with one of the senior barristers, such as myself.

And in light of the recent siege situation at your home, may I offer my sincerest hopes for your quick and full recovery.

All best wishes,

Dan

A sort of apology from a barrister. Maybe it was time to buy a lottery ticket.

Veronica Slater had been exposed and was now facing the consequences of her actions. Her little performance might even have gone some of the way to enhancing Anya's reputation. Even more demeaning, Veronica's own colleagues had reprimanded her.

Maybe the good guys did win sometimes, after all.

She propped the card on the desk next to the cactus, sat back and felt in control for the first time that day. Life was anything but normal. And at moments like these, she wouldn't have it any other way.